BLOOD·BOUND·BOOKS

I0670958

Presents

D.O.A.

Extreme Horror Anthology

EDITED BY

David C. Hayes & Jack Burton

Visit us on the web at:
www.bloodboundbooks.net

Available now from Blood Bound Books:

Night Terrors: An Anthology of Horror
Unspeakable: A New Breed of Terror
Seasons in the Abyss: Flash Fiction

Coming Soon:
Rock is Dead: Dark Tales Inspired by Music
Steamy Screams: Erotic Horror Anthology

The Blood Bound Staff:

Marc Ciccarone
Joe Spagnola
Karen Fierro
Theresa Dillon

CONTENTS

Cherry Clubbing

Kenneth Yu

Hey. Hey!

Francis? You're—Frank, right? It's me, Richard. Ricky! We met in Bangkok some years back. We joined that private beach tour group to Thailand together.

Smooth sand, clear water, blue skies? Tropical sunshine to die for? Ring anything? No? Heh. Can't blame you for pretending. We've got to be careful nowadays, but there's no need to be coy with me. I *know* you.

You really don't remember? Heh, sure. Okay, I'll play. I was the one who lost his balance and fell off the boat when our group went off to chase dolphins. You had to come back and get me, re-member? We lost the dolphins after that. I probably scared them away. Everybody got pissed at me.

Yeah! Yeah, me! That's right! I'm Ricky, Frank! Good to see you! Geez, you weren't shitting! You *really* didn't remember me! So how've you been, you dumb hairy fuck?

Me? I'm fine. A little less hair up top, a bit more of a paunch, but never been better. I'm still up to my old tricks. Same ol', same ol'. And you? Same too, huh? Busy as ever, like bees, that's us.

Hey, man, you got time? I'm not doing anything right now, just hanging around, looking. You, same? People like us, we're al-ways looking. Let's park our asses somewhere and catch up, what do you say? Guys with our 'shared interests' don't get to jaw often, so this is a special occasion!

Yeah, this is a pretty big mall. Open air, too. Smells funky without air conditioning, but that's the way it is here. You know another thing about the Philippines? Their beer is excellent. San Miguel, they call it. Saint Michael, in English. Heavenly when chilled in ice. Let's get a couple of brews, my treat.

Come on, let's try that place. It looks cheap, good and clean. So does the waitress. They don't hire our 'types' here, but she still looks like she hasn't developed yet. Perfect for the both of us.

But nah. We're just 'reading the menu,' 'kay? Here, grab that

1

table. We're not 'ordering.' I want to make that crystal. Let's just say that we shouldn't shit in this backyard. Here, as with most places, it's either 'to go' or forget it. S'funny, for some reason they say 'take out' instead of 'to go' in this country. Anyway, we shouldn't send out any smoke, if you know what I mean. I'll tell you why later. Special reason. Trust me, it'll be worth your while.

That got your full attention, didn't it? I knew it would. Anyway, later.

Two San Miguels, chickie. No, not the light stuff, the ones in the brown bottles. Yeah, the Pale Pilsens. And hey, cutie, you sure you're over? Aww, don't give me that look. I'm sure you're fine. Just sayin', that's all. You're cute, you know. You're *fresh*. That's a compliment, chickie.

See, she's smiling! It's in them, Frank. It's in them, I tell you, like it's in us. I don't know why only we can see it and the rest of the world can't.

Aww...I'm sure she understands English, c'mon! Maybe she doesn't get everything, but this is the Philippines, baby! They speak English well enough. Funny-sounding, but fine. They love Hollywood here! To them, anyone from where we come from is a fucking movie star!

Even with our "shared interests" I didn't expect to bump into you. What're you doing here? Hell, I mean I know what you're here for, same thing as I am, but a classy someone like you runs in different circles than I do. If not for that Thailand tour, I doubt we'd have ever met. What're you *technically* here for? Trade convention, huh? Buying the native handicrafts? Cool. No? Boring? Hey, sorry man. Then you're lucky you got away for some time off.

Alone? Sucks. Your company's running on the cheap, sending their best man halfway around the globe without help. But that's just the way we like it, eh? And you're not alone anymore. You've got me!

Thanks, chickie! Here's the cash, with a little something extra for you. Keep the change. Remember me kindly when I come back. And I *will* be back. For *you*. Promise.

See? See? She's still smiling. Love her dimples. Drink up, pal. Good, eh?

Don't you just love the pointiness of their ears? Makes their eyes bigger, doll-like. So sweet, especially when they're at just that right height. They're perfect that way. That's how you started out,

I'll bet. That's how I did. Hell, that's how we all did. We started with one of them pointy-ears, then there was no turning back, and it was on to greater things. Better things.

It's fate, Frank. Fate. There's a reason we met today, here of all places. You're looking, I know. 'Cause that's the way it is. People like us, we're always looking.

What happened to who? Scarface? Oh, you mean Ronald! You remember him? Hey! Why'd you remember Ron but not me? Oh, his scar. That's right, he had that scar down his cheek, that's why the nickname. Of course, stupid me. Evil-looking cut, made him look like a crook, but he was the complete opposite. As big and as strong as a bull, but what a great guy. The best. He was a good friend.

Yeah, *was*. Got caught, he did. Sad. Shit happens, even to the best of us. How'd it happen? Long story, but we've got time. You ready for a long listen?

Ron and I had been traveling together for years, even before Thailand. They finally got him about two years ago when we were in Cambodia. And of all things, he got caught with some pointy-ears. Yeah, just the pointy-ears, same as that waitress, nothing more, but enough to bring everything down on his head. What a way to go. He was with several of those elves, in fact. It was his own damn fault, really. I like to say it was bad luck, but Ron, he was the reckless type. He always was. Once the mood hits him he forgets to be careful and just goes for it. Shoot from the hip. Damn the torpedoes, full speed ahead. He even forgets to lock the door sometimes. It's not good to be that way. It's never good. You always got to keep some kind of control going until you're sure you're safe and alone.

Scarface...Ron...was living on borrowed time. The only reason he lasted as long as he did was because of me. I was the one watching his back, making sure we did things safely, that we didn't rush. It was his fault, I know that, but I sometimes blame myself for what happened. What if I had been there that night to watch his back as always, instead of sick in bed with the flu? He'd be here with us now, that's how it would've played out. But I couldn't lift myself out of bed back then, and the dumbass couldn't keep himself inside. That jerk-off followed his hormones and he just had to go and do it without checking that all was clear. I warned him to play it safe, to make sure that everything was clean. I knew he wouldn't listen though, and there was nothing I could do. "Yeah, sure," he said, then he smiled at me, closed the door to our room and left me alone with my virus. Those were the last words I ever heard him say.

The next time I saw him it was on TV. Bad, real bad. They showed the full raid on prime-time news. A raid! Yeah, I can smell your fear right now. I can see you sweating. A fucking raid. There must've been a dozen warning signs but Ron walked right into it blind.

I still remember exactly how I felt when I found out. It was a few hours after Ron left. My fever had gone down and I was thinking of going out after him. I switched the TV on for some noise—it was too quiet for comfort—and the news was on. I froze and nearly puked when I heard the reporter say, "We are broadcasting a live raid here from Svay Pak, Phnom Penh." Ron was headed there. He had been eyeing a group of pointy-ears the night before, fresh from the provinces.

It's our worst nightmare. I watched it unfold right there on the TV, and I couldn't wake up because it was all real. I remember how the screen shook as the cameraman followed the policemen up the narrow wooden stairs to the "safe-rooms" behind the bar and restaurant. I remember the heavy pounding of their running feet, shit to them. They banged on the door twice then kicked it open. Ron got caught red-handed in the full glare of the lights. His eyes were large and white when he turned to face the camera. I can still see the shocked expression on his face. His scar stood out like a black shadow, and with his long hair plastered to his head with sweat and blood he looked like some kind of pirate. He was holding his favorite riding crop, the brown one—you remember it from Thailand, don't you? Yeah, that one—he was holding his crop up in mid-stroke, about to bring it down again. He was licking blood off his other hand at the same time.

Everything stopped. I swear, no one moved and everything became quiet, like hitting the pause button except I could still hear the whimpers and the moans in the background. Then someone off-cam swore like a sailor and it was like a signal to act. The camera shook again, followed by more cursing, shouting, and crying. The screen blurred. I could hear Ron's screams through it all. I heard breaking glass, falling furniture, and whacking. A lot of whacking.

When the TV cleared up, Ron was crouching on the floor. His hands were cuffed behind his back. Someone pulled his head by his hair and showed his face to the camera. One eye was half-closed,

4

puffed, and it looked like his mouth and his ears were bleeding. A policeman spat in his face, and another kicked him and he fell and hit his head with a sick thud. "Let him know what it feels like to be on the other end of the stick," someone said.

They panned to show the elves on the bed. There were five of them, two boys, three girls, naked as a brand new sunrise and fucking beautiful. Clearly our 'types,' all of them. Man, if Ron was reckless he made up for it with his energy. Terrific work. He's the only one I knew who could do five at a time in one go, and then be ready for five more not an hour later. And he knew how to work them, work them hard and work them well. Ron did a great job. They were gorgeous.

Of course the damn cameraman played it up for all it was worth. Sensationalism rates, that's the law of media in any country. He showed close-ups of their bare backs and chests, their tight butts, their legs, their faces. I loved the way they looked into the camera, the lights glowing in their wide eyes. The tear streaks on their faces were precious, and their sniffling and whimpers turned me on, in spite of everything. Ron had raised these lovely, long, criss-crossing welts all over their hard, tight, little bodies. So red with blood, so angry. I ran my hands over the TV screen and I could almost feel the bumps. Mmm.

This is how I think the story went down: our dumb friend leaves me and he forgets everything except for the fun he's going to have. He heads straight for Svay Pak, probably pays the cabbie double to run the red lights and get him there quick. He has the cab stop right in front of the bar and he gets down. He doesn't tell the driver to stop some blocks away so he can walk and check the area out like we've always done. Any news cars around? Anybody who may be watching the place? Hiding in the shadows? Nope. He just walks in all excited and big and goes directly to the boss and asks in a voice as loud as he is tall for the elves he met the night before.

The bosses, they never know anything either. It's all money-money-money to them. They're more reckless than Ron. If I was a boss...well, later. So Ron, he's told to go out back to one of the rooms and to wait there, and he does. Then the boss brings in the elves. None of them know that it's all a set-up. The news crew has been waiting, probably saw the whole thing from their unmarked van parked outside. Or maybe it's their man inside who sees Ron walk in the bar, sees him talk to the boss, sees him go out back.

Then he sends a signal—tips his hat or something while sitting by the window—the cops and the crew move in and it's all over.

When Ron left me that night, I prayed hard that nothing would go wrong. The percentages were on our side, after all. What are the stats? Ninety-nine times out of a hundred, nothing happens, right? Ninety-nine times out of a hundred you're left alone and you get to do what you want as long as you've got the cash. That's my personal rule number two: always have enough cash, because if you've got enough you not only get to do what you want, but if something goes wrong, you can always pay your way out with no questions asked. No problemo. But there's no way you can pay your way out of a live TV camera in your face. Not enough cash in the world for that.

What's my number one rule? Well, it's two rules in one, my friend. It's that important. Always, always play it safe, and always leave no trace. Better that than sorry. Keep my rules to heart, you hear? I'd hate to see you go down like Ron.

The newscaster ended her report by calling us criminals and monsters that needed to be hunted down and brought to justice. Bitch. She just didn't get it early enough, otherwise she'd know what it's all about. She'd love it the way we do. You and I know better. There are more of us out there every day, and I'm sure that one day we can all come out and not have to worry anymore.

And it's not like we're hurting anyone, right? I mean, these elves and those like them, they live forever! They just go on and on and we, we're old and our years are numbered, but they'll still be around. Nothing hurts them, or if it does, they've got years and years and years to get over it. We don't. Their whole lives are ahead of them, and they love it. It's in them, and we...we need this. It's in us as much as it's in them.

I beat it out of there faster than a bolt of lightning, flu or no flu. Spent the night at the airport shivering in a jacket. Took the first available flight out to somewhere, I can't even remember where. I played it safe. I couldn't risk Ron not ratting me out, not with what I knew the police had in store for him. Poor guy.

Aww, shit, Frank. All this reliving is painful. I miss Ron. He was great to be with. Why'd he have to go and be all stupid?

Remember what he did in Thailand? On the beach that night when the fishermen brought in that fresh catch of mermaids and merlads for us? Remember what he did? Yeah, you do. Hahaha! I'm glad you remember. I'm glad I've got someone to share that memory with. That guy really couldn't control himself. Heh. Careful there. You're snorting beer through your nose. Heh.

The night was so clear, the moonlight and starlight were so bright on the water when the fishermen came, do you remember? What time was it? Midnight? No? You're right, that's too early. Maybe two or three in the morning. I can still see their boat gliding through the waves. I can still hear the crunch when it hit the sand and they pulled it up onto the beach.

The lead fisherman came to me first. The old guy reached into the boat and he lifted out a bundle wrapped in wet canvas. The bundle was wriggling when he brought it to me. The fisherman grinned as he pulled the canvas aside and revealed the most delightful sight. My first mermaid, you know, my very first. She looked up at my face and I could see the stars reflected in her eyes. Her hair was stringy and long and I pulled it aside so I could see her small, precious breasts. Exquisite, my friend.

You got a merlad, you say? Golden scales on the tail? Who-ah! You lucky bastard! Well, we were all lucky, weren't we? That tour was expensive but worth every cent.

Ron, that bastard, hahaha, he couldn't wait for his catch to be brought to him. He ran up to the boat, reached in and lifted two bundles up all by himself. Carried them under each arm, walked to the nearest stretch of open sand, threw them down, pulled off the canvases and went at them with his crop, his fists, his elbows, his knees, and his teeth like there was no tomorrow. The sounds they made were intoxicating.

That broke the spell for all of us, didn't it? I brought my mermaid to the space beside Ron, pulled off my belt, and began to do my thing. The rest of you were all over the boat like sharks in a frenzy. Massive, man, massive. Our cries and theirs were crazy wonderful, all around us, all over the beach. Shit. Loved the way they mixed with the sound of the surf. I got off real good, more than three times, I think. Best group action I've ever had, hands down. Haven't experienced anything like it since. Gawd, we all needed to help each other back to the huts before the break of dawn. I couldn't walk straight. My body was that sore. Ron had that goofy smile on his face too. What? Me too? No kidding? Hahaha! Then you too, you sonofabitch!

Hahaha! Oh my, good times, those were. *Great* times. We

7

need more of those. Oh my. Oh my my my. Sometimes it's really worth it to be alive.

Hey, hey, which brings me to this. I'm about done with my beer. Are you? Good, hey, I think it's time I share with you my little secret. Bend over closer, will you?

Heh. I'm a boss now. Yeah, well, one of them. I have me some partners. Been here in the Philippines for a bit more than a year, and my job is to bring people like you, who don't have a clue in this country, to where you want to be.

We've got everything. Elves, mermaids, nymphs, satyrs, dryads, you name your type we have them. They have different names for them here, but it's all the same, it's all good, and I can do the translating for you. You want to go wing-pluck some sprites and fairies as a teaser? I can show you where. You want a dwarf, or a satyr or two, either with full beards or shaved smooth, just let me know. Since we're old friends, you get yours at a special rate, the wholesale rate. I guarantee you it's all safe and hidden. You know how I work. The rules, man, the rules. You won't have to worry.

I've sampled all the merchandise, one of the perks of being a boss, and they're wonderful here in this country. The local varieties of the elves and nymphs and what have you, man, they're great! And there are a lot of them. There's a different taste to them, too. Delicious! Exotic! This place is a goldmine, a fucking paradise, I tell you.

Come here, get closer.

It's so wonderful here, we were able to find something extra special.

Angels.

Yeah, you heard me right. Our stars. The demand for them is high. We got lucky, found them, and caught them. Pretty easy. You take anyone or anything by surprise and it's all easy. You want seraphim? We've got them. You should see, no, *feel*, what they can do with their wings. It's like nothing you've ever felt before, I promise you. And their blood, flows like liquid light and tastes like rainbows.

You know what? We have cherubim too. No kidding. Yeah, I know. Hard to believe, eh? We've got them. We're the first in this part of the world to have them. I tried one of them cherries myself. A nice, plump, rosy-cheeked one. Beautiful dark-brown curls. Oh, wow. Heaven. You should try one. Highly recommended.

Elves and mermaids sound like old car engines coughing exhaust compared to an angel when it sings. If we could set up some mass action like we did in Thailand, I'll bet we could experience an entire choir. It's the heavenly host treatment, baby!

I hope you're feeling strong. These angels, they may be smaller and lighter, but they're twice what any elf or dwarf is made of. Takes a lot just to hold them down, and a lot more to get them to sing. I doubt if even Ron could take more than two of them at a time. His riding crop would be useless. You need something heavier and harder, but the effort's worth it, believe you me.

Me? I took an aluminum baseball bat to mine. Needed two hands too, like a caveman with his club. Some of my customers prefer crowbars. But I think a stiff plank of wood would be fine, as long as the wood is the tough kind and you've got strong enough arms. Yeah, wood is good if you want to, you know, savor it. To make it last longer. If you've got the endurance, go with wood!

So, you want to give it a try? I can take you to our place right now. Like I said, wholesale price for you, pal. You high-rolling, jet-setting executives have got all the cash, anyway. What do you say?

Great! Let's finish up. Fate, Frank. It's fate. We were meant to meet here today. Bet you had no clue where to go before you met me. Bet you were just taking your chances.

Ahh, that San Miguel beer is sweet, as sweet as cherry blood. *Almost.*

Hey, chickie! Thanks for the beer! Remember me, and remember what I said. I keep my promises. I'll be back for you.

Smiling. They're *always* smiling. Damn gorgeous. I swear I'll never get tired of them.

Come on! Let's go get you some cherry!

To be Filled in by the subject:

Your name: [redacted]
Sponsor: J. GRANT
CASE ID #: 013396
Re: Randall Chronic Pain Scale

All fields must be filled out unless instructed otherwise by front desk.

1. When did you last consult a physician?
02/11/2008

2. What diseases, ailments, or injuries have you had in the past five years?
SEE ATTACHED

3. Are you currently taking any medication? If yes, please list.
N

4. Are you allergic to any medication? If yes, please list.
ALLERGY TO SULFA

5. Have you been hospitalized in the past two years? If yes, please describe.
N

6. Have you ever been treated by a psychiatrist, psychoanalyst, or psychologist for any mental, emotional, or nervous disorder? If yes, please explain.
N

7. Are you currently under treatment or observation for any physical or emotional conditions?
N

8. Have you ever experienced:

a. difficulties in relations with parents, authority figures, peers? Y
b. behavioral disorders? N
c. fear of wolves or Scandinavian leather apparel? Y
d. symptoms such as mood swings, depression, severe sleep disorders, unusual degree of anxiety, fear, or guilt? Y

9. Are all ten of your toes original/real, and not prosthetic?
Y

10. Are you currently on a restricted diet?
N

11. Can you hum the first three bars of the third movement of Han-
del's Messiah?
N

12. Will your family require any additional medical documentation?
N

The answers I have given are correct to the best of my knowledge.
Subject Signature: [signed and dated in blue pen]
==

2358: Study begins

0100: Subject Blood Pressure (**BP**) 114/86 -- temp 98.9 -- pulse 115
Beats Per Minute (**bpm**) -- pupils dilate normally -- brick placed on
stomach -- restraints OK -- saline drip started

0113: Subject falls asleep -- upon waking indicates Randall Chronic
Pain Scale (**RCPS**) scale rating of 0 -- Second brick placed -- BP
114/86 -- temp 98.9

0119: Subject falls asleep again -- states that normal bedtime is 2230
most nights -- RCPS rating still 0 -- 0.5 mg Pipradrol administered

0121: Third brick placed -- BP 114/86 -- 112 bpm

0124: Fourth brick placed -- subject notes discomfort -- still states
RCPS of 0

0128: Fifth brick requires duct tape to keep on subject's stomach -- first needle inserted in subject's right arm -- subject indicates Randall Chronic Pain Scale (RCPS) 1 -- 10 mg Buspirone administered

0134: Second needle inserted -- subject indicates RCPS 1 -- requests one brick removed -- brick not removed -- 115 bpm

0144: RCPS 2 -- third needle inserted -- temp 98.7 -- subject requests bricks removed -- bricks not removed -- 5 cc saline solution administered -- subject notified that placebo is actually painkiller

0145: Subject becoming profane -- raising volume of voice -- BP 120/90 -- 140 bpm -- refuses to indicate RCPS rating -- 5 ccs saline solution administered -- subject notified that placebo is Demerol

0148: Subject actively struggling -- two bricks dislodged -- hammer administered to subject's left hand -- BP 124/90 -- 184 bpm

0149: Subject indicates RCPS of 5 -- subject questions legitimacy of several staff member's lineage -- temp 99.1 -- fourth needle inserted

0150: Fifth, sixth, seventh, eighth, ninth, tenth, eleventh, twelfth, thirteenth, fourteenth needles and one (1) pair of nail scissors inserted -- RCPS 10

0152: BP 132/100 -- temp 99.0 -- RCPS 4 -- subject crying

0155: Hammer applied to bottoms of subject's feet -- RCPS 7

0156: Subject indicates RCPS 5 -- questions sanity of several staff -- apologizes

0200: One (1) slice of apple cobbler administered -- RCPS 3 -- temp 98.9 -- minor eye dilation in left pupil

0202: Subject requests ice cream

0207: 4 oz. Breyers Vanilla All Natural Ice Cream administered

0209: Subject is verbally praised in Cantonese -- BP 130/90 -- temp

98.5 -- RCPS 3 -- 128 bpm

0214: Subject's left hand amputated with bolt cutters -- RCPS 10 -- subject falls unconscious during procedure -- cauterization of stump successful

0217: BP 120/88 -- temp 98.4 -- 88 bpm

0220: Subject regains consciousness

0222: 0.5 fl. oz. Muriatic acid administered to skin between subject's third and fourth toes of right foot -- subject falls unconscious again

0224: Subject begins to show symptoms of hypoperfusional shock -- blood transfusion started -- third toe of subject's right foot falls off

0233: Subject regains consciousness -- repeatedly indicates RCPS 10 -- solid blow to mouth applied with iron pipe -- 17 fire ants administered to subject's chest area

0238: BP 140/106 -- 170 bpm -- temp 98.9 -- RCPS 10

0241: 10 cm incision made to subject's left side -- 4 oz. ice cream inserted -- subject demands mother

0244: 4 additional oz. ice cream administered to replace meltoff -- incision successfully closed

0255: Subject continues to indicate RCPS 10

0257: 10 cm incision made to subject's left inner thigh -- seven (7) 4" aluminum nails administered to sole of right foot

0301: Badger administered

0309: Badger euthanized

0310: BP 145/110 -- temp 99.1 -- RCPS 10 -- 210 bpm

0312: Sutures finished -- damaged left optic tissue removed -- second unit of blood administered via transfusion

0315: 19 random passages from J. R. R. Tolkien's The Silmarillion read aloud by Russian female volunteer

0316: One (1) liter bleach administered to subject's face

0322: BP 140/106 -- temp 99.0 -- RCPS 10 -- 204 BPM

0323: 3 oz 89 octane rating gasoline administered to subject's groin

0324: Fire applied to subject's groin

0326: Fire extinguished -- caramel chocolate bar administered

0331: Bandsaw administered to subject's leg -- Nine (9) members of Las Vegas All Castrati Barbershop Choir sing Star Wars Original Score a-cappella -- subject falls unconscious and wakes several times during amputation

0338: Sledgehammer applied

0339: Sledgehammer applied -- second and fifth bricks lose integrity -- subject's ribs lose integrity

0340: Sledgehammer applied -- remaining bricks/ribs lose integrity

0341: Sledgehammer applied

0342: Sledgehammer applied

0343: Subject is dead -- resuscitation attempts fail -- intravenous feeds stopped -- prayer in Hungarian administered by family friend -- remaining cobbler distributed to family -- all volunteers dismissed

0411: Sledgehammer applied

0412: Study ends

Demons Lie

Atris Ray III

The sedation is starting to wear off and the demon slowly wakes. Its extremities move first, flesh rattles on the stainless steel coroner's table. Its feet and hands tug against the tight leather straps but the attempts are useless. The restraints have been blessed by a priest and the creature is not going anywhere. Not while I'm here.

The basement's single florescent light flickers and hums above me as I assay my tools. Surgical steel blades, hooks, and separators laid out in glistening rows on the table. Each one sterilized in holy water, they are the perfect implements to open the demon's chest and remove its withered heart. I've been in this fight for years. I know the game. They feign pain from the bindings, but only holy objects can hurt them.

Demons lie.

I look at the creature for the first time in hours. Demons are full of illusions, and this one has conjured up an extraordinary replica of a teenage girl.

She lies naked on the icy table before me. Auburn hair cascades down over lily white, smooth shoulders and pulls my eyes down toward perfect breasts. Despite my better judgment, I feel my vision drawn past a tight stomach and diamond stud belly button ring to the fine patch of pubic hair between pale thighs. The illusion is beautiful. I want to see more, feel more of her warmth. I wish to be inside her beauty, and I feel my groin respond almost on its own.

Willing myself to turn away from the creature's lies, I shake my head and pull myself back to reality. I can smell the demon's overpowering sweat in this tiny room. Its filth is so strong that it's practically tangible. I run my hand along the tools, and the pristine feel of surgical metal under my fingertips reminds me of my task.

It wants me to think it's a girl, a woman ripe and ready for me, but I know the truth. I see the signs. The mole under her left nostril. The way she looks at me. The way she writes and drinks her mocha lattes with her left hand. I have smelled her from across the hallway of our apartment building, moisture, warmth, and raw sex trailing behind her in a hot cloud. She tried to draw me in with a smile and a seductive walk, but promiscuity is a sin. I know the truth.

It deceives. It lies.

The demon is fully awake now. It thrashes about on the table in wild, spasmodic movements, threatening to upset my table of sterile tools. Spitting and growling, the creature is biting the gag like a rabid dog. I would have expected no less from such a foul fiend.

When I pick up the number fifteen scalpel, its eyes grow wide. For the first time, I see irises of deep brown and dilated black pupils. It sees me and knows me. I can read its gurgling pleas. It is trying to call my name.

Demons lie. Demons placate. Demons reach out toward the weakness of men.

A wise man once said that the eyes are the windows to the soul, so I take those first. My scalpel skates across the eyeball for a second before plunging into the meat. It takes nothing more than a tug, a moist popping sound, and a toss to remove the demon's eye. It screams behind the gag and sends a stream of bloody spittle flying across the table.

When I cut out the second eye, it arches its back and pulls so hard against the restraints that, for a moment, I think it's going to break free. In the throes of agony, the beast manages to work free of the gag.

"Noooo!" It screams. "Please stop. Why are you doing this? Please, Mr. Br—"

I quickly block out its demonic voice before it can call my name and try to replace the gag. Yes, demons lie, but I see through the glamour and illusions. I haven't been wrong yet. As it stands, I see right down to the soulless heart of the beast, and I've got to rip it out before the demon spreads more of its deceit.

It's a challenge, but I finally get the gag back into its mouth and make sure to tighten it properly this time. Another large dose of the horse tranquilizer calms down the beast. One of the downsides of taking human form I suppose.

I pick up the bone saw and feel its satisfying weight in my hand. Filling the room with an insectile buzz, it whirs and vibrates to life as I finger the switch. The demon is passing out now, but it will wake when I start to cut. They always do.

Caterpillar

Craig Saunders

Jack pulled the cord tight around Mr. Davis' neck. Veins bulged in Jack's forehead. He could barely hear the screams coming from around the office. The prim women, the tight assed men strutting; each and every one of them was screaming for him to stop, but he was the one holding the gun. Jack could hear the blip-blip-blip of the dial tone from the receiver dangling against Mr. Davis' heaving chest. Must have dialed nine for an outside line, he thought, and laughed. The laughing just made them scream more.

Fuck 'em if they can't take a joke.

Davis dropped to the ground and Jack kicked the dead man in the temple. Then he turned the gun on the rest of them. Fuckers, the whole lot. Meeting in car parks, prim bitches giving head to their spiky haired colleagues...he would show them. How's this for a cock? Put your lips around this. Watch me blow.

"Jack! Jesus Christ, Jack, would you pay attention?" His boss was red in the face. Jack blinked. For a moment there he had wigged out. He shook his head clear and tried to concentrate on Mr. Davis' droning, soul-destroying voice.

"Sorry, Mr. Davis. You were saying?"

"If you'd listen to me instead of daydreaming, you'd get your work done on time and I wouldn't have to ride you all day."

Davis prodded a thick ream of papers on the table. "I want those figures punched by lunch. Get a move on, ok? There's a pal."

Pal. Jack's gall rose. He swallowed and smiled. "Of course, Mr. Davis. I'll have them done by lunch."

"Good man, less of that daydreaming, eh? You know I try to be a pal here. Makes the day go quicker, eh?"

"Yes, Mr. Davis."

His boss thumped him on the back, knocking Jack forward. The back of his chair gave out and he flipped, whacking his knee on the table. Jack swore under his breath and rubbed it. He looked around. Sarah and Emma from the secretarial pool were laughing at him from behind their hands.

His face reddened.

Jack pulled his cock out and Sarah bent over the photocopier. Her ass stuck in the air, her skirt bunched around her waist. She was wearing the stockings he liked today, just for him. His trousers fell down around his ankles. Her eyelids fluttered.

"Fuck me, Jack, fuck me where I like it."

He stepped closer, pushed the tip of his cock against her wet slit. That was all the lube she was worth. He put it against her tight ass.

As he was about to ram it home, he felt a hand reach between his legs, cupping his balls. He turned his head to look down and saw Emma smiling up at him.

The phone rang. Jack turned his red face away and crossed his legs. His trousers were suddenly uncomfortably tight. The girls carried on laughing. Sarah said something to Emma, and they giggled as they walked away, looking back over their shoulders at him. He picked up the phone.

"Jack, it's Johnson. What's happening with the Pickman accounts? I was expecting them in my inbox at six yesterday, and all I got was zilch. Accounting, that's what you do, right?"

Was everyone in this place a snarky asshole or a prim bitch?

"Sorry, Mr. Johnson. Mr. Davis pulled me off that. I'll get it to you as soon as I can."

"ASAP, Jack, and I mean today. It can't wait all fucking week."

"Yes, Mr. Johnson."

He hung up the phone before Johnson could say another word. Fucking bastard.

Jack pulled up the spread sheet and began entering the figures. £169,076.09.

£45.94 – photocopier paper. £3,705.90 – travel expenses. Fuck, he could travel round the world on that.

He tapped at the keyboard. His wrist ached. It had been aching like a bitch for a week now. Jack shook his hand free. He took some time out to stare at the ruby walls of his tiny cubicle. His troll doll, sitting on top of the monitor, looked back at him expectantly. *'When are you going to waste these fucks?'* it seemed to say. Perhaps that was just Jack's imagination.

He checked his wristwatch. Ten minutes had passed. Page one, done. He flicked through the sheaf of papers. Sixty to go.

Jack cracked his back, looked around. All he could see was the top of twenty other people's heads. He didn't even know who half of them were. They seemed to come and go, day in, day out, there was a different man, a different woman. They all had exciting jobs, working with computers. Is that what people get told these days? Pick a great career—use a computer.

He rubbed his sore knee and swore quietly to his troll. He hadn't had any career advice. If he'd have had his way, Jack would have joined the army young and learned interesting ways to kill people. Then he would have come to work here. It would have stood him in good stead.

Can you work an Excel spreadsheet?

No, but I can strip an SA-80 in twenty-two seconds, and put it together again in another thirty-three. Plus, I can break your wrist with one hand.

He drifted and tapped.

He looked up. Thirty minutes.

Time for a coffee break. Jack stood, his back creaking and aching like a set of balls on a month long hiatus from fisticuffs.

He strode to the coffee machine, took a plastic cup and poured himself another dose of humble juice. He added two sugars. Jack's waist could look after itself, pretty much. He'd never be fat. Instead he was gawky. That was what it was called. Gawky.

He did push-ups every night. Jack had a chest these days. He hadn't had one at school. Stupid fuck kids who thought they were cool giving him wedgies, pinching and punching. Made his life a living hell. But what did that matter now? Jack was a man now. He had a job.

One day, he'd show them.

Chris Kitchener came up behind Jack and startled him. He slopped some coffee on the cuff of his shirt.

"Steady there, mate. Sorry I made you jump."

"Didn't make me jump, I just slipped," Jack mumbled. Fuckers. Everyone here called you mate, or pal, or chum. Everybody pretended to be your friend, when all they really wanted to do was suck you dry, turn you into a useless husk of a man so their bitches could come along after and fill you with their piss and bile.

19

He took the coffee pot and smashed the glass into Chris'
face. The coffee burned his face and he screamed. Chris' left eye
popped as a shard of glass entered the juicy orb, his skin melted in
the heat.

Jack stood over Chris' writhing form and put his finger in the
eye juice, watching with delight at the horror on Chris' face as he
took that juice and put it on his tongue.

It tasted like jelly babies.

Chris touched his shoulder. "You alright, man?"

"Yep," Jack forced a smile. "Fine. See you."

It was all he could manage. He walked away, coffee cup in
hand, the coffee burning his hand as he walked. Plastic cups. Just
one more torture.

Jack walked in a daze back to his cubicle with his ironic
chair, the chair that hated him. He twiddled with the handle underneath and got the back to stick in the upright position. He scooted it
forward so he was at his desk and took a sip of his scalding coffee.
Jack's lips burned and for a moment he savored the pain. That woke
him up more than the coffee itself.

He set it aside and worked on figures. An endless stream
of figures, dancing before him like sinners at the Gates of Hell. He
wondered which figure represented the Area Manager's tryst with
his secretary. Which figure represented the sneak trip to McDonald's
for breakfast, or who was waxing his travel expenses with a trip to
the shops to buy his wife some lingerie? Let's spice things up a little,
Mavis, you go on top tonight, in this bra and panties set from Vic-
toria's Secret. Don't tell anyone, but it's bought and paid for by the
share holders. How'dya feel now, huh? Do you want it up the ass?

He chuckled to himself, then took another scalding sip of
his coffee to wash away the imaginary image of Mavis, folds of fat
seeping free of her 44DD bra.

Ouch.

Figures. Figures. Jack began tapping. By twelve, he had
reached page thirty. He took out a banana sandwich his mom had
made him. Jack ate while he worked. He pushed numbers around,
and it felt good to bully something. It set him free for a time. He
dreamed, but only on the surface of things. He didn't let it go too
deep. He had work to do.

"Jack! Pal! How're those accounts coming?"

"I'm on it, Mr. Davis," said Jack, biting back a grimace.

"I'm relying on you."

"Yes, Mr. Davis. Working through my lunch," he told him, and hated himself for sucking up. Fuck off, he thought, but only to himself.

"Good man. Just as soon as you can. Mail 'em to me, eh?"

Eh, fuck.

"Yes, Mr. Davis."

Jack's boss walked away, and Jack turned back to his screen. All work and no play. His troll sneered at him. It called him a pussy.

"Shut up," Jack told it, and flicked his screen up. Numbers. It was all done by numbers. Everything could be reduced to numbers, or so the mathematicians said. But Jack knew the truth; numbers reduced *you*.

He set to tapping, and the pages flew by. For a few blissful hours Jack had no daydreams. The clock ticked past, marking off numbers on the face. People passed his cubicle—seven. He went to the toilet. Twice.

His phone rang. Twice he picked it up. More work. Demands from Mr. Davis. Twice he didn't answer it.

Then, it was just him and the numbers, sucking his soul out through his eyeballs.

By four, he was finished. Five cups of coffee down.

Jack hit send. See if Davis could wiggle his way out of that one.

He looked up. There were fewer heads. It must be cigarette break time. He wished he smoked. Those bastards took up half the day developing cancer. If Jack got cancer, it would be for free.

He almost wished he had cancer. A day off wouldn't hurt.

Johnson. Fuck Johnson.

Jack stretched his legs out. The back of his chair chose that moment to pussy out on him. His legs flipped in the air again. He whacked the same knee.

"Fuck!"

Heads turned in unison. He wanted to put his fingers up to them. Jack knew one of those bastard bitches stayed late and switched the chair back on him every day. No matter what he did, he always got the same chair.

He put his face down.

Fuck Johnson. He brought up the Internet. Click, click. What a beautiful variation from tap, tap.

Variation, Jack realized, was why people kept on living. They waited for their shows to change, they tried tea one day instead of coffee, hot chocolate instead of tea, a mistress instead of a faithful wife.

But they would never be free. They wanted variation, but within a strict set of boundaries. They wanted it to be comfortable. They wanted parameters.

There were no parameters. You didn't have to put up with the same old dross. Jack knew that. If you just had the imagination. You could go anywhere.

Click, click. The sound of an empty chamber. Flick knife opening. Hammer on nail.

Tap, tap. Brought to mind a drip. Endless. Rhythmic. Crazy-making. The sound of every day.

Click…clickclickclick…click. New patterns. New rhythms. Alien and new. Nothing familiar about the sound.

It relaxed Jack. A flood of pictures poured over him. Words. Stories, news stories, alien abduction stories, stupid-people stories, conspiracy stories. He washed in it.

Four fifty-five p.m. Time to get his jacket on. He looked around him. People were standing up, stretching out their aching backs, pulling on jackets.

Jack caught a nameless drone's eye. A dead, soulless eye. No imagination.

Put him out of his misery. Go on. Take the axe. Look down. The axe is already in your hand. A swing, a hit. A cracking sound, and the axe is stuck. The rest of them look around. Perhaps they can all jump you before you pull the axe out. Perhaps you can beat them to it. Nothing to it, but to try.

Jack grabbed the handle of the axe, and pulled. The sound he could hear was screaming. His. They were silent. Silent, waiting for freedom. Waiting to break out.

The axe came free. For a moment, he thought he saw them smile.

He shrugged his jacket on.

A nod to a co-worker. No words. There is no room for words in a world of figures.

Jack shouldered his way out the door, his phone ringing behind him.

It would be Johnson. Too late.

He walked slowly to his car. Put the key in the ignition. Pulled away, then a second before it was too late, slammed on the brakes as Sarah pulled out in front of him.

She threw him the finger and *he accelerated into the side of her car, staving it in. He leapt out of the car and ran around to the driver's side, put his foot through the window, smashing the glass. He reached through and grabbed a handful of her pert, prim hair and rammed her head into the steering wheel, again, and again, and again.*

Jack mouthed 'sorry,' even though the stupid bitch had pulled out on him.

He drove sedately home.

Put the key in the lock. Pushed open the door.

"Jack!"

"Yes, mother. I'm back."

He took his jacket and hung it on the peg. Only then did he go into the front room. It was his rebellion. Great things start out small.

"You're early. You can do my feet before dinner."

He looked at the obese woman before him, splayed out on the couch. She couldn't reach her own feet. It was a miracle she could still get out of bed. Her mouth held a cruel smile, maliciously bent.

"OK, mother," he said meekly.

He walked to the shed, took the saw out. He oiled the blade lovingly, running a finger along the jagged teeth. He walked, sedately, back to the living room. He could afford to take his time. The fat, sick bitch wasn't going anywhere.

He did her feet. He always did as he was told.

He tidied the kitchen, wiped the crumbs from the sofa.

And that, thought Jack, was another perfect end to a perfect day.

He turned on the computer in his bedroom. For a few blissful hours, it was just words and pictures. No demands. Instant access. He dabbled with some sedition, dallied over a little porn, did a crossword. Words and pictures. The sheer joy of it eased his shoulders.

He wound his neck in, went to the bathroom and washed the blood from his hands.

Then he stripped and changed into his pajamas.

Jack brushed his teeth carefully, taking time over each separate tooth. He squeezed some blackheads from his chin. Before he lay down, he got on the floor and did forty push-ups.

Panting, he threw himself into bed.

Jack lay perfectly still for a while, just staring at the ceiling, with a smile fixed on his face. Just another day of holding it all in. It was amazing, he thought, what you could do if you set your mind to it.

He turned onto his side and closed his eyes.

Cold Air

Edward R. Rosick

Helen and I became friends during our 4th term of medical school. On the surface it seemed an odd relationship: Helen was forty-five and divorced, with three grown children; I was twenty-eight, an overweight ex-molecular genetic technician and bored with my job and my life.

Relationships have a way of bringing people to new and unusual places. But the joining of our odd couple, was to take both of us down the very stairs of hell.

Our final anatomy class of the winter semester was *Anatomy 700: Advanced Dissection of the Human Nervous System*. We spent countless hours in the anatomy lab huddled around stinking cadavers as we shifted through the brachial plexus and all its branches, and searched for the tiny chorda tympani and their hundreds of kin.

It was a tedious project, one that taxed our bodies and minds to their limits. During those days, standing hour after hour over the cadavers, our own bodies reeking of formaldehyde, Helen and I learned about each other as we took solace in our shared burden.

I still remember quite clearly how she expressed her abhorrence for the anatomy lab. We were in her apartment during a rare free afternoon, sitting in front of a small gas space heater that struggled against the cold winds that battered her cramped upper-floor apartment. I sat on the couch and let the currents of heat work into my skin while Helen made hot chocolate for us in the kitchen. When I heard her mutter something under her breath I left my warm enclave and walked over to her.

"I hear talking to oneself is the first sign of insanity," I said.

Helen, dressed in blue jeans and a thick wool sweater looked at me with her emerald-green eyes. "Sometimes I think that next time I walk into that stinking anatomy lab all the cadavers will sit up from their tables, form a big circle around me and start giving a discourse on life, liberty, and the pursuit of happiness."

"We'll be done in there after this term," I said after we had walked back into the living room with our hot chocolate—liberally fortified with 100-proof bourbon—and sat down on the couch.

"Once we're out you'll probably decide that you miss the place."

She shook her head. "No way. When we're in there hour after hour teasing out those tiny nerves and vessels, I start to feel…" her voice trailed off and she gave a deep sigh.

"Feel like what?"

"I start to feel like them. I start to feel so fucking old and tired. I bet that if I lay down next to one of the cadavers no one would notice."

"I would notice." I put my arm gently around her shoulder. "You're not alone. I feel just as tired."

She managed a weak smile and laid her head on my shoulder. "Douglas, you're so young. Sometimes I wonder why we're still friends."

I pulled away for an instant, thinking she had grown tired of me, thinking she had found herself another man.

"Oh, don't worry, I'll make it through." She got off the couch and turned up the thermostat.

"Of course you will. We both will," I proclaimed, realizing she wasn't talking about leaving me at all.

It was at that instant, that I saw in her eyes a dark, vacuous glimmer before she suddenly leaned down and kissed me full on the lips. Just as quickly as she had kissed me, Helen moved away and stood by the heater.

"Haven't you ever wondered about the cadavers?" she said in a soft, far-away voice. "Haven't you ever wondered who they were, where they were from, what they did with their lives?"

I was still shocked at the kiss. "No," was all that I managed to mutter.

"I have." She came back over to me, squatted down and placed her hands on my knees. "All the energy those people once had, all the life that once flowed from their pores, now all gone. It's like a giant vacuum in that lab, a huge cold maelstrom of dead, and I swear I can feel it drawing me in. That's what I hate about the lab. Not the smell, not all the inane, worthless details we're forced to memorize. I hate the death."

"We'll always have to deal with death," I said. "All of our patients will eventually die."

She got up with a frown on her face. "But that's different."

26

I was utterly perplexed. "How is it different?"

She frowned. "It's just different. When people die there's still that spark, still a core of life in them. Even now we can bring people back from the dead four, even five minutes after they have clinically died. And who really knows what happens after that, how long their energy, their soul is with them."

"Then where does the soul go?"

Helen's eyes sparked and danced, and I told myself it was just a reflection from the outside setting sun, just too much bourbon in the hot chocolate.

"That's the question, isn't it?" She smiled fiendishly. "That's the one we'd all like to know the answer to."

After that discussion, we didn't talked about the subject of death again for months. The second year of medical school quickly turned into the third, and we were thrust into our hospital externships.

Helen and I picked the same hospital to work at, and managed to schedule our first two rotations of pathology and emergency medicine together.

I witnessed the first step in her decent to madness one morning after we had finished up an autopsy in the pathology lab. The body was that of a fifty-two year old man, an alcoholic and drug addict who looked more like one hundred and fifty-two. His liver was rotted and his intestines were filled will large chunks of feces. After one hour I left to go get some coffee in the cafeteria. Helen stayed on, finally meeting me in the cafeteria an hour later. Her blue scrubs were stained brown and red, her graying brown hair was frazzled, and there were dark circles under her bloodshot eyes.

"You look tired," I said.

She blew across her steaming cup of coffee and looked at me over the edge of her glasses. "I was on call last night. I haven't had any sleep in thirty-one hours. I should be fucking tired."

"What was it down there in the path lab?" I asked. "Why did you stay so long? We had already done everything we needed to."

"Do you really want to understand?"

"I want to try."

She looked around as if scanning the cafeteria for spies. "Last week I got a chance to do an almost instant autopsy. The guy wasn't dead for more than fifteen minutes."

27

I shrugged. "So you did one yourself, we've all—"

"No, that's not it," she interrupted. "I felt it. For the first time I really felt it."

As her eyes burned into me, and her hot breath smelling of coffee and unbrushed teeth washed over my face, I wanted to leave, to run from her and never look back. But instead I asked the very thing she wished me to ask. "Felt what?"

"Cold air." She giggled a bit, a small, high-pitched sound, like something that would come from a small, wounded animal. "That's what I call it. The leaving of the soul. Cold air. It's—," She stopped and looked around again. "I shouldn't say any more. There are too many people here, too many ears."

I reached over and held her hands. "We all know bodies get cold after a person dies. That doesn't mean it's their soul leaving them."

"No!" she exclaimed, then quieted her voice. "No, it's not just the body getting cold. I can feel a real current, a movement outward from the body. I don't know just yet what it is exactly, but I will, Douglas. I will."

Even now I ask myself how I couldn't have noticed what was happening. How couldn't I see the dark, swirling kaleidoscope carrying me away in its awful wake into Helen's private world of insanity? Perhaps I didn't want to see. Perhaps I did see and decided not to care, for it was also during that unholy time when the change in our physical relationship occurred. It happened without any notice and it happened with her in control.

We were at my apartment a week after our initial talk about her 'discovery.' I was sitting on the floor going over some notes, when she came over and we playfully started wrestling as we had done many times in the past. She pinned me down then suddenly thrust her hand between my legs, rubbing my penis into a hard erection. She said nothing as she pulled off my clothes and began kissing my chest, biting my nipples, constantly moving further down until her mouth began to work up and down my shaft. Her tongue swirled over my balls while she jerked my member and turned my most erotic fantasies into dull imitations of this real life pleasure. She continued this relentless assault until I came.

"Now you learn how to do me," she said victoriously, then firmly pushed my head down between her legs to her wet, shaved vagina, and proceeded to teach me about things I was too ashamed to even think about.

For everything we did do, we never made love. I clumsily tried now and then to enter her, but she was strong and quick, and since I, being a virgin, did not really know what to do, I acquiesced to her hands and mouth. I really never complained, yet still I yearned to be one with her, still dreamt of being inside her, being on top, being in control.

During this new time, this time of joy and love, I almost believed she had forgotten her dark questions. But she was not done yet. Her next "discovery" proved to be more insane than the first.

"I've found it!" she exclaimed one evening in her apartment after a brutal day in the ER. I was in no mood for another monologue on death and the soul.

I got one anyway.

Helen ran over to me as I stood in her kitchen making coffee. She placed her hands in my pockets and began to run her tongue lightly underneath the lobule of my right ear. "The final piece of the puzzle. You know where I found it?"

I took a deep breath and slowly exhaled. "No, Helen. Where?"

"Here." She rubbed the glans of my penis through my pants pocket.

I reached down with my right hand and put it on top of hers. "Helen, don't you think that, that maybe you should stop with this obsession about—"

"Obsession?" she said. Her voice rose in intensity with every syllable. "This is no obsession. This is a discovery of the ages."

"What is it now?"

"The life, Douglas, the power of life. The heat opposite cold air." She unzipped my pants, and pulled out my cock and began to jerking it into an erection. "I knew there had to be something more. I knew that the cold air was just a screen, a veil put there by God or nature or whoever controls it all to conceal the real truth."

I said nothing while she continued to masturbate me and talk softly into my ear.

"It's the life-force Douglas, the chi, the essence of what we are, the primeval spark of life glowing brightly before it's extinguished forever." She dropped to her knees and began working the head of my dick with her mouth and tongue. I came in less than a minute.

"Here, Douglas," she said as she stared at my softening dick, "here from where our life begins, here is where life breathes its last breath, is where it ends and begins. I've seen it, Douglas, and it's the most beautiful sight in the whole damn universe."

I knew what she was going to try next. And maybe because I knew, because it scared me like nothing else ever has, I did nothing. Nothing except wait and try to force the disgusting thoughts from my mind, tried to bury them deep underneath mountains of facts and logic.

The denial lasted all of three days.

Helen had worked in the ER late into the early morning hours. Her car was in the shop with a busted timing belt and I offered to pick her up. She was reluctant at first, but then accepted my offer. She said her shift ended at five in the morning. Of course that night I could not sleep, so I arrived there at four.

I walked into the ER to find the nurse, Marvin Sanell, a rail-thin man with a face like a ferret, sorting through charts and drinking coffee in frantic sips. "Where's Helen?" I asked.

"Down in the path lab," he mumbled.

"What's she doing down there?"

He finally looked up at me with beady eyes. "I don't know. She took a patient down there about an hour ago."

I sighed, trying to control my growing impatience. "Who was the patient?"

He flipped through some patient files. "A MVA victim we got in last night." He closed the files then again looked over at me. "To tell you the truth, I really don't know why she was so hip on getting into him. I mean, except for having that half-ton pickup turn his liver and kidneys into cheap ground beef, the boy was in fine shape."

His last phrase, 'the boy was in fine shape,' kept running through my mind as I rushed down to the path lab. The basement was cool and silent, the halls dimly lit by a few hissing fluorescent lights. I almost called out to her, wanting to warn her to stop whatever she was doing before I entered. But I remained quiet as I walked in.

Pathology was partitioned off into four cubicles, and from the end of the lab I could hear sounds I knew were wrong. I walked down and saw that the third cubicle was closed off. I could hear Helen's heavy breathing, and, God forgive me, while one part wanted to run, another part of me wanted to see.

I got down on my hands and knees, the tile floor cold and greasy, and crept through the curtains partitioning off the cubicles. At the third I hesitated, only for an instant, then parted them.

Helen was half-nude, her skirt, pantyhose, and shoes off, crouched on the table directly over the cadaver. From the corner of the cubicle I could see only one side of her face, but even that view showed me a dark facet of her that I never imagined could exist.

She hungrily placed the young man's penis, which was surprisingly fully erect, into her vagina; her feet tightly clenched the slippery sides of the steel table. She began to pound her ivory-white ass up and down while she placed one hand on the man's hairy chest to steady herself and used the other to rub her clitoris. Only when she was finished, only after she emitted a loud, orgasmic moan and collapsed on top of the cold, dead body, did I leave.

I don't remember much of the next few minutes; there was just a vague sensation of movement up stairs and through antiseptic corridors, past questioning faces and wheelchair bound patients. Walking outside, I was hardly aware of the biting cold. My car sat waiting, a rubber and steel chariot that could take me away, and I believe I would have left and never come back had I not heard her voice.

"Douglas?" Helen called out. As she came closer, I could see her face. She was smiling.

I stood by the car, afraid to say anything. Without another word she walked up to me and kissed me deep and hard, her hands caressing my back, chest, and crotch. I was totally repulsed as the bright, painful images of her impaled on the corpse screamed in my mind, but in my loins my sexual urges were at full force. My penis was hard despite my mental disgust and my hands worked on her body, clawing under her skirt, finding her vagina hot and dripping with desire.

With one hand, Helen reached behind me, opened the car door and shoved me in. After she had my pants down to my hips and her skirt hiked up she guided my aching member into her vagina. The same vagina that just minutes before had contained a corpse's penis. The thought of it almost made me lose my erection, but then she started to buck and rock on top of me, and I let myself go, forced

31

myself to forget it all. I tore her bra off and squeezed her nipples hard, and she responded by pulling my dick out of her vagina and placing it in her ass before pounding up and down even harder than before. I felt flesh give, tear and didn't care as I felt myself explode inside her.

Helen never asked that morning if I had watched her in the path lab and I didn't ask. During the next days and weeks I played a game with myself, a great and horrible game called denial. It was a game that I was becoming very good at.

She was just getting ready to take a shower one morning, standing in front of a full-length mirror in my bedroom. Suddenly she twirled around to face me. "It's working, Douglas," she said excitedly. "It's really working!"

"What are you talking about?" I asked, trying to hide the fear in my voice.

"I've wanted to tell you," she said finally, in a voice like a child who has been caught in a lie, "but I didn't know exactly how to say it."

"Say what?" I asked instead of saying: *I know, Helen, that you've had a little fetish these past few months called necrophilia, but I don't want you to say it because I love you and if you say it I might start to realize that you are totally insane and by loving you that makes me part of that insanity.*

She sat down on my bed with a mischievous grin on her face. "Remember what I told you two months ago, about finding the opposite of the cold air, about discovering the source of the life force?"

I nodded.

"I want you to look."

"Look at what?"

"At me," she said, a hard conviction in her voice. "I want you to look and tell me if you see anything different."

She stood up and I saw her nude body as I had many times before, but then I began to see more. Her breasts seemed fuller and her hips no longer sagged. Her stomach was flat, and with that flatness came the realization that her stretch marks, the scars of childbirth, were gone.

She could tell from the look in my eyes that I had seen what she had hoped I would see. "I'm younger, Douglas," she blurted out. "I'm younger, and it's from—"

32

"Your discovery," I quickly intervened.

"Yes. My discovery." She said it in a clear monotone voice as her eyes locked hard on mine. "You were there in the pathology lab last month, weren't you?"

"Yes."

"I'm sorry you had to find out that way," she said to me in a soothing, caring voice. "Dear Douglas, I know it must have been hard for you to see, but—"

And it was at that point, at that phrase of hearing how hard it must have been for me, when I lost my composure. I pushed her back violently onto the bed.

"Helen, this has got to stop. This has got to stop now!" My voice was high with emotion, fueled by my anger and humiliation. "We can get you help. We can go to someone outside the hospital, someone who can help you realize just what's been happening to you."

Her eyes opened wide and she shook her head. "What's been happening to me is a literal re-birth, a new lease on life. Haven't you believed one word I've said?"

"It's not about believing you."

"What is it about?"

I stepped back from the bed. "It's about a perversion, a disgusting act that you can't even see as disgusting."

"But look!" she cried, standing up from the bed and running her hands over her own body. "Look at what I've gained, what I've discovered! Think what this means!" A defiant look spread across her face as she got up and placed my hands on her breasts. "Feel these, Douglas. Feel these and tell me they're the tits of a forty-five year old mother of three."

I backed away, my anger gone. I was unable to meet her gaze, unable to find a passage through her insanity.

"I know it's hard to believe. I know my methods are, well, strange, but I have found something. Something that poets and philosophers have dreamed about since we were banished from the Garden of Eden. I'm not quitting my search, Douglas. Not for anything."

Or anyone, I knew she meant. I walked into my small living room, feeling very alone and helpless, and the sudden loud ringing of my phone did not help my attitude.

"Yes?" I answered curtly.

33

"Is Dr. MacGuin, there?"

"No she's not," I lied. "Can I take a message for her?"

"Yes, that would be good. She said it was pretty urgent."

"Go ahead."

"This is Chuck Herbright, the nurse on the first night shift. Tell her that one of her patients she admitted through ER a couple days ago—"

"Name of the patient?"

"Leon Means. She wanted to know when he was crashing. I was just down in CCU and he's pretty much had it. They expect to bag him in the next couple hours."

"I'll give her the message if I see her." I hung up without another word and tried to stop my hands from shaking. Now she was getting information on when they died. Or almost ready to die.

I'll go see our staff psychiatrist, I thought to myself, *I'll go see him and tell him that Helen is not adjusting well to our externship and if only he could get her some time off—*

"Did someone just call?" Helen stood in the cramped hallway separating my bedroom and the living room, dressed in a conservative skirt and blouse, her hair still wet. "Was it from the hospital?"

"Yes."

"What did they say?"

I walked over to her and put my hands around her waist. "It doesn't matter. Let's sit down, have a drink and enjoy the evening."

"The call was about Lean Means, right?"

I nodded.

"I have to go now."

"Damnit, Helen, don't," I pleaded. "Just stay here. There are things about us that we need to talk about."

"What things?"

"I thought maybe we should think about moving in together."

"I don't know," she said coolly, and I knew she was really saying: *I don't need you anymore, Douglas. I don't care about you anymore.* Without another word she put on her shoes and coat and was gone.

I believe she knew I would follow her. Perhaps I thought I could stop her. Yet there is still a small, dark voice inside which whispers to me at night that perhaps I just wanted to watch.

I waited in my apartment for fifteen minutes, drinking and cursing, before I finally left for the hospital. I didn't really think she would come back to me, but I still had hope. Even as I pulled into the hospital parking lot, my car next to hers, I still had hope.

The CCU was quiet. I recognized Chuck Herbert as he sat watching the soft glow of the bank of heart monitors in front of him.

"Did Dr. MacGuin come through here?" I asked.

He looked up and nodded. "Yeah. About fifteen minutes ago." He said nothing more and looked back down at the monitors. Before I consciously knew what I was doing, I grabbed the front of his lab coat and pulled his face close to mine. "And where is she now?"

Chuck looked at me as if looking in the eyes of a lunatic. "She's in room A-206 with Means." With his eyes never leaving mine, he pointed to the sixth monitor to his right. Its EKG line was flat and noiseless. "Leon Means flatlined five minutes ago."

I let him go and walked quickly down the hall, not caring that I was acting like a madman. As I reached A-206, I stopped for a moment at the door, then slowly turned the handle. It was locked, as I knew it would be. And as I unlocked it, I was sure that Helen was aware, that like her, I had a master key to all the patient's rooms.

I opened the door, then locked it behind me. As I stood with my back to her, I could hear her talking to the just-deceased Leon Means.

He was a young black man, nineteen or twenty, tall, muscular, and even though I was alive and he dead, I was filled with jealousy. Helen stood on the left side of the bed, totally nude. She looked at me only once, our eyes locking for an instant, and in that tiny window of time I was looking at my Helen, the woman I had loved. Then she was gone, replaced by a stranger, a predator of souls.

With a victorious yank, Helen pulled the clean white sheet off of Leon's body and grabbed his dark, flaccid penis. Like a lover in heat, she stroked and licked Leon's member, and to my utter amazement, it became long and hard.

I tried to convince myself the next sight I witnessed was only the lights of the machines reflected off Leon's penis. It was a bright glow, shimmering rainbow waves like heat off black summer asphalt that danced and hummed around Leon's manhood.

With a dark, feral smile Helen climbed into the bed and

35

placed Leon's dick inside her eagerly waiting vagina. She bucked and rocked on top of him and bit the back of her hand to silence her cries of pleasure. Watching, I pulled my aching penis from my pants and began to masturbate. Like a wooden toy soldier I stood silent, aware that the woman I had loved had gone away to a dark and secret place from which I was forever barred entrance. After I had spilled my seed onto the room's carpeting, I locked the door behind me and left Helen in orgasmic throes of ecstasy.

I called in sick the next three days and kept myself in a constant alcoholic haze courtesy of a gallon of cheap bourbon. With all the drinking came frequent trips to the bathroom, and with all the urination came the pain. It was a minor irritation that I attributed to too much booze and masturbation. Yet the pain steadily increased and I began to notice a yellowish, stinking discharge.

I have gonorrhea, I thought. Helen had infected me with gonorrhea. With the realization came anger, a thick layer of hate that began to infest all corners of my soul.

It was sometime during the fourth morning that she came over. I noticed her car was still running in my parking lot. "I came for my books," Helen said as she stood on the porch. "I must've forgotten them the other night."

The other night she said, as if we had been out bowling and eating pizza. I stepped aside and let her in. "You know where they are," I told her.

I stood and watched as she pulled various medical texts from my bookshelf. "You could have asked me at the hospital," I said. "You didn't have to come over here to humiliate me."

"I didn't come over here to humiliate you. I just came over to get my books and to say good-bye. I've quit medical school."

"Quit? What are you going to do?" I asked, my rising rage in stasis for a moment.

"I'm moving out to California," she answered as she packed up the last of her books. "I'm going to work with a cryogenics team that I've been corresponding with."

In perfect lucidity I realized why she was going. Access. Access to dead bodies, dead young bodies that she could commit her perversions on until she was full and gorged.

She finished collecting her books and walked toward the door. I stepped directly in front of her, inches away from her face.

36

"You gave me gonorrhea."

"What?"

"You gave me gonorrhea," I repeated. "I've had pain and burning with urination the past three days, and now I have a discharge."

"I couldn't have given you gonorrhea or anything else, Douglas. I check all of my contacts thoroughly before I unite with them, plus I would have it and I don't. It's probably just a case of idiopathic urithitis, if you just—"

"You gave me gonorrhea and who knows what else, you perverted *bitch*!" I slammed up my right fist into her left cheek. The blow surprised her, and with the clarity of unbridled rage I knocked her down and wrapped both my hands around her throat before she could react.

I don't remember how long I was on top of her. I only remember that when her struggling ceased I was still choking her. Only when her eyes rolled back in her head did I release her. Yet as I lay on top of her, panting with terror and excitement, I realized I still had one more thing to do.

Trembling with fear and anticipation, I walked swiftly over to my desk and pulled out a small-bladed scalpel. I knelt down beside her and cut through her expensive slacks, her panty hose, and finally her black-lace panties, and if I had doubts about seeing what Helen had talked about, they were gone. For above and around her vagina was a dancing kaleidoscope of colors, a spectrum rich and full with vibrant hues of primeval life. I finally knew what she had meant, knew the joy she had felt as my tears fell freely onto her face. I quickly pulled off my jeans and jammed my cock inside her. I was finally on top, finally in control, and I realized even in death that Helen could still give me her love for a long, long time.

Artistic Subject

Adrian Ludens

Her pose brought to mind the timeless beauty of the Venus de Milo, but her thoughts dwelt strictly on the mundane.

The woman in front of me must be feeding a family of ten, Cassie thought. She shifted her grocery basket from one hand to the other and stretched her free fingers, letting them relax.

As the beleaguered cashier slowly scanned the items, space opened little by little for Cassie's modest selections. She carefully lined up two tins of Vienna sausage, eight packages of Ramen noodles—you had to buy eight to get the sale price—and a half gallon of skim milk. The milk wasn't the generic brand; Cassie had let herself splurge on 'the good milk.' The woman in front finished paying and pushed her heavily laden cart toward the exit. For no real reason, Cassie thought of an old west trapper, coaxing and prodding a pack mule along a desolate mountain pass. She giggled.

"Five seventy-eight," the cashier said in a monotone voice. Cassie handed the woman four ones, and four quarters.

"There's five," Cassie said, flashing her best smile. The cashier offered no visible response. Cassie dug in her pocket. As she retrieved her remaining change and began counting it out on her palm she silently prayed that she had enough. Counting out change was no big deal; money is money. But the milk had been thirty cents higher this week and Cassie secretly felt terrified at the prospect of coming up short.

That had only happened once, almost two months ago. She'd been daydreaming as she shopped and was startled to hear the total. Upon realizing that she was a full dollar and thirteen cents short, she stammered that she'd have to put something back. This announcement had been met by tightlipped indifference from the cashier, a snide smirk from the teen behind her and a clucking exclamation of sympathy from the woman two places back.

Isn't this delightful, Cassie had thought bitterly. She began to ask the cashier if she could put back the head of lettuce when the loudly sympathetic woman spoke up.

"Don't you put anything back! I've got a few dollars to help you along," she said in a voice loud enough for several lanes of shoppers to hear.

Cassie had felt her cheeks start to flush.

"That's really not necessary," she began.

"Just take it lady," the teen interrupted, "I don't wanna stand here all day."

Cassie's slight flush blossomed into a deep blush. She'd never shopped without keeping a running total in her mind ever since.

Still, she felt her heart beating faster as she counted the dirty change out on her sweating palm. She needn't have worried though. Cassie ended up with fifty-two cents to spare.

"And seventy eight," Cassie said, handing over the money. The cashier wordlessly gave her the receipt.

"Thank you." Cassie said then added tentatively, "I hope you have a nice day."

The woman looked surprised and stared at Cassie with watery blue eyes, as if noticing her for the first time.

"I hope you have a nice day too," she said, sounding sincere.

Cassie smiled and turned to go.

The cashier had begun scanning the next customer's items, but she continued on, raising her voice over the scanner's electronic chirp. "Let's meet here again tomorrow and we'll compare notes," she joked and Cassie laughed.

It was a nice idea, but it didn't happen.

As Cassie passed through the store's first set of automatic doors, she glanced at the bulletin board. Once she had noticed a want ad from someone asking for help housekeeping. It turned out to only be temporary—the woman had a broken wrist—but it was a great opportunity for Cassie to pick up some extra cash. Ever since, her eyes automatically went to the board.

Today, someone had lost their cat and was offering a reward for its return. Another person was giving away kittens 'to good homes.' Cassie thought it ironic and somehow sad. She smiled when she saw the business card of a real estate agent with the unfortunate name Guy Mann. Then she saw an ad on plain white paper, with black type. It read:

Artistic Subject Wanted

Will pay.

Please call:

The simple message concluded with a phone number. Cassie plucked the stick pin from the board and deftly caught the floating piece of paper with her other hand. Then she fished in her pocket for her last two remaining quarters and stepped to the pay phone. This sounded interesting. *And maybe I won't have to eat Ramen noodles every night next week*, Cassie thought. The phone rang twice in her ear and then:

"Hello?" A man's voice. Quiet and calm.

"Hi, I'm calling about the ad for an artistic subject..." Cassie trailed off, not sure what to say next.

"Of course," the man said. His voice was very soft. Cassie found it oddly comforting. "Are you interested in the position? I have an immediate need."

"Well, I'm certainly interested in seeing what it is that you do," Cassie replied.

"I would be happy to show you," the man replied agreeably, "Might you be able to stop by right away?"

"I think so. I mean, sure," Cassie amended.

"You'll want to bring along the ad itself," the man said.

Cassie was puzzled. "Why?"

"Turn it over."

Cassie did. Directions from the grocery store to the artist's home were printed on the back.

***

The large house looked like a mansion by Cassie's standards. She parked her car on the side of a large circular brick driveway. Lush hedges hid most of the house from the street. Cassie felt a twinge of jealousy at the home's beauty and seclusion. She rang the doorbell and unconsciously held her breath.

Please let me get this job, she thought, *but please don't let his idea of an 'artistic subject' be a girl who'll pose naked while he gets off.*

The door swung open and Cassie came face to face with a well dressed little man who smiled at her, bowed cordially, then beckoned her inside. Charmed, Cassie entered and surveyed the interior.

The sitting room was tastefully furnished with rich mahogany furniture. Gorgeous paintings of nature scenes decorated the walls. A polished coffee table squatted near the center of the room in front of a large black leather couch. Hundreds of books filled an

40

enormous bookcase. Cassie marveled at the man's home.

"Won't you sit down?" the man invited. He gestured toward the couch and Cassie perched on the edge.

"Can I offer you a glass of ice water?" her host asked.

"Yes, thank you," Cassie replied automatically. The artist poured her a glass from a crystal pitcher sweating in the middle of the table. Cassie sipped her water and glanced at an elaborate art tableau situated on the far side of the room.

"You live here in the city?" the man asked.

"Yes."

"From here originally?"

"No. I'm from upstate. I was going to school at the community college, but needed to take a semester off. "

"You are saving up for tuition to continue. Am I right?"

"Yes," Cassie admitted and sipped her ice water. She hoped it would cool the embarrassed flush from her cheeks.

"And are you working currently?"

"The job market has been less than ideal," Cassie replied.

The man threw back his head and laughed. If Cassie felt rattled by the man's line of questioning, he put her at ease again with that reaction.

"Perhaps I can help you," the man remarked.

Cassie nodded took another drink. As she did so, she glanced again at the art piece against the far wall.

"Would you like to take a closer look?" the artist invited. "That is one of my favorite pieces."

Cassie stood, swaying briefly. She felt a little lightheaded from standing up too quickly but carefully crossed the room.

It was a sculpture, Cassie saw, composed of seven ivory colored forearms reaching upward. Above, a small spotlight was mounted on the ceiling, casting a heavenly glow down on the cluster of reaching arms. A lush red velvet tapestry covered the base of the display. Cassie noted that the 'fingernails' were painted a shade that matched the velvet base. The effect was striking and, in Cassie's opinion, completely original.

"I call that piece 'Supplication'," the man said from behind her.

From the sound of his voice, Cassie knew he was still on the far side of the room, yet his words swirled around her shoulders and into her ears like smoke.

"To me it conveys the relationship between mankind and a higher power." The man continued, "Or, you may find it symbolic of a victim and their oppressor."

His voice had taken on a rather egotistic tone that Cassie didn't much care for. She was mesmerized by the piece however.

"So you take plaster casts?" Cassie heard herself asking. "Or do you do all the sculpting by hand?"

She felt another wave of dizziness wash over her. The hands blurred, as if waving goodbye. Despite drinking the better part of a glass of ice water, all the saliva had dried up in her mouth.

When the man didn't answer Cassie turned around to look at him. He stood at his front door. Both her host and the living room appeared fuzzy and drifted in and out of focus.

"My dear, though I am an artist, I am not a sculptor at all," the artist replied as he padlocked the door leading back the the safety of the outside world. "I am a taxidermist."

***

Cassie could smell a pungent chemical odor. She felt like a cork bobbing in water, but realized that though her body seemed to be in motion she could not move her arms or legs. Cassie heard soft footfalls, a rhythmic squeaking and someone's rapid shallow breathing. She realized the breathing was her own. Her mouth felt stuffed with cotton balls. Cassie tried to open her eyes but they seemed glued shut.

Her forward momentum suddenly ceased and Cassie's head drooped forward so that she could feel her chin on her chest.

"We shall begin our tour here," a male voice quietly announced. Cassie's brain reeled in confusion for several moments then the events of the afternoon snapped into focus.

Get up and run from him! Cassie mentally commanded. She might have told herself to burst into flames or sprout wings and fly with more success. Surrounded by darkness and unable to move her limbs, Cassie could only wait. The hands of her captor caressed her shoulders and she shuddered.

"Allow me to show you what no other living person has ever seen," the little man invited. Cassie felt his fingers slide up her cheeks and she cringed.

Light flooded in, drowning all other sensory information as she squinted at the sudden change. The self-proclaimed artist had removed her blindfold. He had apparently brought her to the end of a long hallway. To Cassie's left a beige wall retreated away from them. To her right she saw what looked like a series of holding cells as in a prison, but without bars. She glanced down and saw that her captor had removed all of her clothing and had used leather straps to tie her arms, legs and torso to a chrome wheelchair.

The initial shock from the brightness began to wear off and the man's carefully enunciated words gradually rose back to the surface of her consciousness. "As you will soon see, my museum is a work in progress."

Cassie looked again at the 'holding cells' and realized they were actually a series of small shallow rooms designed to house her captor's artistic creations.

What did he say he was? Cassie thought. *A taxidermist*! She remembered. Cassie considered him to be a kidnapper, murderer and madman. But her captor obviously thought of himself as an artist above all else. And now Cassie shuddered again as she realized that he was about to force her on a guided tour of his 'artistic' creations.

"I adore literature," the man was saying. "And I try to convey my appreciation with my art. Each tableau is a representation of a key moment from one of my favorite novels. This first one for instance—," her captor abruptly wheeled her chair forward and two figures seemed to lurch into view. Cassie gasped. The artist beamed.

"Your reaction is exactly how I felt when I read the passage where Lennie kills Curley's lovely wife by trying to stroke her hair yet accidentally breaks her neck instead!" Cassie gaped at the green glassy eyes of the slumping woman. Her gaze traveled up to the face of the hulking behemoth that held the dead woman. His bright blue glass eyes were set imperfectly in their sockets.

"That's by design," the artist quickly announced after following her gaze. "The man I used as my subject was the right size physically but had no mental defects. I had to compensate by adjusting the eyes to convey Lennie's shortcomings."

Cassie remained silent. These *were* human beings. A man and a woman who had been lured here, murdered and then stuffed to recreate something this madman had once read in a book. Their unnatural poses and contorted faces were a mockery of humanity.

"Haven't you read Steinbeck's *Of Mice and Men*?" her captor asked. Cassie shook her head. His lips pressed into a thin white line and he stepped back behind her chair. "This next display was actually my first creation."

Cassie's eyes swam with tears. A little boy of perhaps ten reached out with one arm into the pocket of the other figure, a man in a black cloak and top hat. The boy's face and hands were dirty and his clothes were shabby and threadbare.

"The irony here is rather humorous and worth mentioning," the artist prattled. "The wealthy 'mark' was actually a homeless transient, while my street urchin was obtained on his way home from a prestigious private school." He grinned at Cassie as if waiting for her to share his enthusiasm. Instead she felt nausea threaten to overwhelm her. Obtained on his way home from school? Cassie didn't want to look at the abomination on display so she gazed at her captor instead.

"Surely you must recognize this one," he said and raised his eyebrows. "The boy is the Artful Dodger! Dicken's *Oliver Twist*! Ring any bells?"

Cassie shook her head and the little man made a show of groaning aloud. Then he sighed and pushed her forward to the next exhibit. Cassie wrinkled her nose in surprised disgust. Two large hogs stood on hind legs on either side of a small table covered with playing cards and shot glasses. The swine's lips were curled into malicious smirks that made them look surprisingly human. "And here are Karl and Dick," the artist announced.

"At least they're not humans," Cassie whispered. It was the first time she had spoken since regaining consciousness.

The little man only scowled. "That was a joke. They're obviously Napoleon and Snowball from George Orwell's classic novel *Animal Farm*."

"I don't know what you're talking about and I want to go home now," Cassie told him.

He gaped at her, mouth hanging open. Finally he shrilled, "For God's sake! It's an easy read!" Spittle flew from his mouth and Cassie felt convinced that he would lash out and strike her. Instead he angrily shoved her wheelchair forward.

Cassie saw that a wall of stone and mortar hid the next exhibit from view. "I hand-sewed the jester costume for this artistic subject myself, then hid my handiwork behind this wall that I built stone by stone," the artist complained, "But I suppose the ingenuity of my homage to Poe's *The Cask of Amontillado* is lost on a blond zero like yourself."

They moved forward again and Cassie cried out, clenching her hands into helpless fists of impotent fury. A hairy, naked man sneered in glassy-eyed lust from his position on top of a grimacing teenage girl. The bed sheets lay crumpled at the foot of the bed. "I needed help getting this one just right," the madman admitted. "So I let my 'Humbert' get into character first before I took his life—"

"You're fucking insane!" Cassie shrieked. Hot tears scalded her cheeks. Fueled by vindictive rage she struggled against the straps that held her down. "This is not art! This is garbage excreted by a diseased and depraved mind!"

The little man staggered back as if she'd struck him. All the color drained from his face. For a moment it looked like his knees might buckle and her captor would sprawl onto the concrete in a dead faint. Any glimmer of hope Cassie had was immediately snuffed out as the little man instead leaned forward until their noses were almost touching. His skin was ashen but his eyes glittered with the juices of insanity and cold fury.

"You ignorant little pinhead; how DARE you criticize my art!" He straightened abruptly, chin up and chest out. "I thought you might appreciate what I have created, but I see now that I was gravely mistaken."

He moved her chair forward for the last time. The next display was incomplete. A thirty-something man in a business suit posed awkwardly in one corner.

Her eyes skimmed over an array of liquid-filled jugs, scalpel blades, heavy duty scissors, knives, fleshing tools, and tumblers neatly arranged on a large rolling tray table without really knowing what they were. She guessed their purpose however.

The artist lifted the footrests of the wheel chair into the air and locked them into place. Did he intend to break her legs? Cassie struggled vainly and watched as he strode across the tiny room. He retrieved a large metal tube from the table. The man shook the tube, held it up to his ear and listened. Cassie heard a faint sound that reminded her of nails on a chalkboard and a squeaking that wasn't coming from the wheelchair.

"Here's another instance where I want to make this display as authentic as possible. I will recreate the most shocking scene in the novel. I'll film the process for reference and that way I'll be able to preserve you and your attacker in the most realistic pose possible."

45

A sheen of sweat glistened on the artist's forehead. He grinned like a hyena.

"Your facial expression, how much exposed organ tissue is created as a result, how your body will contort; I won't have anything less than perfection in my final creation."

The artist stepped forward and stood between Cassie's outstretched naked legs. His sweaty hands struggled to twist the lid from the shaking metal tube.

If Cassie had realized what waited inside the tube and where the starving creature was headed next, she might have started screaming immediately. But Cassie disappointed the artist one final time.

She hadn't read Bret Easton Ellis' *American Psycho* either.

Plague Hulk

Glynn Barrass

When the ship was first sighted drifting into port, the small harbor town fell into an uproar. But talk of calling in the Army or the Navy became nothing but that... talk. Town officials finally decided to alert the European Center for Disease Prevention and Control, but, until such representatives arrived, the town's general consensus was to stay away from the port.

Ash and his gang, however, formulated a different way to deal with the problem.

Using a stolen boat and dressed from head to toe in oiled leather boiler suits, their intention was to board the ship and liberate its passengers of their valuables.

Not necessarily a solution to the town's terrible problem, but it provided a means to address the gang's cash shortage issues.

They'd brought no weapons with them. None were needed. The ship's occupants had been dead some twenty years. Bundled off to die in shame, their carcasses haunted the ship, one of hundreds sent adrift on the Atlantic after the plague had decimated the majority of the South East of England.

The three thieves: Ash, Terry and Will, proceeded with their mission unperturbed by anything as mundane as moral decency. Leaving the harbor's breakwater behind, the boat was hit by one swell after another as the sea revealed *its* distaste for their mission.

"Keep it steady," Will said, seated at the bow. In answer, the swell tossed the boat angrily in its wrath. At one particularly high leap, Terry emitted a strangled gurgle from behind his divers mask. He barely succeeded in removing it before he began to divulge slick gobs of vomit down onto the deck.

Ash, looking down at his friend's steaming deposits, had to hold back his own rancid expulsion.

The swell continued, bumping them about wildly as they left the breakwater far behind. From his spot at the stern, Ash suffered the least from the tumult. But despite his position, Ash took his mask off in order to laugh as he witnessed Terry slip and fall over in his own vomit. His giggling fit mingled with Terry's exclamations of disgust.

Ash's mask fell to the floor. The respirator crackled, making the earpiece in Will's hood shriek loudly. Will screamed.

Ash continued to laugh.

Will added his mask to those already discarded, his expression filled with dark-eyed hatred. His hair protruded comically after being restrained beneath his hood. Ash turned his appearance into another reason to laugh. Will and Terry glared; Ash hid his tear-stained face in his hands.

Will spat and swore.

Ash's problem was that everything around him appeared far more entertaining than it actually was. Earlier he'd downed LSD and vodka with the goal of gaining the euphoria he thought he'd need to board a ship brimming with the dead.

Unfortunately, his actions also had the effect of infuriating his already nervous companions.

"How many pills did you take, dipshit?" Will said, scowling.

"Yeah, you silly, fat fuck," Terry added, scrubbing the vomit from his leg.

Choking away his laughter, Ash wiped his face before grinning at the two. "Chill out guys, I got us here, didn't I?"

While the three were heckling, the plague hulk had sneaked closer. It floated thirty feet away from the bow.

"Now that's what I'm talking about," Ash added with enthusiasm.

All heads turned to the hulk. The huge, rusted freighter, floated between the roiling swells like a diseased, water-bound pupa.

The engine complained and then roared in frustration as Ash turned the rudder towards the port side. His companions quickly removed gas-powered grapnel guns from their backpacks for use on the hulk's rotten deck.

Will and Terry crouched and discharged their gun's wire-cabled grapples, filling the night air with a pair of loud *pops*. Their jobs done, both grapnel guns were tied under the seats to keep the thieves' escape route certain.

With a quite sensible fear of the plague, the men replaced and resealed their masks.

Throttling the boat down, Ash watched while Terry, then Will, used the wires to straddle up the side of the hulk. They climbed with an efficiency he found quite intimidating; the drugs in his system making him feel unsteady on his feet as he himself deboarded the boat to begin climbing the freighter's side.

Dark, filth encrusted metal, first wet and slippery then dry and flaky, scraped against his feet as he ascended. His muscles strained and he kept his eyes closed as he climbed between rows of sinister, black-eyed portholes. Soon his scrambling climb was almost complete. He tumbled over the guardrails and finally set foot upon the deck of the plague ship.

Faceless heads greeted him, his companions' glass-buttoned eyes staring down as he absorbed his new surroundings.

The deck was massive, dark and rusty and a hundred feet long from bow to stern. Before the bow stood the pilothouse. Dark windowed and topped with twisted aerials, it stood sentinel to the sea but not to the three human violators.

"Wow," Ash murmured.

Side by side against the starboard towered two huge cranes. Looming up from the deck like a pair of giant, skeletal arms, their paintwork lay chipped, their wire tendons hanging limp and exposed.

Ash expected the deck to be littered with corpses. His anxious and hesitant movements were quite apparent as he straightened himself up.

Terry spoke first. "Still tripping?"

"I'm wondering where all the bodies are," Ash replied.

"They pushed them all into the hold." Will said. "I saw it on the Discovery Channel."

Will set off towards the pilothouse, closely followed by Terry. Crossing the deck after them, Ash warily examined the cranes before continuing to question Will.

"What about security locks?" he asked, closing in behind them.

"Do your research instead of popping pills," came Will's sour reply. "The poor bastards were all too weak to fight or even walk when they stuffed them into these things. They'll all be rotted up down below."

Will's deadpan delivery filled Ash with a cold revulsion. Even though he'd been preparing himself for the sight, the thought of actually witnessing the charnel sight below did not sit well with him.

49

Following Will towards the pilothouse, they climbed and crossed two enormous hatchways. Each spanned the width of the ship from starboard to portside. As far as Ash knew, their rusted lids concealed a very grisly cargo.

"What kinda stuff did this thing actually hold?" Terry asked as he entered the shadows beneath the pilothouse.

"Before the corpses?" Will replied, his tone filled with sarcasm. "Look at the size of this thing. Probably trains and bits of oil platforms, jack-ups and the like."

Before it became a haven for the plague, Ash thought grimly.

Within the shadows, the door to the pilothouse lay open to a deeper, far more sordid darkness.

Will disappeared inside, followed by Terry a moment later. Ash tilted his head, scowling up at the sky beyond the jagged roof of the pilothouse. The stars warped and wavered, blinking down at him with sparkling glee. He swore and entered the ship.

Silence and darkness surrounded Ash. The sensation was only momentary for a second later a bright beam of light appeared to push the darkness back towards the room's shadowy corners.

A tall figure loomed before Ash. Slick and shiny, its brown face lay featureless except for a pair of round, glassy eyes. Momentarily taken aback, the fear quickly dissipated when he realized the apparition was merely Terry.

Terry wandered around the room. Will followed, his chest-mounted lamp beaming like a lighthouse beacon.

"Put your lamp on Ash," Will ordered. Ash reciprocated.

Fully illuminated, the room now appeared both bleak and abandoned. A rectangular space of stained white walls, it lay devoid of anything but filth and stagnant pools of water. Three pairs of ladders lined the far wall.

"Down," Will said. Turning, he headed towards the ladders.

A few splashing steps had Ash by Terry's side.

"Take a look at the floor man," Terry said. Ash did so and noticed that within the grimy pools lay a multitude of square indents lined with gaping bolt holes; evidence that machinery and consoles had been removed.

"Seems someone got here before us." Terry said, forcing a chuckle.

"All that stuff was taken years ago." Will replied. "Now get a move on." Already descending, he was halfway down the hole beneath the ladder.

Terry was quick behind him, the sounds of his feet joining the clangs already reverberating through the desolate room.

Not much to look at, Ash thought, following suit toward the ladders. He knew with grim certainty that his statement would not remain true for long.

The ladder felt cold and greasy to the touch. The rungs, bolted onto rusty plates, creaked and complained as they descended into the hulk.

The ladder terminated at another bleak room, leaving them facing a lone, rusted ladder. Another creaky descent and the three found themselves on a wide platform devoid of handrails. Below lay a gaping blackness their lamps refused to penetrate.

Three ladders stood at the platform's edge. Ash headed towards them knowing that he was finally going to witness the horror making him sweat and shiver beneath the pigskin suit. They each took a ladder.

Ash's lamplight shone bright against the dull metal rungs. He gripped them so tight that his fingers ached. The thought of falling into whatever waited beneath was an awful one to consider, and the creaking ladder did little to dispel his fears.

His feet touched something that wasn't floor.

"Jeez!" Terry said.

Ash looked down with trepidation.

Cushioning his steps lay a substance, the upper membrane of which crunched away as his feet sank in. The final rung of the ladder waited somewhere beneath the congealed mass.

"Shit," Will said.

"I think I'm gonna be sick," Terry shuddered.

Their lights revealed a sight both ugly and macabre. Stretching from bulkhead to bulkhead was a mass, a thick layer, of what could only be the congealed forms of hundreds of plague victims.

"Disgusting," Ash muttered.

Brown and red and even hairy in places, lay the ugly outlines of faces and buttocks, chests and limbs. Ash didn't dare look into the hole he made in the stuff after stepping off the ladder. Throughout his life, the plague had been nothing more than a macabre fairytale. It was hard to believe that he was actually standing ankle deep in its legendary aftermath.

Will pushed forward. Turning to Ash, he said, "Yeah, fucking disgusting if you ask me." He removed a long metal tube from his backpack, the end of which was flattened like an adder's head. It was a metal detector, and his companions' backpacks each bore one of the same, as well as folding shovels and rolls of plastic sacks in which to store the stolen booty.

"But," he continued. "We have a job to do and we need to stick to it." He waved the device at them. "There's another hold behind us so I'm gonna get to work."

Will turned and walked away.

As Will trudged off, Terry said, "Good hunting."

Will waved his arm and continued into the darkness, leaving Terry and Ash alone in the sea of molted remains.

"He's got balls of steel," Terry muttered. Then, "Pretty sick isn't it, all this disease just inches away from us. Ash? Hey Ash, do you hear me?"

Ash stood silent and motionless, looking down at the horror with watery eyes.

The mass of solidified death reminded him of a time, years ago, when he'd found a patch of magic mushrooms. Mistakenly trying to dry them in a jar set atop a gas fire, they'd congealed and festered into a filthy mush, coating the bottom of the jar. The ship's hold looked much like the bottom of that jar.

Terry, growing frustrated with Ash's pill induced state, removed his detector and began to search. Although Ash didn't know it, he was experiencing more than just memories.

"Munchrooms," Ash whispered. In the darkness beyond his lamp, a horde of bright purple, stick thin mushrooms appeared.

Wavering unsteadily, they twisted and bobbed, floating towards him.

Ash grinned at the fluorescent shapes.

They drew closer and paused a few feet before him. In a sudden rush of movement, the neon shapes pulled together as one, forming themselves into the shape of a high-browed, sharp-chinned face.

The face smiled. Ash smiled back.

***

Ten minutes of groping through the filth revealed nothing to Will's metal detector; and wading through the sticky, crunching remains had taken its toll on him.

He was disgusted, not so much by the misshapen floor of

52

death but rather at the fact that not a single corpse held anything close to valuable. Since nothing could compel him to scarch by hand, Will's thoughts consisted of leaving the hold, thus abandoning the mission as futile.

He shook his head and flicked the switch on the detector's handle. Its hum disappeared, replaced by the dripping sound he'd first heard upon entering the hold.

Adding a sigh to the dripping echoes, Will turned and began kicking his way through the filth back towards the bulkhead door. Raising his head, Will gasped at what he saw on the door. A fleshy mass now covered his only means of escape.

Somehow, while he was been scanning through the dead, an obscene growth had germinated and sprouted to smother the door in its ugliness.

Filled with disgust, he approached the object while tucking the metal detector into his backpack.

Removing a knife from his belt, he asked, "Where the fuck did you come from?"

The mutation bore no mouth to answer.

Up close, the object resembled a huge, bloated chicken's wing. It hung between the doorframe looking raw in places and rank in others. A greasy looking tendril attached the end of the 'leg' to the top of the frame.

Raising the knife, he experienced a brief revulsion over touching the thing. Fighting it, he pressed the blade against unclean flesh. About to hack into the growth, a sudden movement sent him staggering back.

It was alive.

Pulsing madly, its mottled surface twitched as if something within was attempting to break free.

Will had little choice. Grim curiosity compelled him to discover what lived and festered within the corpulent mass.

He forced the knife deep into the bulk, eliciting a shuddering spasm. The flesh split, sounding slick and loud as he drew the blade down.

The incision left was inches deep, and yellow and porous at the edges. Within, something sticky and pale lay exposed. The blade was three quarters of the way down when the thing inside jerked, flopping free of its own accord

Stumbling back, Will steadied himself with difficulty. Limp

hands sent his knife tumbling to the floor. The newly freed form, trailing chunks of yellow gristle, joined it on the floor of corpses.

Bile rose in Will's throat. He ripped off his mask as he struggled to choke it back. A second later the rank stench around him brought Will to his knees. Still, the awful smell wasn't nearly as awful as the aberration lying before him.

Fetal and unmoving, emaciated and shrunken to an impossible degree, the creature was still recognizable as Terry. Terry, but tiny and pale, hairless and shiny-slick with afterbirth.

Knee deep in filth, Will still found the opportunity to be horrified. Having left Terry only fifteen minutes earlier, he simply couldn't fathom how his friend had been mutilated and deformed to such an impossible degree.

He leaned over, tentatively touching Terry's tiny knee.

The action was followed by an instantaneous reaction: Terry coughing then shuddering to life. Yellow liquid poured out from his mouth and nostrils. Eyelids popping open, he stared up at Will with glazed, rheumy orbs.

"Terry?" The small word seemed to fill the fetid air.

With a scraping, liquid sound, Terry cleared his throat. "Hell here," he said, his words filled with sinister glee. This was followed by a fit of retching cackles.

Will didn't hear him. One moment he was crouched horrified, the next, a pair of huge, scaly black hands were lifting his body up through the air.

Confusion by his sudden weightlessness and the sight of Terry's receding form, Will darted headlong towards the ceiling. He felt neither the snap of his neck or the crushing impact as his skull caved in; the monstrous hands had already crushed him senseless.

***

"Are you the King of the munchrooms?"

The florescent face smiled at Ash's question, new purple lines rippling into life in the form of vivid cheek dimples.

"Some call me that, and others, The King in Neon," it replied. "But to most," and at this, the smile grew wider, "I am the King of the Dead."

Minutes earlier, unbeknownst to the mesmerized Ash, the floor had sprouted a score of misshapen tentacles, engulfing and dragging Terry away without a sound.

Ash wobbled. The strange apparition's presence filled him

54

with confused giddiness.

"Go to your knees," the voice said, "You'll feel better."

Ash obeyed.

The face, sneering, continued as Ash sank into the slippery gore. "You'll feel better without the mask on, son. Remove it."

Nodding numbly, Ash again complied. Pulling the seals open he removed the mask, staring back towards the King's leering eyes.

"Doesn't that feel better?"

Nodding despite the stench, Ash smiled, slivers of drool pouring from his lips.

"You look hungry, son." The voice said. "Pick yourself an apple. They're all around you."

Ash looked down. Seeing nothing but unsightly shapes, he shook his head.

"Do it, NOW!"

The angry tone made him flinch. Reaching down, he fumbled through the muck until he caught hold of something small and round. It took a few seconds of effort before the child's skull came loose from its spine. The eye sockets were empty but the head lay sticky with corrupt flesh. Pressing it to his mouth, Ash bit down. Beneath the wispy hair and flesh, the skull crumbled.

He tasted salt and rank mushrooms.

The voice said, "YOU CAN ALSO CALL ME PLAGUE!"

Choking back tears and nausea, Ash continued eating.

Clang! A noise from the forward hold, that of Will's head crushing against the roof, reverberated through the room. Knocking Ash from his stupor, the sound had a twofold effect. The first caused the neon face to shimmer then disappear. The second, and far more horrifying effect, instilled a full consciousness of what he'd done.

"Aw, Jesus!" he gasped.

Ash dropped the half-eaten skull. It tumbled from his hand, still dripping moldering brain matter, to join the rest of the dead. He gagged, expelling the contents of his mouth and stomach against his chest and knees.

The rank, gamy taste mingled with the bitter foulness of burning stomach acid. The disgust at what he'd done overpowered Ash completely. Realizing he probably contracted the plague, he continued to dry heave long after his stomach was emptied.

Moaning loudly, he lay prone and helpless for a while, until a second booming *clang* forced him to his knees.

Something was coming from the forward hold.

"The King in Neon," he groaned. The clanging continued.

Climbing to his feet, his suit dripping vomit, Ash took a deep breath and gagged for his trouble. Another *clang* became a stomping drumbeat as something huge entered the hold. His lamplight couldn't reach far enough to illuminate the shape stalking towards him.

Retrieving and pulling on his hood, Ash turned away from the invader. He clicked the hood's seals and experienced a rush of clean, metallic-tinged air. Staggering slightly, he turned his slow gait into a run before charging towards the ladders. The thing behind him sped up. It was right on his heels as he jumped at the rungs.

Grabbing rusty handholds, Ash headed up, the thing behind him lunging and cackling loudly. He escaped the last rung just moments before the ladder came loose from its supports, crashing to the deck below.

He continued his escape, charging through creaking doors and down dark passages in the hope he was heading towards the upper deck and freedom. Slick-pooled flooring and rust-rimmed walls flashed about him as he ran. Another rickety ladder followed before he found himself back inside the pilothouse.

Ash continued to run even though the thing from the hold, monster, hallucination, or plague incarnate, had stopped pursuing him, because his fear hadn't. He ran from a terror consuming him from within.

Was the plague still active? His thoughts were manic, his footsteps pounding across the first hatchway.

Without warning, it burst apart beneath him.

The plague-thing had been toying with him; biding its time till it heard him scurrying across the deck like a fleeing rat.

The explosion sent him tumbling through the air, up over the ship's side.

Flying headlong, too winded to scream, he took a short, wistful look at his boat. Breathless tumbling followed, down through the icy waters.

Ash tried swimming, but the backpack's weight, combined with a merciless cold leaching away all body heat, proved too powerful to overcome.

He stared down helplessly as the silty blackness consumed him. In a matter of seconds Ash reached the bottom.

Corpses, more plague victims abandoned to the sea when Ash was only a child, waited for him upon the rocky seabed. White, naked and bloated with pestilence, they showed no mercy.

The Devil and Jim Rosenthal

C.M. Saunders

She was in labor for fourteen hours. I stayed with her the whole time. I held her hand and whispered a few well-chosen words of encouragement while I silently wept at the sight of so much agony and suffering reducing the woman I loved to a pitiful, exhausted, pain-filled wreck.

The miracle of childbirth. A woman thing. Men can only dream of the art of conception, the nine month long adventure as one life slowly grows inside another and the final, ultimate triumph. A celebration of life and living. A moment so bloated with emotion that many women are powerless to describe the event in any meaningful detail.

Unimaginable pain as the pelvis opens and the vagina splits, a rush of adrenaline aided by the ever-plentiful supply of gas and air, one last push—a little like having a shit I imagine—then overwhelming relief and joy as the pain subsides and you are presented with a screaming, shivering, gore-streaked and blood-soaked miniature person. The happiest moment of your life. So they say.

For me, though, it was the moment it all went wrong.

I had been looking forward to it so much, we both had. When I look back at all the planning involved, and then all the hard— yet very enjoyable—graft we had to put ourselves through, I didn't anticipate such an outcome as this for even the briefest moment. I would have considered myself mad for even entertaining such bizarre, twisted thoughts. For this was the stuff of nightmares. It made *Rosemary's Baby* look tame and unimaginative. The worst part is, nobody knows but me. Nobody can see, so nobody believes.

It isn't a baby. It isn't even human. If I told you what my darling wife had given birth to you would laugh. You would think I was joking and laugh until your sides hurt and tears ran down your cheeks. And even if I could prove to you that I wasn't joking, then you'd think I was mad. The victim of a cruel, untimely nervous breakdown or something.

But I haven't lost my marbles. They are all still rooted exactly where they should be. I can still function normally and effectively in every facet of my complicated life as if nothing had happened. The only area where I experience problems is...the baby. And that's only because, despite what everyone else seems to think, it isn't a baby at all. In fact it looks remarkably like a caricature of Jim Rosenthal, the ITV sports presenter.

Told you, you'd think I was joking. Or mad.

I first noticed that something was amiss the moment the thing thrust it's vile deformed head out of my wife's' gaping vulva, brutally ripping and tearing apart the once so delicate folds of secret flesh. The head was huge, covered in blood and entirely out of proportion to the rest of its tiny body, probably even bigger than my own head, with oval, darting yellow eyes, a grotesquely pointed nose and large tapering ears, Mr. Spock style. As I watched dumbfounded, the thing announced its arrival by emitting an inhuman, high-pitched howl and a sleek black forked tongue flicked out of its toothless mouth to taste air for the first time.

I actually screamed. I remember that part vividly. I screamed and struggled to stop my bowels from opening right there in the delivery room. But everyone must have thought that I was screaming out of joy or sympathy. No chance. I was screaming because I was absolutely horrified by what I was seeing.

I remember turning my head and vomiting on the floor. One of the nurses present simply tussled my hair as if I were a ten year old boy and said, "Don't worry about it. You'd be surprised by the amount of men who throw up in here. Some even faint. I'll just get a mop."

The stupid bitch! Could she not see? Couldn't *any* of them see that something was terribly, horrifically wrong?

I could feel myself slipping into shock and fought it desperately. My plight wasn't helped by a young trainee midwife who kept screeching in false delight and chanting "It's a little baby girl! It's a little baby girl!" at the top of her irritating voice over and over again until all my fear and confusion was replaced by a searing rage. I wanted to fly at her and punch her in the face and head until she stopped shrieking. Or stopped breathing.

It wasn't a little baby girl. It was a fucking monstrosity.

Minutes later the chief midwife wrapped the howling, shivering baby-thing in a thick blanket—mercifully almost covering its head—and handed it to me with a smile. The look on her face told me I should be grateful. Trying desperately to hide my revulsion and swallowing back sour mouthfuls of bile and vomit, I smiled back weakly.

As it was our first child, and it had been a particularly fraught and gruesome delivery—not surprising when you take into account the size of the thing's head—the hospital decided to keep both mother and child in for two or three days observation. Over the course of that time I found myself dreading the onset of visiting hours. I would be forced to sit and watch my beautiful wife nurse the baby-thing as its massive head lolled lazily on its frail shoulders and obscene sticky liquids oozed out of every orifice in its pale body. All the time we were surrounded by perfectly happy and normal new families. Laughing, joking, and immersed in their brand new lives.

I put on a brave face of course, but there was simply too much fear and loathing in me to hide all the time. Now and again the cracks in my armour would reveal, to some extent, my true feelings. My wife's brow would crease; she would take my hand lovingly in hers, and ask me what was wrong. So I lied. What else could I do? I voiced non-existent political anxiety and feigned concerned about her health and the security of our financial future. Anything to keep her happy.

Sometimes it's better to lie to protect the ones you love.

Then, they were home. Safe and sound.

Friends, family and neighbors came to visit, all saying what a lovely, pretty little thing she was. I watched closely for any grimace of disgust, any flicker of distaste, any indication at all that someone might be seeing what I saw. But there was none. It was just me. Only I could see the truth behind the disguise. I had never felt so alienated.

I looked on in helpless horror as the bond between my wife and the offspring deepened and their love blossomed. I was in emotional turmoil. Desperate to do the right thing, I unselfishly played the part of the devoted husband and doting father while I secretly struggled to come to terms with it all. My work began to suffer. Feverish nightmares haunted my restless nocturnal hours and I spent the days in a permanent state of disbelieving shock. Before too long a gigantic, ominous question-mark began hovering over my sanity like a vulture over a rotting carcass

The turning point came when I saw her breast-feeding for the first time. My stomach churned as I watched the baby-thing take my wife's swollen nipple greedily into its mouth the same way a new lover would. It stared at me as it was doing it, as if laying down a challenge to a rival. I knew then that things could only get worse. The baby-thing, that devilish product of our divine love-making, would be driven between us like a wedge pushing us ever further apart and soon our relationship would totally disintegrate leaving me isolated in misery. I had to do something.

When the time came, it happened spontaneously. I didn't plan a thing. I thought about accidentally killing it, but would anyone believe me? I would be branded a baby-killer and child abuser and be hated by everyone with such a lethal passion that my life would be permanently under threat. Even if I did get away with it, I knew that my wife would never forgive me for allowing anything to happen to her precious devil-baby. There would always be a burrowing maggot of doubt in her mind.

She suspected that something was wrong for a long time. Like most women she was very perceptive. Women's intuition and all that. So one night she confronted me. I told her that I had met someone else because it was either that or tell her the hideous truth. A girl from the office, I said. Our marriage was over; I was going to live with this young tart despite the baby.

My wife wept uncontrollably for what seemed like hours on end and shouted hurtful abuse at me for a while, and then I left never to return, with only the clothes I stood up in. Like I said, sometimes it's better to lie to the ones you love.

That was an age ago. Don't ask how long because I couldn't tell you. I live on the streets now. One of the many thousands of city dwellers that exist around the fringes of society. I move around the hostels and soup kitchens like your average homeless person. Who knows? Maybe you've walked past me yourself. Maybe you were so kind as to throw me some change.

A few of the people I have met have asked me my life story—we all have a story to tell. But when I tell them mine they either laugh at me or simply shake their heads and walk away, muttering about worthless vagabonds and dangerous crazies.

I can only tell the truth. And, even though everybody else was blind to it, the truth is that my beautiful wife gave birth to a demonic Jim Rosenthal look-a-like. Yes, Jim Rosenthal. I mean, if it had been Des Lynam I wouldn't have minded half so much. But that fucking Jim Rosenthal...

Cena

Chad McKee

Bradley saw the chords of muscle bulge in the dog's neck as it struck, ripping its opponent's flesh with its teeth, shredding skin with its paws. It was surreal, the strike, like something out of one of those brutal nature documentaries. He looked up—as much as he could, anyway—at those in the crowd. The chords in *their* necks were prominent as well, veins popping from the skin, eyes bugged as the action got more intense, bloodier. *Bloodlust*, he thought distantly. He'd heard the word before but never understood what it meant. Until now. Oh yes, he knew now.

The other dog appeared to be struggling, its strength flagging. *No!* Bradley cried silently. The dog must have felt his urgency because it picked itself up a bit, stopped losing ground for a moment, and made an attempt at an offense. Despite being the bigger of the two dogs, it was clearly the lesser trained. Almost from the beginning it was on the defensive, dodging attacks, retreating. Maybe Bradley had seen something of himself in that dog's eyes. It didn't want to be there. It would fight for survival, and only that. He saw a kindred spirit in that poor battered mutt.

A mistake. A terrible mistake.

The dog's keeper kept Bradley's head on the action—the invisible hand gripping his neck made sure of that. Bradley silently cursed himself, blinking away the sweat that dripped into his eyes. Irrelevant thoughts floating though his mind cast his captor as Ares, God of War, and himself as one of the Lotus Eaters, but he shook them away. This was more than a battle between a killer and a pacifist. It also involved the plight of a living conscientious objector, who had foolishly made his opinions known.

Suddenly, the bigger dog, Bradley's pick, lashed out with a speed and force that surprised both his opponent and the onlookers. The match was competitive again. There was a cheer from the crowd, which made a rough circle around the dogs, themselves in an earthen pit of hard clay. It was possibly a foot deep, a foot and a half at most, but not nearly deep enough for Bradley's taste. From his perspective, on its very edge, he could hear every growl of aggression, every grunt and yelp when the dogs met for battle. He could see the rippling of their muscles and the snapping of canines and the desperate look in the eyes of whomever was losing at the moment. He could also see clearly that hollow, beastly expression when on the attack. He took it all in, poised precariously on the lip of the pit, the massive hand forcing him to look upon the grisly scene below.

There was chatter in Spanish. An exchange of money was taking place. The bigger dog, nameless as far as Bradley could tell, was effectively striking now. People were adjusting their bets. A man in a guayabera and khakis was running the betting. A fat cigar hung from his lips as he compiled notes with professional efficiency. He was flanked on either side by men in tight jeans and stern faces. At least one had a gun, a revolver tucked down the front of his jeans. That was part of what put Bradley in his present situation. The other being a generalized arrogance, or stupidity, that led him to question these men and what they were doing.

There were a few women, too, but they stayed far back, sitting on pick-up tailgates facing the dusty road back to Mexico City. A breeze carried the smell of tortillas cooking but Bradley couldn't determine from where. His line of sight was limited to the dog pit and a square of sky beyond it. In a glimpse up from the fight below, he saw the sun steadily dipping into the horizon. He wondered if he would experience dusk. That would be appropriately symbolic, Bradley supposed, dying at dusk. When the light was gone and the darkness took over, he thought. Again he shook the thoughts from his head. *Idiot.* Must be the Lit student in him causing Bradley to think of such nonsense.

There was still sunlight. And his dog still stood, however bloodied. Bradley decided in that moment to call it Cooper, after his own pet when he was a kid. Cooper would have died to save him, he was sure. His old Retriever would have fought valiantly to free his master.

He found himself yelling "Cooper!" over the shouts of the crowd. Most didn't understand the word but traded amused looks anyway. Perhaps only his captor knew. He spoke in English to Bradley: "Your dog fights well. Maybe you can take him home with you." He laughed. It was deep and surprisingly jovial, that laugh, as if lives were not at stake. Perhaps in another world he would have been a used car salesman or an elementary school teacher. But he

63

was from a poor barrio on the outskirts of Mexico City and was not either of those. Instead, he held Bradley's neck nearly down to the dog's themselves, making sure every scent and splash of blood was recorded at the most visceral level.

Bradley found himself less angry with the man than himself. He had known what the men were going to do. It shocked him, a suburban boy from Baltimore, to see animal cruelty. He knew it happened but not to such a blatant extent as this. Perhaps that was what offended him—making no attempt at all to hide this barbarity. It wasn't their fault, he said to himself, these were poor people. They shared the streets with dogs like these, no doubt wild and dangerous, everyday. Bradley knew dogs here were not treated like almost-humans as they were in Baltimore. His own Retriever had spent a large part of its life inside, despite being, in effect, an "outside" dog. But that sense of injustice was strong in Bradley. He had carefully erected it in college and had planned to cultivate it when he started his first job next month with a humanitarian organization.

Even the anger at himself was at a low ebb. Increasingly his mental energy was being channeled to Cooper, returning now to the dog that only a few minutes ago was tired and near defeat. Bradley made eye contact with it, hoping to establish some tenuous mental bond that would push him that extra mile. In spite of himself, Bradley drove the dog forward with thoughts of violence, of ripping his enemy apart, then turning on their captors in a bloody fury.

"Kill him Cooper!" he heard himself yell. It came off his tongue oddly. He thought that he would never utter such a statement and mean it.

His captor provided a patronizing pat on the back. "Good! That's the only way. He needs you. You need *him*."

The renewed threat drove Bradley into desperation. He pleaded with the dog to continue just as he had pleaded with the man to let him go. His captor had simply shaken his head, using that extraordinary laugh as he told his lackey to keep a gun trained on the *gringo*. There had been animosity when he first pushed his way into the crowd, and implored in broken Spanish to spare the dogs and go about their business. That seemed like hours ago instead of minutes. One tiny corner of his mind, the only one not willing his savior to a victory, thought back to his entrance among the people of the shanty town with its picked over land and miserable sloping shacks. He had crested the dog pit like a pretentious twat, the Ugly American, his backpack high on his shoulders like a beacon of civilization. It only took moments to realize his error.

Then he was given a choice. A bet.

"Kill him! Kill him!" Bradley screamed.

Cooper was on the verge of defeat, his ears torn, the fur on his head soggy with blood. His thick body strained for breath in great heaving sighs. There was little fight left in him it seemed, the last burst of energy expended. Like all opponents sensing victory, the other dog strode forward confidently, despite its own severe wounds, taking the fight to Cooper. Bradley doubted that either dog would battle another day; but no other day mattered. No other fight mattered. Escaping the man with the gun and his captor with the impossibly strong hands was Bradley's only concern.

Bradley eyed the possible winner, a pit bull. Its block-like head was huge; its black gums and bloody teeth were exposed as it panted, circling Cooper in short, quick strides. Its body was lean but powerful. He didn't have to imagine that the dogs had been starved or to imagine how fresh meat would taste to the victor. That was the only way to provoke dogs like this, certainly. Starvation was part of their training, like endurance or power. Food was their reward for winning. The punishment was obvious.

Money was no longer changing hands. The fight was nearly over. It only took one more attack to end things. Cooper was on his hind legs, tongue lolling out of his mouth permanently now, exhaustion impeding the survival instinct. Again Bradley's mind railed against it.

"Get up, Cooper. Get up, boy. You can do it. Do it!"

In that moment the pit bull turned its cold, merciless stare on Bradley. He felt a rush of cold adrenaline under that stare. The flight response. It was as if the dog knew, that it understood what Cooper meant to Bradley. He suddenly had an insight of how the gazelle felt when it was separated from the herd and the lion had it sighted. The point where your final breaths could be enumerated in double digits. It was a lonely feeling, despite the other eyes in the small crowd watching him as well. There was an odd mix of sympathy and excitement on their faces. They knew now.

Bradley would be *la cena*. The dinner.

That had been the bet. If Bradley chose the winner he could go free. If he chose the loser, he would be fed to the winner. His captor had not let him know just how long it had been since either had been fed. But there was desperation in their hunger. And they knew whatever was thrown into the pit would be their next meal.

Bradley held the dog's stare, knowing that it could probably smell his fear, even over that of Cooper. Bradley tried to return the look with defiance and hatred. He hoped his anger would overcome any other emotion he might emit.

The exchange lasted no longer than seconds, perhaps only one second, but that was enough for Cooper to rush in with fangs bared and sunk his teeth into the Pit Bull's throat. The dog gave out a surprised bark but all other sounds were strangled as Cooper's jaw snapped shut with terrifying strength. Blood pumped from the pit bull's neck like spray from a garden hose. Sprinkles tattooed Bradley's face, which might have repulsed him twenty minutes ago, but now was as welcome as cool rain in the summer.

"Yes!" he said as the blood pooled. "Yes!" he repeated, the pit bull collapsing into a heap in the clay ring. "Yes!" he screamed when Cooper let go and let loose a howl of victory.

Others in the crowd looked onward in shock. Soon there were shouts of anger. One of the men in tight blue jeans, with the gun, drew it from his side in warning. The man with the cigar shook his head and began counting the money. The spoils. His captor finally let go of Bradley's neck, which was pinched and cramped, but he hardly noticed.

"*Gringo*," he said, with his cheerful laugh. "Your dog won! You have been saved! Celebrate!"

Bradley found himself doing just that, laughing and jumping up and down in a crazy dance. Those in the crowd frowned, then laughed, as the *gringo loco* jumped and screamed and cried like an imbecile. He was alive, he would go free. He wanted to hug Cooper but instead he cried. He couldn't restrain himself; the tears were hardly noticeable mixed with the sweat but his sobs were likes howls. Moments later he sunk to his knees, exhausted.

His captor looked on. His face was on the verge of another cheerful laugh that never arrived. There was coldness in his eyes. "That was my best dog, *amigo*. He should have won. This will lose me money."

Bradley could say nothing. He brought himself back to his feet and stood as straight and steady as he could manage. He glanced at Cooper, who was laying next to his dead opponent, head between paws. No one was giving him a second glance now.

The keeper followed Bradley's stare. "Your dog will fight no more. But now he has something to eat."

The laugh finally did come as he pointed to the corpse of the pit bull. His men also laughed, despite the language barrier. They understood all too well.

"Yes, *amigo*, you have cost me money but I will keep my part of the bargain. I will let you go." He paused. "But I would not stay here long. *They* lost their money today," he said, pointing to the crowd. "And they don't have much to lose."

Bradley did not need to be told twice. The stares of the villagers were hostile now. The looks of amusement at the crying and dancing *Gringo* were gone now. A mob was developing.

Bradley stumbled from his position on the pit and made his way towards the road out of town, towards the highway. He ignored his backpack, full of useless guidebooks and designer clothes. His only concern was leaving and not looking again at the angry locals. The only glance he spared was to Cooper, matted with dry blood, calmly eating his opponent.

Frogger

JW Schnarr

We both grew up in the eighties.

I was a big fan of video games even then. I loved my Atari. Little black joystick, bright red button on the top. I remember it cost my mother a fortune when it first came out.

We had to turn the controller sideways when we wanted to play Q-Bert. You remember that little round guy who jumped on the pyramid?

My sister wouldn't play that one. She always said it was too hard to figure out where to go.

It's *easy*, I'd tell her, and then we would fight about it. There were a lot of games, though, so eventually we'd find something to play. Pac-Man. Combat. Mouse Trap.

I loved Frogger more than anything though.

You remember that game, don't you?

You were the frog at the bottom of the screen. You had to get to the top of the screen where four little frog-holes were waiting. Your home in the swamp.

You only had four lives, so you couldn't die even once if you wanted to make the high score.

And there was traffic. A lot of it.

Large multi-colored rectangles for cars and trucks. Even bigger ones that represented semi-trailers. Four long lanes of traffic, bumper to bumper, humming along at a steady pace. Everybody was watching the car in front of them, and nobody was watching the side of the road for the little frog.

He only wanted to get home.

So busy, these commuters, always driving in one direction, or another. Never watching what was going on around them.

There were little gaps though. Tiny spaces where a smart frog could gain some ground.

And so he'd begin.

If he was smart enough, and quick enough, he would make it out onto that first lane.

If he could make it through two lanes, he might even catch a breather in a thin little strip of grass between the two sections of busy commuters.

Eventually, though, he would have to go on.

So he'd jump.

Sometimes he'd be crushed flat under the rolling tires of the traffic.

Sometimes his head would hit the windshield of a commuter car and burst like a melon. His broken body would sail through the air as the shocked driver hit the brakes and swear to God that the little frog hadn't been their but a moment before.

Of course, there were times when he made it.

He would be so close to the swamp that he could smell it. He knew once he got there he would face other problems, of course. Like logs in the water, and crocodiles.

None of that mattered at this point.

So he'd watch. And he'd wait. Eventually, it all came down to guts.

Was this little frog fast enough to take the plunge and jump into traffic? Of course he was. Even stuck in that little frog position like that, he could move as fast as he wanted. Was he smart enough? That's tough to say. Certainly he was clever enough to recognize the patterns in the traffic and react accordingly.

But was he brave enough?

That's the big kicker, isn't it? That's all the tomatoes, right there. Eventually it all comes down to whether you have the guts to hold your breath, close your eyes, and step out into that wall of speeding cars.

Could you take that step knowing full well that you might end up in the grill of some speeding commuter with a big fancy truck? How about being mashed under the tires of a semi-trailer, with twenty thousand pounds of speeding weight mashing you into a pulp?

Sounds like hell, docsn't it?

Doesn't it?

Well, you should have thought of that before you made her break my heart. Fourteen years together, and my heart broke like a hot glass filled with ice. I cupped the pieces in my hands and they bled and bled. Now stop talking about her or I'll make you wear a blindfold.

There's no sense crying about it, my friend. There is absolutely nothing you can do now. Those ropes on your hands and feet aren't going to let you escape, and this shiny nickel plated handgun is going to make sure you don't try anything stupid. Because if you are thinking of being a hero, I'm going to put a bullet in your head right here by the side of the road.

Then I'm going to go to your house and shoot your wife and children, before putting the gun in my mouth and pulling the trigger.

Maybe I *am* crazy. Maybe I've just had enough of this place to keep me full for a good long while. Maybe she was the only thing in the whole world that mattered to me, and you took that away when I found you two in bed together.

It's just about time for you to start your journey. The ropes on your feet are so tight, aren't they? You'll have to hop, just like the little frog.

You never know. You could make it across all those lanes of traffic safely. Do that, well, and I might just let you walk away.

Why not? You'll be free to get back to your little frog-hole in the swamp. Sounds fair to me. Are you feeling brave?

Good.

It's almost time to go.

And don't ask about her again.

Let's just say that this time I won't be getting a high score.

White Out

KJ Moore

Frosted white beneath a stream of salty smoke, the two men watched each other as one chewed a leather apron. The oils that seeped out were thin and bare.

Close to the fire that popped and spat hot blubber, Don hugged the long leaning knife he'd found to his chest and held the apron to his cracked lips with the heels of his hands. Curled and blistered, his hands were yellow and throbbing.

"They won't come," Graeme said, touching his right hand to the pool of lukewarm water about his feet. He hissed as he tried to nurse life back into his shiny fingers. "They'll go for each other first. Then a bear'll probably get them."

Don watched the fire as he chewed. Both sleds had been lost. The first dog team had been dragged through a crack in the ice by the sled laden with medical supplies. The others had barked hoarse warnings when the men tried to whip them back into line to free the remaining sled. They then dug in the ice for the drowning team. But it was no use; the ice froze around the second sled leaving it and the remaining dogs half submerged.

Stirring at the memory of their stiff distrust and mournful howls, Don nudged the alight rags gathered from across the whaling sheds with the tip of the knife.

Graeme fidgeted loudly, coughing. "Can't believe you just left them."

Around the apron, Don grunted back in wet sounds. "Just have to go push on without them." The remaining distance to Aleknagic was a long and likely fatal walk. The thought of staggering across miles of white wilderness made them both shift on the rotted floor.

A long silence of deliberation as Graeme worked his thick tongue about the tight words. "You would say that: Push on. Push on when we should've been stopping to eat, and push on when we should've been checking the ice. God damn, Don, it was a soft winter."

He jerked his head, the deep lines about his eyes shifting

together. "Storm should have toughened it out more. And no good getting there if we can't get there in time."

The heaviness of the air felt like night, though the light reflecting off the snow outside was still sharp and clear. Thick time passed. Don watched as Graeme slept and woke to stir the fire back to life, then swirled his hands through the water. Graeme noted the stare. "How long's it been now?"

Don swallowed in long convulsions, thinking. "Three, maybe four days."

There was a mouthless low groan and Graeme pressed his elbows into his stomach, sitting back down. He breathed through his teeth. "Oh, God."

They had been expected tomorrow in Aleknagik, three days away, and the window to treat with the post-exposure prophylaxis was gone. Once the first symptoms appeared, ten days after being bitten by the rabid dogs, there was no hope. It had taken four days from after those bites for the dogs to turn paralytic in their hind legs. They suffocated hours later, and then rabies had been suspected. With the storm grounding the few Alaskan planes available, the infected people at the head of Wood River had had to rely on drugs being brought in by sleds. The drugs were now beneath the ice and there was no chance of more getting out in time.

Don continued to grind leather between his molars, saliva welling about his lips. "Don't talk to me about God."

Slipping the apron from his lap, Graeme sat back against the wall and watched the black smoke peel through the gap in the roof. "We should go back. Maybe something—"

"Something nothing," Don barked around the hide in his mouth. He levered his body up with the wall then paced Graeme in a jerking arc. "There's nothing there, just the dogs and a hole."

"We can't just sit here."

They both knew it but didn't know what more to say, so they didn't say anything.

Silence pressed. "How's your hand?"

Don raised his curled right hand, overlooking the frostbite as Graeme was. Four puncture wounds slid into tears, dark purple and hard at the edges. "Alright. Wont matter much if this keeps up, but it's healing fine. Ain't the first time I been bit."

The wind pressed about the shed again, holding them inside.

Graeme finally asked the lingering question. "How do you

72

think it happened?"

Don looked about to sit down but seemed stuck on his feet and swayed, clutching the knife like a new baby and tonguing a piece of leather. "Think the dogs ran off a wolf or a fox with it. Chewed it up a bit, probably, then bit on the handlers when they went wild."

Graeme shook his head. The ice coating on his hood scratched his face. "Should have just killed them when they first got wild. Can't do nothing with a dog that wont get beat into line. They should've shot 'em or beaten their heads in if they didn't want to waste the bullets. Then them handlers wouldn't have got bit and wouldn't be dead in a week."

A week was optimistic and Don smiled at the naivety. He sat down. "If they'd killed the dogs then they wouldn't have gone dead in the back legs and frothed, and no one would've known different. Got to treat a person before they start getting sick, and couldn't have guessed they'd get sick if the dogs had died before they themselves got sick."

They let the wind speak for a while, feeling their eyes crust and freeze close and their hands burn with cold. Don quit the leather and scooped handfuls of snow, offering it out to the smoke until it turned soft and then drunk the grey slush as if each swallow was the first.

Graeme's gut hurt more than his hands. "We can't stay here. They got no reason to look for us here."

"They won't look for us." Don scratched as his beard, slick with salty water.

"We should go back to the sled. Dogs might have settled enough to work 'em now, and some of the crates might have floated up. If we're lucky."

"Ain't nothing there to find. We stay here and we got fire, so we let our hands get better off then we go and find someone who might be looking in a few days. Too far to Aleknagik like this."

"We ain't got nothing here," Graeme croaked through his teeth, running his boot along the rotted floor. All the sheds were rotting on the inside from the summer whaling seasons, but because of the cold they didn't smell. "We can't keep going without food. Leather ain't gonna help us much longer."

"There's food plenty if we looked."

Graeme started to stood up. "We looked all around here,

Don, and there's nothing. Even the hooks and winches been picked clean by the birds. We gotta go. Dogs might have died now and we can bring one back and cook it, then go on to Aleknagik when we got some strength to do it."

"No way the dogs'll be dead yet," Don said to his wet palms, greasy water running out from the sides of his mouth where he couldn't swallow fast enough. "They'll last longer than us. It's only been a day or two."

Graeme shook his head and the wind moaned, finally empty of falling snow. He started for the thick door. "I'm going back. You coming?"

Don looked up and down the height of him, settling on the blistered fingers held like overgrown claws. With the knife between his elbow and chest, he took a last handful of slush into his mouth and got to his feet. "Think we could kill a dog if it came to it?"
***

Out of the shed and over the inlet of the sea ice, they walked through the snow that had frozen stippled with salt. It clutched their boots for half a mile and then turned clean and powdered for the rest of the walk.

Graeme followed Don, pausing when the older man stooped for handfuls of snow, thirst outweighing the pain in his hands. "How long can we go without food?"

Don squinted at the watery sun. "Couple more days, maybe."

They kept walking, the snow rustling so that either of them could pretend they were alone. "When that plane went down a few years back, think the survivors went six days before they started starving to death," Graeme said.

It had been the last time a plane tried to fly out here through a snow storm. "Guy I know found two of 'em," Don said, stopping to take more snow into his mouth. "Froze to death with full bellies."

"Hope the dogs are dead."

Time passed and snow fell, filling the footprints leading back to the whaling sheds to shallow indents. The wind carried past them and dogs started to bark up ahead. More time passed and they could see the dark shapes howling and jerking at their lines as they approached.

Graeme stopped walking and looked at his hands, breathing the other man's name like a prayer.

Don kept walking and stopped when he was just out of reach of the dogs. They watched him with bright eyes and hot mouths. The lead dog was rent into bloody portions, and Penine was bowed over something slick, rasping at the lump with his tongue whilst watching the returned man. Chest tight, Don could feel the pit of his stomach throbbing.

He looked across the animals to the sled trapped by one sunken end in the fissure in the ice. Past it the ice was cloudy, still freshly frozen and still weak. Like before, Don couldn't see the other sled or the crates that had been lashed onto it. There was a shape in the snow, though, and he moved towards it.

Graeme was trapped half out of the ice, arms stretched out and raw fingers grasping. There were sharp pits in his waxy face, red flecks from where birds had tested his stiff flesh. Don looked back to the wandering line of his lone footprints, holding the leaning knife harder to his chest. His gut churned, caved inwards. Graeme was in the ice—went down with the sled.

The pit of his stomach throbbed anew, twitching his body and shaking his head. He clumsily eased to his knees, shifting the leaning knife to bring the blade to the heels of his ruined hands. Eyes wide and away from Graeme's face, he chipped at the coat on one of the reaching arms. By the time he'd gotten through the fabric the dogs had fallen silent and watchful, noses twitching when the smell of blood reached them.

Cleaving away thin slices, Don stacked the meat in untidy piles between taking mouthfuls of snow. The short hairs of the arms were stark against the pale hide, and he sheared against their grain to take long, stiff planes of meat. When it was too much agony to keep using the knife, Don bent to take one of the scraps into his wet mouth and bunched the rest against his chest. Ignoring the dogs, he followed his tracks back towards the whaling sheds and the waiting fire.

To his right there were mountains of broken ice, and to his left the curve of the Earth against the milky blue sky. Graeme matched his steps on his left side, and he hunched his body over the flayed strips.

Graeme didn't try to take it. "They'll be dying by now," he said, watching Don eat the freckled skin that had covered the bicep of his right arm. "Window for the vaccine's gone."

Don's face twisted and he coughed, choked on the stiff meat

75

with slow heaves. It cleared after his knees sank into the snow, and he dipped his face to chew up the powder. Graeme remained standing, and the man in the snow watched his frosted boots with a curled lip.

"I ain't gonna take any," Graeme said, scuffing his toes in the snow. "I think someone's coming."

"No one's coming," Don said, dropping the meat strips to pick through them with the side of his better hand.

Graeme crouched, reaching but stopping short of touching. His eyes were framed with thick white crystals. "It's alright, you know."

Don grunted, but it wasn't unkind. Saliva rolled at the seam of his mouth.

The barking grew loud enough to be a curiosity, and he looked up to see Graeme staring back towards the sheds. Unseen, he found the biggest slice of meat from the lot and took the edge into his mouth, tonguing the slick underside as he watched.

The closing dog sled bore one man wearing a Caribou coat with tight Aleknagik stitching. Graeme vanished. Don sat up at the voice that came up coarse from the man's gut. Between his stomach and the humming in his ears, he didn't understand what came after the cautious pause.

Mouth full and overflowing with saliva, Don couldn't speak and breathed through his nose. He watched the man's eyes travel to his hands and at the sharp exhale, he looked too. The half-eaten strip had the seam and crease of an elbow at one end, and a shrunken mole in the middle.

The dogs whined, wanting to eat the vomit that fell and sank in the snow. Don swallowed the mouthful and took another whilst the man wasn't looking.

Spiric Satisfied

John McNee

All Fiona saw as Franco led her into the master bedroom were machines.

Mr. Spiric's bed was lost somewhere behind a wall of monitors, regulators and breathing apparatuses—and the machines created a lot of noise. The heart monitor kept a constant electronic beat, while the other devices chimed in with *whoops* and *pings* like some kind of clinical rhythm section. In addition to the noise, the room stunk of strong disinfectant. It wasn't exactly sexy and it definitely wasn't what Fiona expected when she took the job.

Amongst the machines were two others, a doctor and a nurse. The doctor appeared middle-aged, and wore a gray suit and overcoat. He was bent over machines checking read-outs and recording data. He looked up briefly when Fiona entered but didn't nod or speak and returned to his work just as quickly, grim expression unchanged.

The nurse, on the other hand, didn't seem to be doing anything. She was about twenty; slim, pretty, and blonde, dressed in a tiny white nurse's outfit that appeared to have been bought at an adult boutique. There was no way the flimsy material was NHS regulation. When Fiona and Franco entered the 'nurse' was checking her nails and hopping from toe to toe, apparently cold.

Fiona had registered the chill in the room, but she was used to that. They liked to keep it cool in the club so the girls' nipples were always pert. Now that she was here in this makeshift hospital room, the club felt so far away.

She had just finished her shift, gotten dressed and was ready to go home when Janet had called her out by saying: some guy asked to speak to you and he looks fucking loaded. Fiona was exhausted and sick of being propositioned by heavy-breathing drunks with too much disposable income, but she did her best to perk up when she saw him—a tall, dark, Latin stranger—and prayed that he wasn't planning to offer her a role in a porn shoot.

The stranger introduced himself as Franco, gave her a card with no surname on it and bought her a £7 whiskey at the bar, proceeding to tell her how talented and beautiful he thought she was. Overall he had been very charming. Then he asked if she ever gave private performances.

"Sure," she replied. "All the time. It's what the back rooms are for."

"I don't mean here," he had said. "Home visits. Parties. Anything like that?"

"Not really," she answered, hesitantly. "Some of the other girls do. But I'm not sure I'd be comfortable…some of the stories they come back with—"

"I'm not proposing anything wild," he said. "It's just that the man I work for can't leave the house."

She smiled. "Why? Probation? Does he have one of those ankle bracelets?"

"Just old," Franco replied, humorlessly. "He misses… all this." He waved his hand around the club. "He misses attractive women. You'd have nothing to fear. It would be strictly one on one. Private. You wouldn't have to do anything you didn't want to. And you'd be paid very well."

Fiona had thought about it a moment, then asked: "How well?"

The sum had been enough to persuade her to change clothes again and follow Franco into the back of a chauffeur-driven Mercedes. Half an hour later she found herself in the cold room, surrounded by machines, the doctor and the inappropriately dressed nurse.

As she walked deeper into the bedroom, the click of her heels on the black-and white tiled floor announced her presence.

"Who's that?" Mr. Spiric rasped from behind the machines. His voice was sickly but loud and what he said was clear enough.

"It's just me, boss," Franco answered, following a step behind her. "I brought a guest. Fiona."

"Fffiiiooonaaaa…" The unseen Mr. Spiric echoed, drawing out the vowels, making the most of the consonants with his elderly tongue. "Well don't be afraid, sweetheart. Come say hello."

Fiona had been making her way slowly to the foot of the bed, getting her bearings, taking a good look around the room. The walls were white and glossy, almost reflective, like the walls of an art gallery. There were a lot of paintings and sculptures. Abstract things— psychedelic images she didn't recognize or understand. There were

78

also a lot of bizarre ornaments that looked like they came from far-off lands and peoples. And books. Shelves and shelves of books about mysticism and myth, folklore and legend. Hefty-looking text-books with words in the titles like 'Astral,' 'Meditation' and 'Psychic.' A lot of books on tape, too.

The bulbs in the ceiling fixtures were fluorescent and cast a fierce light over everything. She wasn't too happy about that. In the club the girls had softer lighting to work with. Black light, dry ice and shadow were all their friends. Patrons had to squint to get even half their money's worth. In this room there was nowhere to hide. Every inch of her body would be illuminated in cold, perfect detail. She presumed Mr. Spiric was a man who didn't like to miss a thing.

That presumption was cast to the wind when she finally laid eyes on the old man.

She navigated the bank of life-support equipment and came face-to-face with a desiccated husk. Spiric was a mummified skeleton in white bed-sheets. His limbs were wasted twigs. His arms hardly seemed thick enough for the doctor to make injections without skewering his flesh straight through. In spite of this, they'd somehow managed to fix maybe ten or fifteen IV drips to him. His legs—if he had any—were invisible, not even making a bump underneath the bed-clothes. The skin over his bones was pale and dry, stretched so thin that it looked like yellow cellophane. He had a jagged grinning skull for a face. It looked fragile and cracked, like a shattered porcelain mask, pieced back together with bandages. No lips, near as she could tell. No hair…

And no eyes. The gaping sockets were stuffed with cotton wool.

"Nice to meet you," he said. The grinning skull mouth clicked open and closed with his words, like an animated ghoul. She choked back a scream at the sight of him. "My name is Mr. Rembrandt Spiric."

Fiona looked to Franco, searching for some indication that this was a twisted joke. His smoldering South American eyes were vacant.

"Don't be *shy*," Spiric wheezed.

"H-hello," she squeaked, hand clawing self-consciously at her neck.

Spiric's grin widened and she feared for a moment that the skin across his cheeks might split. "I know," he said. "I'm not as handsome as I was in my younger days. Alas, the ravages of time and ill health…" He coughed. "That's why… I try to surround myself with beautiful things…" His bandaged head jerked a little. One finger twitched.

The nurse read his subtle signals, quit her hopping and fetched him a cup of water. She had to lean over the side of the bed to place the cup to his lips, her fancy dress uniform riding up as she did so, exposing her bare pale buttocks to the elements. Fiona wasn't surprised to find that the girl wasn't wearing underwear. Surreal as it was, in the context of this room, it made absolute sense.

The doctor turned his head to check out the nurse's ass. Fiona caught his eye and he ducked back down again.

Spiric gasped after two swallows, water spilling out from his lipless mouth and down his chin. The nurse pulled some tissues from her cleavage and dabbed him dry. When she was done she leaned in a little closer and gave him a soft kiss on his cheek. Spiric quivered as though shot through with electricity and all around him machines began to blare. The heart-rate monitor suddenly cranked up to flamenco tempo. The doctor swore quietly, head snapping back and forth between screens.

"Thank you, dear," Spiric breathed.

When the nurse rose and sashayed away from the bed Fiona read a smile on her scarlet lips that seemed to say: *Top that, bitch.*

The doctor swore again from between his cluster of machines and fished a stethoscope out of his pocket, hopping over cables to reach his patient.

"Franco…" Spiric whined, as the doctor put his hands upon him.

Franco nodded to the blind man and snapped his fingers for attention. "Come on guys," he said, indicating the door. "Let's go." With that command, they all departed—the doctor, the nurse and Franco, the bodyguard—leaving Fiona alone with Spiric. Franco spared her not a glance as he pulled the door closed behind him.

And suddenly Fiona felt desperately uncomfortable.

"My physician," Spiric groaned, "Seems to think that the slightest whiff of excitement will do me in. You can imagine what he must think of *you*. Thinks my frail old heart can't take it. I've tried to tell him… I'm far stronger than any of them realize."

"I'm sure," Fiona replied, eyes still on the door.

"You have a lovely voice," he said. "You're not from London…"

"Cheshire…"

"Ah. Redhead?"

That took her by surprise. "Yes."

Spiric nodded, very slightly. "An informed guess," he said. "Franco knows what I like. Describe yourself to me."

This is how he gets his kicks? She thought. *We could have done this over the phone.* "Um… Five-foot six. A hundred and five pounds…Slim…Athletic, I suppose. I work out."

"Of course you do. Breasts?"

"Two of them," she said.

He chuckled. "Size," he said. "What size are they?"

"34C," she said, resisting the temptation to embellish the truth. "Long legs, a small waist, flat stomach, and round ass."

Spiric nodded and she could see him painting a picture in his mind. "What would you say is your best physical feature?"

"Well," she said. "I do receive an awful lot of compliments about my arse. And I am quite proud of it. But others say my eyes."

"Green?"

"Hazel. Some say my hair. Which is shoulder length, incidentally, and wavy."

His heat rate had been slowly climbing throughout the exchange. He sighed blissfully. "You had better not be lying to me."

She grinned and realized she was beginning to enjoy herself. "Certainly not."

"Age?"

"24."

"Young," Spiric remarked, a little drool escaping from the corner of his mouth. "Good."

That seemed enough to provide him with a picture. She was glad she didn't have to go into more detail about the length of her fingers or the contours of her face. "So… How does this work?" she asked. "You still want me to dance for you?"

"I do," said Spiric. "You'll have to describe it to me, of course. *Every* detail."

"Ok," said Fiona. It didn't sound to her like such a bad deal. "Music?"

"You brought some?"

"Yeah."

"Well then. Be my guest."

81

Fiona took the CD from her purse, crossed the room and inserted it in the stereo.

"Not too loud," Spiric wheezed. "I need to be able to hear what you're saying."

She adjusted the volume, treble and bass, and found her favorite track. Then she checked her hair and make-up in the cabinet's glass front, without for a moment considering how pointless it was. "I'm just taking off my coat," she said, as she did so.

"What sort of coat?" the blind observer groaned. "Describe it."

"Black fur," she said. "*Fake* fur," she added, so as not to be misleading. "Ankle length."

The music began to play and the room was filled with the soft, deep sounds of acoustic guitar, double bass and slow drums. Fiona liked tango music when she danced privately. It was warm and passionate and she didn't have to try so hard to be sexy. It came naturally to her with the rhythm.

"I'm wearing a strapless, satin dress, tight around the waist and bust, in a dark shade of purple," she said. "The hemline's just above the knee. I'm also wearing black high-heels with purple bows... and simple black stockings. There's a split down the right side of the dress, so you can see a couple of inches of thigh above the stocking. I'm taking a step forward and bending my knee a little to show that off..."

"Yes," said Spiric, the image clear in his mind. "Continue..."

"I've got my hands on my hips," she said, speaking slowly, trying to add a little sexual emphasis to the words. "Just swaying in time to the music... Raising one arm, running it over my stomach and chest... Up above my head... Still swaying..." She closed her eyes, listening to the female singer's beautiful voice. "I bend forward to reach my toes... Hands grab my ankles... And I rise, slowly, running my hands up the length of my legs..."

Spiric was silent now and completely still, deep in concentration. The noise of the monitors had slowed to a steady, unobtrusive beat, almost in time with the tango music.

"I turn," Fiona continued, voice lowered to a purr. "So that my back's to you, and I repeat the move. But this time my hands are on the back of my legs and as I rise, I'm running them along the back of my thighs. I pull the skirt up... just a little... so you can see..." She maintained her precise narration as she unzipped her

82

dress, brushed it down over her hips and let it fall to the floor.

She turned to face Spiric once again, offering him a detailed description of her strapless black and white laced bra and matching thong. "I drop to my hands and knees," she said, as she did so. "And I crawl like a cat across the floor… All the time I'm looking straight at you."

It had become a game and Fiona was enjoying it now. She felt in absolute control of the room. His blindness had gifted her an extra level of confidence. She didn't seek the root cause of it, but there was something about dancing for a blind man, teasing him with image—she felt *powerful*.

She spun about on the floor, turned her back to him and un-hooked her bra. She raised herself up onto one knee, then stood, hooking the thumb of her left hand in her g-string, while holding the bra in place over her breasts with her right. She played with the thong a little, twisting her body in time to the music like an enchant-ed cobra, then dropped the bra, covered her breasts with both hands and turned back to face the bed. She described each move as it was performed and offered him a detailed illustration of her breasts as she revealed them: "Very round and soft…Small nipples. Very red. Very hard."

She turned again and thought she heard a noise at the door—the click of a lock. She stole a glance, but saw nothing amiss. In any case, the key was on this side of the room, and Spiric was hardly in any shape to turn it.

He didn't stir. No movement and no sound. It was almost like he was hypnotized. She liked the thought.

"I've got both thumbs hooked in my thong now and I'm bending… just sliding it down… over my hips… thighs… knees…"

She felt a hand on her back. Icy cold palm flat against her skin. Thin fingers pressing between her shoulder blades. No sound escaped her lips, but she jolted with fright and stumbled forward, almost tripping on the panties snared about her ankles. She caught herself, kicked off the thong and spun about. There was no-one near her. Spiric, in his bed across the room, looked like Lenin's corpse in its mausoleum.

Mother fucking Christ, Fiona thought, still breathless from the scare. *What the hell was that?*

She found her place again quickly, ignoring the fright for the moment. There was only a minute or so left of the song and she

83

couldn't waste it.

"I...I've turned back to you," she said, starting to swing her hips again, a little half-heartedly. "I..." She stopped. Stood still. "I..." She was looking around her, eyes searching the room for the source of her discomfort. Something was dreadfully wrong. She could sense it. Her hands dropped to her sides. She looked back to the bed. "Mr. Spiric?"

An invisible hand snatched at her left wrist.

"Oh God!" She cried.

A second clawed at Fiona's right arm, pulling it back. Something kicked against her knees and knocked her to the floor. She hit hard, face smacking against the tile. Hands grabbed at her ankles. Fiona tried to kick them away, but it was like kicking at mist. One of her shoes went spinning into a corner. Fingers dug into her thighs, prying her legs apart. She thrashed her arms, trying to break free, but felt more invisible hands, descending like a swarm of monkeys to smother her. One wound its way into her hair, snapped her head back and thrust it into the tile. Her bottom lip split, blood rolled down her chin.

"Spiric..." she cried, as fingers prodded between her legs. "Somebody...Help! *Mr. Spiric*!!!"

"Shhhhhhhh..." came the calm reply. "I am in complete control."

She felt fingers at her throat stretching, winding their way around her neck time and again... and tightening. "Ple—!" She spat without enough air in her lungs to finish. She gasped wantonly, unable to take in another breath.

Spiric smiled, slowly. "Took me for a weakling, did you? An old man. A *piece* of a man..."

Fiona's head was tugged up by the hair, her body raised up off the floor, arms pulled up to her shoulders and out, so she was dangling like a marionette. She was held aloft—a naked Pinocchio without strings—toes scraping against the floor, while she looked down at the stuffed eye-sockets of Spiric, still lying peacefully in his bed.

"But I'm stronger than you," the old man hissed, the voice emanating from his mind rather than his mouth.

Fiona was choking to death. Mouth agape and tongue flapping, eyes bulging, tears on her face... She wanted so much to breathe. Wanted to flail her arms and kick her legs, but every instinct was held in check by Spiric. Movement was impossible. Escape impossible. There was a thick pounding in her skull. Her vision began to cloud and she knew she was going to pass out.

Spiric's awful voice echoed across the room. "I am in complete control," he repeated. "And you... are powerless."

At that he dropped her. The binds holding her aloft faded to vapor and she collapsed, crumpling to the floor—a gasping, quivering wreck. She breathed deeply and desperately, air burning in her windpipe as it flowed into her lungs. She rolled onto her side, pulling her legs into her stomach, folding her arms over her chest. The places where he'd touched her stung as though his hands had been soaked in acid. The pain was fierce.

Spiric cleared his throat and spoke again. "I suppose you're wondering how all this is possible..."

"I don't give a FUCK!" she screamed in reply, surprising even herself with the volume of her voice. Spiric's heart-rate monitor spiked a little with the shock.

"Well," he replied, after they'd shared a passing moment in silence. "That's a shame. It's a fascinating tale..."

Fiona wasn't the least bit interested. All she cared about was survival. Even now, as the old man was speaking, and before she truly felt capable, she was dragging herself up onto her hands and knees, inching towards the door.

"There's a great many, I'm sure, who would love to know the secrets of unlocking my power," Spiric continued, as Fiona slinked past his bed. "It's somewhat inspirational... A testament to how much can be achieved by the human mind. Thought over flesh. And all it takes is money, patience, a little knowledge... and *will*."

Fiona was shivering as she crossed the tiled floor, her body still reeling from the shock, aching from his touch. Her nudity, and the temperature in the room, only compounded her discomfort.

"But perhaps you're right," said Spiric. "Enough with the foreplay..."

And then his ghostly hands were upon her again, colder than before and just as eager. They gripped her limbs and spun her about, onto her back. She cried out and a flat palm pressed down over her mouth. Fingers gripped her throat, but there was no pressure.

"Don't test me," Spiric warned her. "Play *nice*... And perhaps I'll let you live."

She tried to nod and relaxed her muscles, relenting to his icy embrace if only he let her keep breathing.

"That's good," he said.

His hands were rough on her breasts, squeezing and tugging her nipples. She could imagine the outline of his arms by the indentations his invisible fingers made on her skin. Fingers curled through her hair, caressed her brow, cheeks and lips. Each touch felt as though it were searing her flesh. She bit into her lip and tried to keep from making a sound.

He grabbed her under her knees and pulled her legs up. Fingers cold enough to burn spread the lips of her cunt and sank inside her like wriggling worms. Fiona told herself not to cry. Not to think. If she could will her brain to shut down, she would have done it. A moment later and the fingers withdrew. Hands forced her legs wider apart in preparation for the main event.

"Yes," Spiric groaned. "Yes, *indeed.*"

The head of his psychically-projected penis nuzzled against her vulva. Fiona tasted acid and Franco's whiskey in the back of her mouth and feared she might puke.

Franco! That FUCK! He knew. He KNEW!

Spiric entered her slowly, struggling to force himself into her modest opening. His mental dick was fiercely hot and rigid, with a touch like hard leather, and grotesquely oversized in both length and width. Fiona felt her flesh straining against his monstrous cock and was certain he'd make her bleed.

With his first thrust he knocked her back across the tiles. With his second, her head hit the wall. She grit her teeth against the pain and realized her hand was flattened uncomfortably atop an awkward object. She clutched it, turned her hand over and found she was holding her discarded shoe.

Fiona could sense Spiric's projected presence was repositioning himself to resume intercourse. His hold on her was considerably weakened while he navigated. As strong as he was when projected out of his head, the man was still *blind.* He couldn't see her or what she held. He lay on the bed, motionless as ever, a pathetic impression of a human being.

Fiona took her shot and hurled the shoe at the bed. The thick heel struck him hard on the temple. He blurted a shocked cry as his head snapped to the side, his bank of life support machines blaring madly.

Fiona sank to the floor again, her legs falling through claw-

ing hands turned to ether. She dragged herself to her feet—
against her body's agonized protests—and hurried towards the door.
She could feel a hysterical wail rising up out of her throat as she
placed one hand on the doorknob, the other on the key in the lock.

"NOOO!!!" Spiric cut her off with a cry of his own. His
phantom hands grabbed her at the door. His arms wrapped about her
waist and hauled her back.

She was lifted into the air and thrown backwards, landing
with a crash against his bed. The door key—knocked out of her
hand—bounced across the tiles into the far corner.

Fiona gripped the side of Spiric's bed and tried to heave herself up, not wanting to go another round with him on the floor. She
looked up and blinking through tears, saw him in the bed looming
over her. He was sitting up, sheets ruffled, his eyeless sockets cast
down towards her, seeing her without sight. There was a dark smear
of blood on his temple where her heel had caught him. "Just for
that," he said, "I'm going to play *rough*."

"Oh please…" Fiona replied, her eyes following him as he
calmly lay back down. "Please no…"

Hands grabbed her wrists, holding them almost hard enough
to shatter her bones. Her arms were bent back and held firmly in
place as she was raised up and forced to bend forward over the bed.
Her feet were spread far apart. Hands clawed at her buttocks. His
fingers toyed with her anus.

"Nooo…" she moaned, voice muffled by his bed-sheets.

She felt the blunt, rounded head of his penis pressing against
her, preparing to force his way inside.

He's going to kill me, she thought. *He'll kill me!*

She fought and thrashed as best she could but every attempt
was rebuffed as she was slapped, thrown up and brought down
against the bed with such force that she was almost knocked unconscious.

When she opened her eyes… she found her head was in his
lap.

His lap. Not phantom Spiric. Not unstoppable mental Spiric
of the thousand hands and monster cock. Old Spiric. Infirm Spiric.
The withered husk of a man she'd almost managed to off with a
high-heeled shoe. The man hooked up to a hundred monitors, checking every beat of his ancient heart. Because too much excitement
can *kill*.

She felt her legs drawn up, ass spread wide as he attempted to force himself upon her.

She was pinned. Couldn't move her arms, legs, hips... All she could move was her head.

You want satisfaction? She thought, and bit into the bed sheet. She jerked her head and tugged the sheet down with her teeth to expose his naked belly and groin. His antiquated penis was revealed to her in all its flaccid, withered glory. *I'll give you satisfaction.*

She sucked the shrunken organ into her mouth, taking it fully down to the base.

Spiric howled suddenly and she felt all coordination drain from his supernatural attack. The bank of medical equipment shrieked. She heard his heart-rate rocket to dangerous heights.

"Stop..." he wheezed, raising a weak hand to push her head away. "Please..."

Blood rushed into his prick, enlarging it in her mouth as she licked and sucked, coiling her tongue around the tip, her lips working the shaft.

"P-please... God..."

His phantom self gradually came undone. Invisible fingers unwound from her limbs, hands slapping limply against her naked flesh like empty gloves.

A new alarm sounded, pitch and volume greater than any before it. Fiona could hear people running down the hallway outside, but she let nothing distract her from her task.

"P-p-please... N-n-n... Oooh..."

When she finally managed to free her arms she put her hands to work pumping Spiric's dick and massaging his balls. She could feel the blood pumping in his flesh, his pathetic little prick fast approaching climax.

People were hammering at the door, trying to get in. She heard muffled cries about the lock and confusion regarding the location of the key. None of it mattered to her. She had but one goal in mind.

"Dear...G-G-GOD!!!" Spiric's hands slapped pathetically against the mattress as his whole body arched upwards, head rolling back beneath a plume of spittle he'd sent spurting from his quivering lips.

Someone was throwing their full weight against the door.

One thud. Another.

In Fiona's mouth there was a shudder of movement and a modest spurt of lukewarm fluid. She swallowed, drew her head back and gasped for air.

Behind her, Franco broke down the door in a flurry of splinters. He ran to the bed, grabbed Fiona and threw her to the floor. Spiric's doctor followed, cradling an emergency kit in his hands and rushed to his patient's side.

Fiona lay where Franco had thrown her, making no effort to move. Exhausted, body wracked with pain, she lay sprawled on the cold white floor and watched the duo as they struggled valiantly to save their employer.

There were injections. Tubes were attached. Medicines and electricity administered. They pounded on his hollow old chest like it was made of iron.

But in a few minutes it was all over. Decided. Case closed. The doctor shook his head, grimly. Rembrandt Spiric was gone.

To a far worse place, Fiona hoped.

Franco said nothing to the Doctor. He stared a long time at Spiric's body, expression imperceptible, intentions impossible to gauge.

And Fiona began to tense, knowing that her ordeal might yet not be complete. What kind of men were these? What were they capable of? To what lengths might they go in order to preserve the reputation of their employer, even after death?

If she were able, she'd run. She'd hurl herself out of the room and out of the building and run naked down the streets screaming for help. As it was, she had hardly enough energy left to keep her eyes open. There was nothing but to wait, watch and accept whatever gruesome punishment was handed out.

"Well," Franco said, at last, turning to fix her with his forbidding gaze. "You did it. You killed the boss. You know what this means, don't you?"

Fiona made some attempt to raise herself up on one quivering arm, cleared her throat and tentatively asked, "What?"

Franco held out his hands apologetically and sighed. "No tip."

Everyone Has Their Own Sound

Piper Morgan

> When I hear music, I fear no danger. I am invulnerable. I see no
> foe. I am related to the earliest times, and to the latest.
> -Henry David Thoreau

The simple phrase, which served instead of a company logo, was stamped in elegant gold leaf letters across the ornately wrapped box that was being handed to a withered gent—bowed but unbroken by the constant crush of years. As the severely dressed, but noticeably relaxed woman handing him the box would have readily told anyone who bothered to ask, was that some products and services don't need a flashy logo or a catchy jingle. The right product inspires brand loyalty on its own. The right product amazes and entices us enough to serve as its own brand without the mundane, empty identity found in a name.

"Are you sure that Elise is ready for this?" she asked him, her smile failing to mask the concern that draped her like a caul. "I realize that she's not a little girl. Hell, she's almost twenty-one, but age doesn't mean a whole lot. I'd hate for you to end up being known as the grampa that set her up with a few years in the rubber suit at ye olde Planter's castle. Especially since you've just paid a good year's worth of my house payments buying this."

"You worry too much," he replied with a soft pat on her shoulder, every bit the comforting old patrician. "She's ready. Not just ready, but she needs this. It's the only way that she'll be able to move on, to get past all that she's been through. That cocksucking little bastard... Well, that's why I came to you in the first place. The money is nothing." A single tear worked its way along the myriad crevasses that lined his face. "There's no way to repay you for what this will mean to her."

"Nonsense. I told you before this isn't just what I *do*, it's what I am. I only charge because I'm so damn good. It'd be a shame to waste such natural skill on a hobby."

"Speaking of that, well, I don't want to pry, but... I've always wanted to know..."

"How I got started? That it?"

"Well, yeah," the old man replied. "How does anyone get started in a line of work like this?"

The woman laughed. "I guess it isn't exactly something you pick up in a few classes at the rec center, now is it?" She paused, the smile left her face and was replaced by the expression of deep thought. "Like all decent stories, this one happened way back in my youth, during those miraculously fragile days of first love."

The man nodded solemnly as if he could relate. He waited for the woman to continue, but she remained lost in the memories of her own story.

***

"Can we go see the new Neil Watson movie for my birthday?" I asked.

"No," Brady snorted. "He's stupid, and you're a dipshit for thinking he's funny."

"Well, I just thought..."

He cut me off without even looking up from his video game. "No, that's your problem, Sophie, you don't think." He looked at his watch. "Look, you have to go." He grabbed my upper arm and pulled me off the couch.

"Why? You said we could spend the afternoon together. Ouch, you're hurting my arm."

He didn't loosen his grip. "I changed my mind. Chris is coming over to play his new game with me, so you have to leave."

"But—," was all I got out before he slammed the door in my face.

I walked a few of blocks before I realized my backpack was still at Brady's. I went back to his house and knocked lightly on the front door. When no one answered, I reached for the doorknob. The unlocked door swung open. The television in the living room was off, and the rest of the house was silent expect for the noises I heard coming from Brady's bedroom.

I quietly pushed the door open and that was when I saw her, Marta Jones—the perfect slut. She was fifteen going on twenty- five, perfect lips, boobs, ass...perfect everything. And she was having sex with my boyfriend. Their sweaty, naked bodies intertwined on the sheets as the bed banged loudly against the wall in rhythm with their movements, their moans drowning out the sounds of the radio. I felt the color drain from my face and love melt from my heart. My world seemed to be crashing down on me like a sledgehammer; everything was moving in slow motion as I watched the horror before me. Waves of nausea forced bile into my throat. I went out to Brady's front porch and puked in his mom's flowers before running the six blocks to my house, hot tears stinging my eyes the entire way. I ran upstairs to my room and started playing my drums.

He can't get away with this, I thought. *He isn't going to survive breaking my heart. Even if it kills me, too.*

A couple of days later, I invited him to my 'secret' place by the locks and dam. "I've got a surprise for you."

"Tell me what it is, Sophie. I don't have time for games."

"Just come with me. I promise you won't regret it."

We got on our bikes and raced toward the dam.

"I beat you! You suck!" He let his bike fall to the ground.

I just smiled and took his hand. The murky water was still; water skippers and occasional air bubbles were the only movement. I took my backpack off and set it on the ground in front of me. I took out my portable CD player, pushed play and put it on the bank. Tribal drumbeats echoed through trees and bounced off the water.

"What are you doing?"

"Shh." I took out the pair of white satin gloves and slipped them on. I ran a gloved finger along Brady's forearm and then down his neck. "I want to give you something special," I whispered. "Close your eyes." I grabbed his hands and led him toward the edge of the bank.

"What's going on?"

"Keep your eyes closed. Trust me; this is going to be the biggest surprise you've ever had." I looked around, making sure we were alone. "Sit down."

He plopped into the muddy water. "Great. That's just wonderful, Sophie. You just ruined my new jeans."

I closed his eyes again with my gloved hands, straddled his lap, and leaned in close to his ear. "Brady, I want you to know."

"Know what? You're stupid; what are you talking about?"

"I saw you with Marta."

Surprised by my words, his eyes sprang open.

I grabbed him by the throat and shoved his head under the water. As he flailed and fought, his head struck a large rock just under the surface. The swirling mud devoured the blood just as quickly as it escaped from the wound.

Brady grasped at my arms, yanking at my long sleeves; I pushed my thumbs further into his windpipe and squeezed tighter.

After what seemed like forever, everything stopped.

Quickly, I grabbed a small bag from my backpack and took out the fillet knife. I unzipped Brady's precious new jeans then stopped.

My heartbeat synced with the resounding drumbeats. My original plan changed and I smiled. This one was way better.

Putting the knife back, I reached for Dad's sixteen inch bone saw instead, happy that I thought to bring it along.

I grabbed and held onto Brady's right hand, the very hand that I saw squeezing Marta's boobs in my memory. I began sawing at the hand, right below his wrist, in the tiny space before his ulna and radius started. I smiled as tendons and nerves popped and tore. I didn't care about a clean cut; I just wanted the bones.

After finally getting through all the muscles and skin, his hand fell to the ground. I picked it up and placed his last gift to me inside my bag.

I rinsed the saw, tossed my gloves in the water, and toed Brady's bloody, lifeless body away from the bank as the dam opened. I watched him float down the river before getting on my bike and going to my Dad's shop.

I had just replaced the saw back on the table when he stuck his head in the back room.

"Hi little lady."

"Hey Dad." I gave him a quick peck on the cheek. "How are things going?"

"Kinda slow. Care to keep an eye on things while I run to the bank?"

"Sure."

He smiled down at me and patted the top of my head before grabbing a deposit bag from his office.

After I heard the familiar jingle of the bell on the front door, I went to work. I pulled Brady's hand and the fillet knife out of my bag. Leaning over the large stainless steel sink, I started shaving away as much skin as I could. Tossing the hand in the sink, I put the strips of skin and muscle on the cutting board and diced them into smaller pieces before throwing them into the running meat grinder.

I bagged what remained of the bloody stump and cleaned everything. I poured ammonia on the cutting board then put it and a few other dishes in the sink as it filled with hot water and suds.

A month later I had a beautiful set of handmade maracas. The shattered bones make such a pleasant rattling sound, reminds me of that special day.

***

"It's okay," the old man smiled, interrupting her thoughts. "I guess some stories aren't meant to be told. Thank you for everything, Sophie," he said, holding up the box.

Sophie nodded as he headed toward the front door. "Elise will love it."

The familiar jingle of the store bell broke her concentration. As she came from the back room, Sophie saw a twenty-something man standing near the counter. His pink puffy eyes were rimmed with tears.

"Can I help you?"

The man's head snapped toward her and he sniffled. "My wife... she..."

Sophie closed the distance between them and placed a reassuring hand on his shoulder. "I'm very sorry. Please have a seat; I want to hear your story." She followed him to the plush navy couch and sat down after him. After pouring him a cup of tea, she looked into his heartbroken eyes. "You know, everyone has their own special sound."

Les Sperme Vampire

Michael Bracken

The overpowering scent of the man's testosterone intoxicated me and made me quiver with anticipation before I even saw him, and when he rounded the corner at the unlit mouth of the alley, I wasn't disappointed. A big man in every sense, at least six-foot-two, with thick, muscular arms and a broad chest that tapered down to a firm waist, a tight ass, and muscular thighs. He wore a half-unbuttoned, long-sleeve blue work shirt with the sleeves rolled up to reveal his powerful biceps, a faded pair of Levi's so tight at the crotch that even in the dark I could see the bulge of his massive cock and heavy nutsack, and a pair of thick-soled black work boots. He wore his hair in a military flattop and his left earlobe sported a tiny gold hoop. A scar bisected his left eyebrow and his nose had been broken at least once. The tattoo on his right forearm read "Semper Fi" and the tattoo on his left forearm read 'USMC.' Up close he smelled of bourbon and breath mints, masculine sweat and hot coursing blood.

And testosterone.

I had been waiting, since nightfall, at the dark mouth of the dead-end alley for the arrival of someone like him. Finally, it was time. I stepped from the shadows.

He stopped, looked me up and down, and said, "I haven't seen you around here before."

I shrugged.

"How old are you?"

"Fourteen," I lied.

Though I could pass for a teenager in the shadows of the alley, I had left my teen years behind many decades earlier. I appeared barely pubescent and a touch malnourished, with paper-white skin, enticing bee-stung lips, heavy-lidded eyes, and dark, shoulder-length hair. Constantly evolving fashion trends had ultimately worked in my favor, allowing me to adapt a quasi-Goth appearance that made my pale skin seem a fashion choice and not a quirk of fate. I dressed all in black. From the knee-high lace-up boots, that added two inches to my height, to my tight leather pants, and sweat-stained hoodie that clung to my emaciated frame, right up to the dog collar, and eye shadow.

The big man standing in front of me thought he knew what I was and what I wanted. He removed a well-worn leather wallet from his hip pocket. "How much?"

I looked him up and down. "Twenty."

"Ten," he said. He opened his wallet and removed a crumpled ten-dollar bill.

I eyed the money as if it were important to me and tried to put a touch of desperation in my voice. "Fifteen?"

"Ten," he repeated.

When I hesitated, he started to put Alexander Hamilton back into his wallet. I snatched the bill from his hand and stood holding it. "Ten is okay. Ten is fine."

He returned his wallet to his pocket and I shoved Alex into mine.

I had him committed, but I needed more. I ran one finger along the inside of his muscular arm and coyly asked, "You got a name?"

"Call me John." He grinned as if he'd just told me the punch line to a great joke.

All my men were Johns. I smiled, though, pretending to enjoy the joke as much as he did. "OK, John," I said huskily, "you want to do this here?"

John glanced around and then did what I'd hoped he would. He took my hand and led me deeper into the dead-end alley. As soon we reached the brick wall that sealed the far end, he stepped behind an overflowing Dumpster, unbuckled his belt, and unbuttoned his fly. I grabbed the waistband of his jeans and his boxers and pulled them to his knees, revealing a long, thick cock already half-swollen with desire. Before he could complain about his restricted movement, I dropped to my knees in front of him and took the head of John's cock in my mouth, hooking my lips behind the spongy-soft mushroom cap. His cock responded immediately by rising to its full stature.

I teased his cockhead with the tip of my tongue and then slowly took his entire length into my mouth, careful not to scratch him with my razor-sharp incisors or pierce his skin with my needlepoint canines. When I grabbed his nutsack with one hand and kneaded his walnut-sized testicles with my fingers, he moaned with pleasure.

Under different circumstances I might have toyed with him. I might have dropped my own pants and let him take me from behind before I went down on him. I might have let him wrap his powerful hands around my hips as he drove his cock deep inside me, but not this night. Too much time had passed since my last meal and I was hungry. Starved. So I had immediately gone for his meat and he hadn't resisted.

John hadn't groomed in quite some time and his thick thatch of pubic hair tickled my nose as my head bobbed up and down the length of his turgid cock. He leaned back against the Dumpster and took my head in his hands. Soon his hips began moving back and forth, his crotch meeting my face in a steadily increasing rhythm, his heavy nuts bouncing against my chin.

I glanced up. John had closed his eyes and was rapidly approaching *la petite mort*—the little death.

Marcel had taught me about *la petite mort* and about *la grande mort* and about *les sperme vampires*—and that blood alone is never enough. He had made me what I am, and for several years I had clung to him like a remora, surviving on his scraps until I learned how to fend for myself. How to hunt, how to feed, and how not to create competition. We'd been—or I thought we'd been—orphaned by the events of the Great Depression, forced to survive on our own when our families could no longer care for us, but I'd later learned of his emigration from France years before the Declaration of Independence was signed and how he'd survived through the years. He had taught me about love, had awakened my sexuality, and had given me an eternal appetite to which I would forever be enslaved.

I'd been wrong about Marcel's love for me, though, and I soon realized he was using me to satiate his own sexual desire and as bait to satiate his blood lust. Once I could survive on my own I turned on him, driving a stake through his heart three days after the Japanese bombed Pearl Harbor as he slept in the basement of an abandoned building in Chicago, love and hatred driving me equally.

Since then I had survived on my own, finding lovers and meals with equal aplomb, rarely distinguishing between the two. There were always men interested in sex without commitment, men who found my youthful appearance enticing and were willing to pay for my companionship, men who came and went without ever comprehending what I really was. There were other men who wanted me exclusively and thought they could save me from life on the streets by taking me into their homes, a situation that only lasted until I felt the hunger and simply left my host or worse, left my host dead.

For many years I had remained in the shadows, unable to pass for an adult, despite my age, and thus unable to avail myself of the simple pleasures of a home address, a motor vehicle, or a bank account. Occasionally I stumbled across others like me who could pass. A few had driven me from their territory; a few others had encouraged me to move along by offering contacts to the underground world of forgers, petty thieves, and information brokers. By the time William Jefferson Clinton took the oath of office, I had established legitimate bank accounts and had a small, but steady, income from my investments. Even so, I still had no easy way to satiate my sexual desire or slake my thirst. My physical appearance prevented my admission to the nightspots, the bathhouses, and the private clubs that men of a certain sexual proclivity were known to frequent. I was forced by circumstance to troll the streets, taking risks that might otherwise have been unnecessary, in my search for food and fulfillment.

John wrapped his thick fingers in my hair, holding the back of my head as his cock slid in and out of my oral cavity. As his nutsack slapped against my chin, I stroked the sensitive bit of skin between his scrotum and his anus, causing him to moan with pleasure. When my temporary lover's rhythm suddenly increased and I knew he wouldn't last much longer, I pressed the tip of my middle finger against the tight pucker of his sphincter and pushed, driving it deep into him.

As John's cock throbbed with orgasm and he came in my mouth, the scent of his testosterone overpowered my senses and I sank my canines into his dorsal arteries. I sucked hard. His cum and his blood mixed in the back of my throat and I swallowed again and again and again.

The orgasm clouded his mind, and the unexpected rush of blood to his groin further weakened John. He didn't realize what was happening until it was too late. When he did, he tried to pull away. My razor-sharp teeth tore at his cock, ripping open the arteries and veins, allowing his blood to flow freely, so fast that I couldn't swallow it all and it leaked from the corners of my mouth onto John's jeans and the pavement below.

He began to struggle and tried to kick his legs, so I wrapped my arms around his thighs, holding him tight. He punched the top of my head so hard he might have broken a knuckle or two, but I had been hit before, many times and by men far stronger than John. He hit me a second time and then a third and a fourth, but his ineffectual blows grew progressively weaker as he rapidly lost blood and slowly collapsed to the filthy pavement of the dark alley.

I could have stopped sucking at any time and left John just enough life to become like me, but I didn't. I was hungry—malnourished because I had not eaten in weeks—and I sucked him until he stopped struggling. By then he was completely drained and my belly was so distended from all his blood that I had to unbutton my tight pants.

But I wasn't finished. I needed something from John that I could never get from a woman.

I took his nutsack into my mouth and clamped my front teeth together, sawing them back and forth until I snipped his sack free. Then I reached in my mouth, pulling out the hairy scrotum as I sucked the nuts free from the flesh sack. I tossed his flaccid scrotum aside and pushed one testicle into each cheek, making me look like a bloody gothic chipmunk.

As I chewed, I emptied John's wallet, removing $137 and a pre-paid long distance telephone card. Then I stood, swallowed, and picked a long, curly hair from between my teeth.

For *les sperme vampire*, blood is never enough.

The Bogeyman's Key

Calie Voorhis

The key throbbed in Clark's hand as he stood over Melissa, fast asleep in her bed. A poster of Mia Hamm glared at him from over the oak bed like she knew what he was getting ready to do. A row of old teddy bears stared back from their wall shelf, each black-beaded eye fixed on him. The room smelled of dirty gym clothes, strawberry lotion, and a faint hint of stale smoke. Melissa had been sneaking his cigarettes again.

Melissa snored once, then rolled onto her back.

Clark started and a vein began to beat in his temple. He waited a tense moment to see if she'd wake up and wondered what Melissa would think if she saw him standing over her. The old-fashioned skeleton key vibrated in his palm, the copper in the metal staining his skin green.

Only a dream, what he was about to do, Clark told himself. Not like he would ever do it in real life. He wasn't like *that*.

No, he was like his father. Shame flushed his cheeks, but he battered the feeling down into the pit of his stomach. Dreams weren't real. His memories of running endlessly away from the beast that had chased him had never *really* happened.

Dreams were just like the Internet, like the pictures of the girls who were legally eighteen but looked younger in their tight pink dresses. True, Melissa was only sixteen, but her body told him she wanted it as much as he did. Those breasts pointed at him when she came down to breakfast in the morning. Her nipples taunted him over his coffee.

At least she wasn't his daughter, not really. A foster-child was completely different.

It wouldn't hurt her. She'd be dreaming. It would be his fantasy.

With a gasp of anticipation, Clark took the key his father had left him and pressed it against Melissa's forehead with a shaking hand. At first, her skin resisted, then with a pop the key sank deep as it melded with the dreamworld. He turned the key and opened the lock of her mind. A tunnel opened up before him, swirling gray into a void, like smoke sucked in through a straw. Clark reached out a finger. A sensation like grease coated first his finger, then his hand. The cold crept over his arms, covering his body. Clark fell whirling into Melissa's dream.

The soccer field glowed green under a hot afternoon sun. The roar of the crowd beat at Clark as the blue team barreled down the field towards the goal. Melissa had the ball, streaking ahead of the rest of the pack of girls. Her scowl of exertion couldn't hide the pure joy on her face. Melissa faked to the inside then cut past the last defender. Her auburn hair bobbed, catching the rays of the sun to gleam red, then brown again as she passed into the shade of a cloud.

The faces of the cheering parents were blurry in the dream mist, except for two Clark recognized from the creased picture Melissa carried everywhere with her. Her real father pumped a fist in the air as Melissa swerved to keep the ball, while her mother stood with her arms crossed, face tight, as if she could will her strength to her daughter.

Melissa scored. It was her dream, after all.

Clark's cock pressed against his jeans. His chest tightened. It had become hard for him to breathe, now that he was here. Melissa's face looked so young, so innocent. His cock softened.

He concentrated, tightening his eyes as he took control. The crowd vanished. The teams wavered out of existence. Melissa's father turned towards her and her mom reached out a hand, but Clark forced their memory away until only Melissa and the soccer ball remained, along with the scent of fresh-mown grass, and girl sweat.

"Hello, Melissa." He walked towards her, at first each step a hesitation. As he gained confidence, he took the time to tighten his paunch, rippling the muscles to the structured cut of a weight-lifter, so that his t-shirt clung to his chest. His feet sank into the soft grass and the sun rested hot on his shoulders. The sense of power had him throbbing with need.

She stopped the soccer ball under a grimy sneaker and looked up at him, curiosity tightening the corners of her eyes.

"Hi." She picked up the soccer ball and bounced it off her knee. "Want to play with me?" Her stained soccer jersey fell past her waist, and her blue shorts sagged down her thighs.

That wouldn't do, Clark thought, even as his heart clenched

101

at her trust. He made a small adjustment, replacing the worn-out shoes with a set of bright red pumps, changing the knee-high socks and shorts to a mini-skirt and thigh-high stockings. With the adult garments, she looked younger, he thought. His cock bounced free as he let his worn clothes vanish. After a moment's consideration, he adjusted the size.

Her eyebrows tightened, forming a small set of wrinkles over her nose. Clark could see the future, how those small shifts of skin would one day form crags in her face. He smoothed them away with a thrust of thought.

Her body was all he could have asked for, all he'd hoped for through long nights lying sleepless next to his cold wife. Puzzlement opened her eyes wide. Her hand flew to her mouth. She hesitated when their eyes met and Clark knew she could see what was coming. He held out his arms.

Melissa ran, clumsy in the tight skirt. The heels of her pumps foundered in the grass. The combination made her awkward and banged her hips from side to side as she struggled to keep her balance. The faster she ran, the slower Clark let her move, until she was right before him again.

A rip of her blouse bared her breasts to him, the pink aureoles exposed. Clark took her there, on the soccer field of her dreams.

She screamed, beating at him with useless fists. He turned her scream into a moan of passion, and her fists into a clutching hug.

When she tried to draw away, he made her respond. Her hands caressed his smooth face, the acne pits banished in the dream.

She struggled to keep her legs tight together. Clark felt a rush of power as he made her arch her back in welcome, spread her legs wide for his convenience.

His concentration slipped as he plunged into her.

Melissa raked his shoulders with short fingernails as she tried to scrabble away, her face twisted.

Clark forced her to wrap her legs around him. She cooed into his ear, a soft, "yes."

He drove into her, until his need was satiated in a rush of exultation, making sure she quivered around him in her own release. In that respect, he wasn't like his father.

The day chilled around him. Clark looked down at Melissa. Shards of horror peered out from behind her eyes, even as she rubbed his back and hummed with pleasure. Clark raised himself off her and staggered back. He needed to go.

Clark visualized the key, then fell into the grass and seeped through the cold earth, back into the reality of Melissa's bedroom.

Clark twisted the key. It slid out from Melissa's forehead with a soft pop. As he turned to leave the room—his pajama bottoms sticking to his crotch from his dream ejaculation—he heard her whimper. He glanced back as he shut the door. Melissa had curled in on herself, clutching her spare pillow like a teddy bear. Her eyes were clamped shut. Her feet kicked at an unseen foe, small waves rippled under the blankets, and her thin hands gripped the worn fur.

Clark blundered down the hallway and back to his own bed with a hot flush in his face and a pit in his stomach. It was just a dream, he tried telling himself. She wouldn't remember it in the morning.

At breakfast, Melissa wouldn't meet his gaze, already dressed in her school uniform, no bra-less sleep shirt for her this morning. Across the battered breakfast table, she hid from him by concentrating on her bowl of cereal.

A pity, Clark thought. A memory of last night, of how tight she'd been, made him shift in his seat. How much did she remember?

"Sleep all right?"

Melissa's ponytail bounced, but she gave no other reaction that she'd heard him for a few seconds. "I slept fine." She began to shovel cereal into her mouth.

Clark watched her mouth close over the spoon. Tiny, kitten lips, he thought and an image of the night ahead flew through his head, sending his thoughts spinning away, even as he promised himself it wouldn't happen again.

The day passed in the usual routine, sitting in his assigned gray cubicle with the gray cloth-covered walls, eating his peanut-butter and strawberry jelly sandwich, scribbling the same words he'd scribbled a thousand times on the same forms, just like every other day. But all he thought about was the key, weighing down his polyester-blend pants. The key and his father.

"This is yours," the old man had said the last time Clark visited. The heavy air of the nursing home, filled with the stench of cabbage and old people, had pressed down on Clark, while the withered face stared up. His father coughed into a tissue. "You can use it to enter the dreamworld. Just don't let them get control." His father's watery blue eyes skipped about the room, looking anywhere but Clark's face.

Weight clamped down on Clark's chest, the familiar feeling of a hot shame he couldn't control, from dreams he knew weren't the truth, but had constrained him just the same. Because they were always, always, about his father, who had hardly ever touched him, certainly not like that, during the day.

He'd woken from those dreams with the taste of stale water in his mouth and memories of snakes surrounding and penetrating him, as his father caressed his skin.

And then the old man had finished explaining. The words drove into his head, his father's voice cracked and thin, but clear. Clark's breathing rate increased and each gasp for air brought the smell of shit concealed by bleach into his lungs. He took the key though, and left.

Clark had blundered down the pale yellow hallways, stumbled past the women and their walkers. The somnambulant slept like old cats in front of the televisions. He exited out the door in a rush of white heat, while static roared in his ears. He never returned, not even for the funeral.

But now it was night, and Clark's dilapidated Honda drove itself home. Where dinner awaited, and then, he could have Melissa in her sleep, just like his father had had him. All fantasies, all of it, and dreams meant nothing.

That night, and many nights after, Clark did everything he'd ever wanted to do. He hunted Melissa through the treacherous terrain of her dreams, as they grew ever darker. He had her in school, bent over a desk with the smell of chalk dust. He made her take him in her mouth in the parking lot of the school prom, while her two best friends in their purple velvet dresses watched.

He woke each morning with a bitter taste in his mouth and a vow he wouldn't do it again.

But he did.

Clark found that he didn't care if she enjoyed it or not. Now when she screamed, he let her. Pushing him away excited him more, made him harder, propelled him to push deeper.

Her expression during the day grew more haunted; her hair

104

fell slack in unwashed strings around her oval face. She changed her clothing to black shapeless garments reeking of cigarettes and a sharper, sweeter smell Clark knew was pot. When she saw him in the mornings, she flinched away, ate her cereal mechanically, and averted her face as she ran out the door.

Clark tried to fight his urge, but every night he found himself outside her door.

The school counselor urged them to get her counseling. Fearing discovery, he did, and Clark watched with a pit burning in his stomach as she went to session after session with a therapist, but it didn't stop him from creeping down the quiet hallway at night, into her room.

***

Clark fell once again into Melissa's dream under the baleful glare of the stuffed bear trio.

He found himself, not on the bright soccer field, nor the parking lot of school, but in a deep wood, heavy with rotting vegetation. Decaying leaves slid under his feet and seeped in between his toes, so he conjured a pair of shoes, along with a sweatshirt to cut the chill. Spiked vines swayed from branches and grabbed at him as he searched for Melissa. He didn't have any particular plans for the evening—this forest with its mossy carpet would serve as well as any other place.

A slim shadow cut across the path in front of him. Melissa darted to the right. Clark could see the white of her bare feet as she slipped round a large oak. He hardened as he picked up his pace. Tonight, he'd play the hunter. Acorns peppered down around him, bouncing against the loam.

When he got to the tree, though, Melissa wasn't there. Clark paused for a second. His breath formed small smoke clouds, white against the ebony green growth.

The ground hissed at him. Clark's chest pounded. Pressure dug at the top of his shoe. Clark looked down to see the mottled cream and brown argyle pattern of a copperhead snake. They're attracted to warmth, he remembered. Just stay still. The snake curled around his ankle, finding the flesh between his jeans and shoe, squeezing him with a ripple motion.

Sweat broke out on the back of his neck. In the distance, an owl hooted twice, sharp against the throbbing of blood in his ears.

"Oh, you idiot." He was in control here, this was his world.

The snake burst into charcoal, falling from its coil into dust. He kicked the remains away from him and leaned against the tree for a moment, hands in his pockets to still their trembling.

A breeze blew against his face and chilled the sweat. With the peaty smell of a swamp, it brought the sound of a girl crying. Melissa sounded as though she choked on the sobs.

Clark chuckled. He followed the wails through the dimness, making no attempt to hide the crunching of his feet on the twigs and branches littering the forest floor. Soon the sound changed to sloshing as the world around him altered, became filled with brackish water. He didn't mind. His heart beat with the chase, the thrill of the look he imagined was on Melissa's face—heartbroken brown eyes, the crease of her forehead, and the twist of down-turned lips.

He stumbled over a submerged root. It caught his foot. He wrenched his ankle free and stepped forward into water as deep as his knees. The sudden shock of the chill stopped him. Anger boiled in his chest.

"Come out, come out, wherever you are." His words shocked the silence and echoed through the swamp. A ripple lapped at him as something moved in the distance. His hand went to his penis and stroked it both in anticipation and to revive it from the effects of the cold. The water surged, its oily surface reflecting the light of a waning moon in rainbow swirls.

Enough, Clark thought. He focused his attention. The cypress and cedar trees wavered around him, but did not change. He pursed his lips in irritation. He was the master here; this was his world. His key opened the door.

He closed his eyes, the better to envision a more pleasant surrounding. Perhaps a girl's locker room, or better yet, the communal shower.

Snap. Teeth closed on his ankle. Clark fell into the swamp. He flailed for purchase. The jaws of the alligator tightened. Pinpricks of pain swarmed through his head. As his head broke the surface, the taste of rot on his tongue, the scaly back of the beast presented itself. His shoulder knocked against a tree. His hands beat at the alligator, to no effect.

He had to concentrate. This was only a dream. Clark took a deep breath. The grip on his ankle relaxed. Water drained away. The swamp melted around him as he regained control. He stood and dried himself, shedding the brackish water. He waited a moment to gain control of his senses.

"Ready or not, here I come." Silly girl, there was no way for her to evade him.

He caught a glimpse of the edge of Melissa's nightgown, glowing white and pure in the dark. His ankle ached, but he forced himself forward, quiet now, as the edges of the swamp faded into the high school's soccer field. Halogen lights rose up from the ground and bathed the grass, leaving no place for Melissa to hide, no shadows left for her to crouch in.

He'd take her as he had the first time, on the grass where she'd thought to be strong, like her idol, Mia.

She cut in front of him, running like a deer across the green, lithe and supple. The nightgown flapped against her white calves as she ran.

Clark took it from her.

Melissa stopped. Her buttocks clenched as she faced him.

Clark smiled. His cock throbbed, filling him with dark need. An image of his father flickered before him. He shoved it aside, but swore he could hear the old man's cackle.

Melissa stood, head bowed, shoulders slumped in defeat. She didn't even bother to cover herself. The peaks of her nipples stood taut and high, the curve of her waist lured him closer.

"Here I am," Clark said.

Melissa swung her hair back. "No. I won't."

Clark giggled, he couldn't help it. She was defying him—so futile, so useless.

"Here I come, ready or not." His ankle throbbing, he stepped nearer, so close he could smell the strawberry scent of her sweat.

"My therapist says it's my dreams. I can control them." Her voice wavered, sounding small to Clark in the enormity of the field.

"But they aren't your dreams, now are they? Unless this is what you've really wanted all along."

Her cheeks flushed. Could it be, Clark thought, could it be she had wanted him, some part of her, hidden away in the day? Perhaps this time, he would be tender. He placed a hand on her shoulder, felt the tremble of her body as she shivered.

"You're cold," he said. "I can warm you up."

When she made no response, he slid his other hand over her breasts. They warmed his palm. Melissa swayed under his grasp.

"I've done my research," she said.

107

His belly expanded back to its normal paunch.

"Shh," he said. He gathered her to his chest and pressed his face in her hair. Melissa nestled into him. Her arms reached around his waist. Clark pressed himself against her. With a brief thought, he let his jeans fade away so he could feel the warmth of her skin, so she could feel the heat of his desire.

She tightened her arms around his waist. He rubbed his face against her head. His acne scars caught her fine hair. The smoothness of her skin contrasted with his scabrous lips.

Her knee caught him square.

Pain lanced through his groin. It radiated up through his stomach. Nausea curdled him to the grass. He cradled his hands around balls swelling into watermelons.

"I found your father."

Through wavering vision, Clark looked up. The man stood there, as he had long ago, tall and proud. One hand jerked on his penis, readying the flaccid member.

Melissa drew her foot back, and kicked again.

"Goal," she said, her face split by a wide grin. "Score for the team." She held up her hand, as if to stop him as he struggled to rise. A green stain marked her palm in a familiar butterfly pattern. "Ever wonder what would happen if I woke up during the dream?"

She darted back and ran forward.

His chin snapped back.

"My dreams. You fucking pervert."

Clark heard a hiss. He forced his eyes open. The copperhead stared back, malevolent yellow eyes fixated on him. He rolled away, still cradling his balls. The movement took effort; his stomach had expanded even further, burying his penis underneath its pendulous weight.

The alligator hissed. Fetid warmth swept over his face.

His father stepped forward. Clark smelled his sour breath. A tide of humiliation made him crinkle his eyes against the tears.

Through the mist of red and the overwhelming urge to vomit, Clark retreated, rolling his bulk with a grunt. The lesions on his skin caught at the skeleton ribs of rotted leaves.

Melissa's foot blasted into his chest. Clark heard a pop and felt something bubble in his throat.

"I wonder what happens if *you* die in your dreams," Melissa said. Her voice echoed through the slamming in his head. "Or perhaps I'll just leave you here with them."

Stoners and Saviors

Quinn Hernandez

So here's the deal: last Thursday night while I was minding my own business, asleep, Jesus Christ spoke to me.

Ok, ok, now don't look at me like that. I know what you're thinking. And no, this is not a joke. This is *not* an attempt at pay-back for you posting my truck for sale in the paper. That was fun-ny though. The guy on the phone was like, '*what's wrong with it?*' Anyway, this has nothing to do with that. I swear. I'm not crazy, either. And no, I wasn't drunk and I wasn't high that night. Matter of fact, I had just smoked the last of my green last Tuesday with you.

What? No, I didn't dream it! Yeah, I said I was asleep when he came, but he woke me up. Look, I understand it's human nature to be skeptical. Shit man, if you were telling me you talked to Jesus Christ last Thursday night, I'd think you were full of shit, too. But I have proof. All I ask is that you hear me out, and when I show you what I have to show, you have to promise me you won't freak out, ok? Promise me you'll stay cool. We're boys, right? I'm only telling you all of this 'cause I love you like a brother, man. I'm trusting you with this, ok? So, please don't get all weird on me. I'm counting on you, alright? I'm not crazy!

Alright?

Alright! Cool! Well, here goes nothing. As I said before, I was asleep minding my own business when I was awakened by the sound of trumpets. Can you believe that? Trumpets! The Son of God, the savior of man's soul, the guy people call on to help them through the toughest times of their lives, comes floating down through my ceiling on a trumpet train like he's James fucking Brown taking the stage in Vegas. I mean, what's that say about the guy's ego? I know he's the Son of God and all, but does he have to act like a total douche and announce his presence with trumpets?

Anyway, he floats down through my ceiling and takes a seat at the foot of my bed. He looks like he does in all of his pictures: like a hippy in a wool robe wearing Birkenstock sandals. Well, maybe they weren't Birkenstocks but you get the idea. He doesn't say anything. He just stares at me with a shit-eating grin and tries not to laugh at me in my pee stained boxers and the tent my morning wood was poppin'. He then asks me if I wouldn't mind helping him out. First let me say, the dude didn't sound like I'd imagined he would. I was expecting him to sound British or some shit. Kinda like that Charlton Heston dude in that *Ten Commandments* movie, but no. He sounded just like you and me, dude. I swear. It was a trip.

So anyway, I'm like, what does the Son of God need from me? Some good weed? Can't he just wave his hand or something and weed will just fall out of the sky? He was like, I'm not here to get high, I'm here because I need your help to return to Earth. And I was like, uh, dude, you're already here. He rolled his eyes at me and seemed to get a little pissy, then began telling me his whole life story like I was his A&E biographer.

He said he got into a fight with his old man. I guess his daddy wanted him to come down here with some Old Testament fury and wipe out the world and take *his people* back to Heaven, leaving the Earth and us sinners to the Devil and his buddies to fuck over. But Jesus wasn't feelin' that. According to ol' J.C., both the Bible and the history books portrayed him all wrong. Sure he was the Son of God, and true, he was meant to be the savior, but what they didn't fess up to was that Jesus didn't *want* to be a savior. Once he got a taste of the good life—drinkin', bangin' bitches, snorting lines off of Mary Magdalene's ass—Jesus wanted no part of martyrdom. Why should he? Why die a painful death and give up all of the pleasures Earth had to offer? Why give up being the rock star of his day? Hell, everyone worshiped him. All the dudes wanted to be him and would do anything he asked. The ladies all thought he was a pimp. If you could miracle booze out of water, would you let the party die so the miserable pricks who couldn't be cool in the first place—who don't deserve redemption—could be forgiven and go to Heaven? Hell no! You wouldn't wanna give it up, I wouldn't, and neither did J.C.

So, his old man was like, either you go down and fulfill your destiny or I'll turn this car right around, and when we get home you'll be grounded for a month. Nah, dude. I'm just playin'. He didn't say that. But he did say his dad would only let him come back in spirit form until he decided to grow up, take his responsibilities seriously and perform his duties. He said Jesus had abused his flesh privileges, that *his* flesh wasn't to be used for sinning. Finally, Jesus got tired of his old man's shit, told him to go fuck himself and split.

111

Before he left, J.C. told the old man he'd get his own flesh. And that's where I come in.

Why me? That's what I asked. You know what he said? He said, *why not me*, and left it at that. Talk about Jedi mind tricks, right?

What? No, dude. He's not gonna possess me. That's demon stuff. He wants uninhabited flesh, not flesh with somebody already living there. Nah! Check it out. Jesus told me he went down to see Satan for two reasons. First: Satan had the pull to help Jesus get flesh; two: Jesus knew how pissed his dad would be if his own son asked the help of his number one competitor and rival, plus, he knew Satan would help because it would humiliate the old man.

Jesus said Satan gave him some sort of incantation to recite. Said he had to get a hunk of flesh, read the spell over it and everything would be kosher. Huh? No, dude, he's not gonna sacrifice me. He just needed a little hunk of skin, nothing major. Here, look! Let me roll up my pant leg and show you my calf. See! It's nothing. Naw, I'd say it's about a five by five-inch patch of skin, that's all. Oh, now, c'mon dude, you promised me you'd be cool! Let me finish, ok? I told you I'm not nuts, all right! Just chill, ok. Can you do that for me? Thank you! Now, where was I?

Oh, yeah, before I cut the skin off, Jesus wanted me to get a tattoo on it first. He said the flesh would need a form, an identity. So the next day, I went down to O' Toole's and had him stitch me the picture Jesus gave me. You know what that weird fucker wanted? He gave me a picture of himself, buck-naked! And he was hung like a Shetland pony! He was all spread out, lookin' like a six-pointed star. Do you realize how hard it was to go down to O' Toole's and tell him I wanted a tattoo of Jesus Christ with a huge swingin' dick? Any idea how embarrassing that is? Well, I did it. I just told them I was a priest new to the area and left it at that.

I know I'm not priest, dude. It's just a joke bro. Anyway, when the tat was done, he said he needed me to free it from the prison it's bound to. Meaning I had to cut it off. I used the filet knife from the cheap set my mom bought me last Christmas to do it. Man, it hurt like a motherfucker. But the cool thing was, Jesus miracled up some good ganja and lit me fatty after fatty until it didn't seem to hurt anymore. Once I finished skinning myself I gave the liberated tat to Jesus, he held it in his palm and read the incantation. No sooner than he finished the last word of the spell, the dude disappeared.

Now this is where the story gets a little hard to believe. You still with me? Cool.

After the patch fell to the floor . . . it stood up!

The naked Jesus-thing stretched out its appendages until it resembled a man shape. The tattoo half was facing me so I could see how the picture grew with the skin: how his new face lined up on what was to be the head, how the blue arms followed the patch's arms, as did the legs and its donkey cock. Like I said, he looked like a six-pointed star. A very angry star, though. He was cussing up a storm in his tiny Jesus voice. He was like, *mother fuck* this, and *lying piece of shit* that, *you've gotta be fuckin' kidding me*! He said he was gonna go see that goat fucker and kill him! I didn't know what the hell he was crying about. I was like, problem? He told me to shut the fuck up then stormed off.

Once the dude got back from Hell, and had time to cool down, he came to me and gave me the skinny. It appears El Diablo played a big joke on him. You see, Jesus, in all his infinite wisdom, was in such a hurry to taste pussy again, he didn't think about what he was asking. He told Satan he wanted to be bound to the flesh once more, meaning he wanted a body, but he didn't clarify that. So, when Satan wrote the incantation, he used Jesus' lack of specification against him to bind him to a hunk of flesh instead of a full-fledged body. What's worse, according to Jesus, since Satan didn't exactly lie to him, and Jesus willingly participated in the deal, there's some kind of bylaw or treaty that prevents his father from intervening. If he did, he'd lose his God license or something.

What's that? Where would Satan find a lawyer in Hell? Oh, jeez man. Real fuckin' funny. What's that? The point? Man, don't rush me. I'll get to it. 'Ere, have another toke. What was I sayin'? Oh, yeah, Jesus is fucked. He told me his daddy wouldn't help him even if he could. Said his father was so pissed off, he pretty much disowned him. Said he's on his own now and he doesn't care what he'd become. But man, he should.

Why? Cause he's not just some hunk of animated skin, dude. He's something worse. You see, the way Jesus explained it, there are actually two creators: God and Satan. God creates all the flowers and kittens and good shit you see on Earth; the Devil creates all of the fucked up, evil shit that runs around in Hell. Jesus went to Satan for a body, instead he gets put into a hunk of flesh. Now, since Jesus

113

did not actually possess a full-fledged body—and a human body is considered a creation of God—J.C. is now *not* considered a creation of his father. Instead, he is a creation of Satan; since, technically, an animated hunk of flesh is not a complete human being it is considered a creature. This creature, which was produced by black magic, is the direct product of Satan, and therefore everything within said creature belongs to its creator.

Does that make sense? In a nutshell, Jesus is now reborn in the image of Satan, kinda. Since Jesus is now a new creation of Satan, one that has never before existed, it states in some kooky bylaw, the creator has the right to decide how it eats, if it sleeps, if it can think, whatever. This creator has full control over his creation, but once said creator decides how the thing is gonna exist, those decisions are set in stone and cannot be undone. If Satan wishes Jesus to be an animal with chronic flatulence, three eyes, green skin and feed primarily on cock, then that's how he'll be for all eternity. There's no do overs.

So what did he decide? Glad you asked. Turned out, Satan doesn't have much of an imagination. He left Jesus as he was, but with one small hitch. You see, he's just a small patch of dying skin, and to keep that skin from drying out, Jesus needs to keep himself wet. That is where you fit into the picture. You see, he needs fresh flesh and blood to maintain his vitality. Yesterday I had Cheryl over. You remember Cheryl, from high school? She's always calling me for weed. So when she called yesterday, I tell her I'll give her some killer weed for free, *if* she gives me a blow job. Being the gutter whore she is, she agreed. She gets here and I sit her down right where you're sitting now and wait for J.C. to unfold himself from under the couch cushions. Dude, it was disgusting to watch. He kinda stuck to her back like a cartoon starfish and kinda...absorbed her.

You could see his shape growing larger as she imploded. I've never seen anything like it. He just sucked away all the blood and meat until she was a dry husk of skin and bones. Man, the sound it made was gross. What's worse was the look on his tattoo face. He looked fuckin' wild, man. Then he was like, get me more. So I called you. Tomorrow I'll invite Mike over.

Uh oh! The look on your face tells me he's already got you. Oh please don't give me that look, bro. You've got to understand, either I bring him people to feed on or he eats me. What would you do? Whoa, dude! Your eyes just popped out! Well, look on the bright side, at least you didn't go from being the Son of God to being a fuckin' vampire.

Digital Media

Michael Cieslak

"Wake him," a voice said.

The body lay slumped in the chair, unconscious. Its head lolled back and to the right. One of the men stepped out of the shadows. A vicious slap to the face did nothing. A bucket of cold water was fetched and dumped on the figure, who came to life with a sputter.

The man, now fully awake, struggled briefly against the bonds which held him to the chair. After a few moments he stopped, hanging his head in defeat. The light from the bare bulb overhead illuminated the man's bald pate.

"Look at me," the voice commanded.

The man in the chair sobbed once, but kept his chin tucked against his chest, either to avoid seeing the surroundings or as a defensive posture.

"Head up, Sunshine." The words seemed warm, but the voice was as cold and dark as the inky blackness which surrounded the small circle of light.

The man in the chair raised his head, squeezing his eyes shut against the harsh light.

"Open those eyes," the voice said. "Remember, you asked for this."

"I never—" the man in the chair started to protest.

A hand shot into the feeble light and caught him, open handed, along his jaw. His head snapped back, teeth clacking shut audibly.

"Do not contradict me, Mr. Johnson.

"But I, I didn't..."

"No, of course you didn't." The voice had moved slightly in the darkness. Johnson, the man in the chair, thought it was coming from his left side. He turned his head to follow it, but he could see nothing outside of the light bulb's illumination.

"Where am I?" he asked. He couldn't remember anything beyond leaving his office that evening. Or yesterday evening? He was not even sure of the time.

From where he sat, the room he was in was utterly feature-less. The darkness could have hidden a warehouse, an airport hang-er, or a closet-sized kitchenette. His whole world was defined by what he could see, what was directly below the bulb. Existence was reduced to his own body, naked except for brightly striped boxer shorts, and the chair to which he was bound. The chair was wooden, sturdy, with wide set legs. His arms were bound at wrists and elbows to its wide armrests. Other straps, which felt like leather, bit into his legs, chest, and waist. That was everything. That was his reality. A chair, some leather straps, and the ridiculous boxers he wished he had not worn.

That... and the voice.

"Do you think that rules are important?"

The voice was definitely coming from the left side of the chair now.

"Um, rules?" Johnson was unsure how to answer.

"Yes, Mr. Johnson, rules. Do you think that rules are impor-tant?"

"Sure, some rules. Others... I don't know."

"An honest answer, therefore a good answer." The voice continued to move—behind him now. Johnson tried to turn, but the high back of the chair prevented his head from moving very far around.

"I think that rules are very important. They are necessary, es-sential. Without rules, all would be chaos. Rules are imperative for the existence of modern society."

The voice was still directly behind him.

"Laws, on the other hand, can be corrupted. They tend to serve the strong and the powerful, to the exclusion of the weak and powerless. Good laws are based upon accepted rules. As such, if one follows the rules, one is safe. Do you agree Mr. Johnson?"

"Yeah, right. Rules are important." He whipped his head from side to side. He craned it to the right, but still could not make out the source of the voice.

"I am glad you agree."

The voice paused. In the silence which followed, Johnson thought that he could detect movement at the edges of the circle of light. Were there others in the room?

"The application of rules allows us to chart our way through

117

life. They define what is permitted and what is proscribed. Of course, there is a dark side to the application of rules. It allows us to punish behavior which breaks the rules."

There was a scraping sound directly behind the chair. Johnson felt someone grab his hair tightly. His head was slammed into the chair back.

"I am glad that you understand the importance of rules, Mr. Johnson." The voice whispered into his ear. Johnson could feel the hot breath on his skin. "Now pay very close attention. I am going to tell you the rules of the most important game of your life. Are you listening closely?"

A squeak slipped from Johnson's throat. He nodded as best as he could with the hand twisted tightly in his hair.

"Good."

The grip on his hair relaxed. The voice began moving again.

"We are going to engage in a game somewhere between Jeopardy and Truth or Dare. The questions may be hard to answer, but I guarantee you will know the answers. There is only one topic—your life. You must answer truthfully. There is no "dare" option. You must also answer correctly."

The pacing stopped. The voice was off to his right.

"You are right handed, correct?"

Johnson nodded.

"For the sake of clarity, please verbalize all of your answers."

"Yes, I am right handed."

"Good, very good. Your answers should be as succinct as possible, yes or no where possible. Do you understand?"

"Yes."

"Good. The rules state that you must answer every question. Now it is very important to remember, you must answer truthfully and you must answer correctly."

The voice had continued to move until it was directly in front of him again. Johnson peered into the darkness still struggling to see the speaker.

"Which is more important, honesty or intelligence?"

"Uh, I am not sure," Johnson stammered nervously. "They are both…"

The voice cut him off.

"Don't worry. We have not started the game yet. I am just interested in your opinion. Let me phrase it a different way. Which

118

is more abhorrent: someone who is wrong, or someone who deliberately lies?"

Johnson's throat dried up. He rasped out his answer. "Lying is worse."

"We agree. It is far better to be incorrect then deliberately deceitful. So, we come to the final rules of the game, the rules regarding punishment. If you answer a question incorrectly, you will lose a finger on your left hand. However, if you do know the answer and provide one which you know to be false, you will lose a finger from your right hand."

Johnson sobbed quietly.

"Now remember, the rules state that you must answer every question. Failure to answer will be considered a lie of omission and will result in the same punishment as a spoken lie. If you are not sure about an answer, it is better to guess. If you are wrong, you will only lose part of your left hand.

"Bear in mind, by answering you at least have the possibility of providing a correct answer. Failure to answer is an assured wrong answer. It is better to chance an educated guess, just like the SATs."

There was a slow scraping sound, like metal being drawn over stone. Johnson looked up. A long cruel looking knife gleamed in the light. The hand that held it was encased in a blue glove made of latex or rubber. The blade rose slowly until it was pointed at Johnson's right eye. He pulled his head back as far as the chair would let him.

"Twenty questions, Mr. Johnson. You have only to answer twenty questions. Of course, if you run out of digits we have to move to other parts."

Johnson turned his head, pressing it into the seat back.

"Let's begin."

"How long have you lived at your current address?"

Johnson blinked. Was that really one of the twenty questions? Were they really going to be that easy?

He squeezed his eyes shut, wondering how accurate he needed to be? He had moved in the fall a few years ago. It had been after he had gotten his new job. He was due for a five year pay bump next month.

"Your answer please."

"I have lived there for four years, ten months—"

He was stopped by a chuckle.

"There is no need to be that specific. Four years will suffice. I would have also accepted 'almost five years.' Don't worry about these first few questions, they're easy. If I need you to be precise, I will let you know."

The voice sounded relaxed, almost charming.

"How long have you lived alone?"

The voice did not ask for precision, but in this case it would be easy to provide. He could answer down to the minute, if he knew the current date and time.

"About 18 months."

"And before that?"

Johnson wondered if that counted as one of the questions. "Um, before that I was living with someone, Linda. She...she left."

"Yes, she did. How long has it been since you have been on a date?"

"A date?"

"Answering a question with a question is a stall tactic often used by people who are about fabricate their answer. Think very carefully about what you want your response to be. How long has it been since you have been on a date?"

"I haven't really dated anyone. I don't go out."

Silence.

"Do you have to go out to be on a date?"

Seconds ticked by, then the realization hit him.

"Well, on-line dating. I have dated in Virtual World, the on-line..." his voice trailed off.

"So you have dated."

Johnson swallowed hard.

"Meaning the answer you provided was incorrect."

The voice came from his left side.

"No, wait! I did not understand the question!"

There was a flash of pain. Johnson looked down in time to see the knife blade, bloodied, retreating from the light. Then a burning pain shot through his arm. Blood spurted from his left hand—his pinky finger now ended at the first knuckle. He strained forward in the chair. On the ground was a growing puddle of his blood. At the edge of it sat the other two-thirds of his finger.

Johnson opened his mouth to scream. He passed out instead.

***

120

This time it took more than water to bring him around.

Johnson opened his eyes just in time to see a slim figure retreat from the light. There was a stinging sensation in the crook of his right arm. He looked down and saw a single orb of blood nestled there. As he watched the orb swelled and burst, releasing a trickle of blood across his arm. Its source was a tiny puncture in his vein.

He had a brief moment to wonder what he had been injected with before the throbbing started. With the pain came the memory.

A quick glance at his ruined left hand confirmed it. A bloody lump of gauze was taped to the side of his hand. He lifted his hand as much as the bindings would allow. It came away from the arm of the chair with a sticky wet sound.

Johnson started screaming again.

There were no words. His shriek was the raw sound of panic, fear, and disbelief. It lasted until he ran out of breath. He tried to suck in more air and begin again, but before he could, a hand connected with his cheek. It was much harder than the previous slap. The hand seemed different, too. Harder, stronger.

"Mr. Johnson, it's time to continue. We still have a lot of questions to go."

The voice was coming from the left side. The slap had been from the right. There were at least two different people in the room with him.

"Now, we have established that you 'date' in various on-line scenarios. We will return to that in a moment. What other internet activities do you perform?"

"The same as everyone else, I guess." Johnson did not know what the voice was looking for, but did not hesitate to answer. "E-mail, look up stuff, pay bills, surf the net."

"And when you surf the net, what do you look at?"

"All kinds of stuff. The usual stuff. What everyone looks at."

There was a glint of steel and a blaze of pain. The flat end of the knife blade rapped down on the stump of Johnson's severed finger. Pain lanced up his arm. The blood begin to flow again, pooling on the arm rest before dripping to the floor. He stifled another scream.

"A non-answer. Tread carefully, Mr. Johnson. You are perilously close to a lie of omission."

Johnson gulped air. The pain subsided to a throb. Each beat of his heart fueled the suffering. He closed his eyes for a moment and concentrated on his breathing.

"Better now?" the voice asked. "Good. Then I ask you again, what do you look at when you surf the net?"

"Amazon," Johnson blurted. "I buy books all of the time. I go to my bank's website. I...I look stuff up, you know, videos, cartoons, funny stuff. I watch movie trailers. I read the news. Sometimes I watch old episodes of TV shows."

"What else?"

"I don't know what else. Honest I don't."

His voice climbed higher, whining, pleading. The knife appeared again. The tip grazed his left arm. It was dragged gently up the arm to his shoulder. The knife was sharp enough that the faint scratch was enough to draw a line of blood the length of his arm.

"What else do you use your computer for?"

An image popped into Johnson's mind. He opened his mouth to speak, but no words came forth.

"Tick, tock."

The man in the chair shook his head. He had an answer. He was just unwilling to give it. It was too horrible to admit. There was no way they could know.

He saw movement to his right. He tried to pull away, momentarily forgetting the leather straps. His hand slipped forward and tightened on the edge of the arm rest.

He felt the knife bite into the meat at the side of his hand. Johnson gripped the chair harder. He watched in horror as the little finger on his right hand was replaced by the knife. Blood gushed over the blade which was wedged partially in the arm rest, partially in his hand. The tip had nicked his ring finger. His pinkie was gone at the base.

"What?" Johnson screamed. "What do you want you dirty, mother—"

What he could see of the room dimmed. The circle of light he sat in seemed to shrink. The edges of his vision became gray. He shook his head to clear it.

When his sight cleared, he saw that his right hand had been roughly bandaged. He did not remember anyone coming close enough to wrap the gauze around it. Had he passed out again.

"Typing has now become significantly more difficult for you," the voice said in a mocking tone. "Before it becomes even harder for you to operate your computer, why don't you tell me what else you use it for?"

"Chatting," said the man in the chair. "Instant messaging, chat rooms, all of that."

Johnson slumped in the chair. Even his voice sounded drained.

"And who do you chat with Mr. Johnson?"

He wanted to say 'friends.' He wanted to say 'family.'

Instead, he answered truthfully.

"People like me."

"And what does that mean, exactly?"

"People who...collect things."

"What sort of things?"

"Pictures."

The voice remained silent.

"Trophies."

No response.

"Bodies."

"Excellent."

"I'll tell you everything. I'll give you names. Please, just, no more. Please."

"How long?"

"How long what?" Johnson asked.

Movement, pressure. The knife was poised for another cut. It rested on the ring finger of his right hand.

"You said people like you. How long have you been like you?"

"I don't know, honestly, I don't know. I never—"

The knife blade moved with the efficiency of a Benihana chef. The finger spun away into the darkness.

"This is becoming tiring. When was the first time you visited the website?"

Johnson did not have to ask which website. The excruciating pain provided clarity. "I read about it on-line, in a thread on another website I frequent."

The words were pouring out of him, gushing forth like the crimson pumping from his ruined right hand.

"I think it was a couple of years ago. At first I only looked at the welcome page. I was too scared to put in my credit card number so I didn't sign up. I just looked at the pictures on the first page."

The knife came down again, severing the two remaining fingers of Johnson's right hand. As the blade descended, there was a squeak and a curse. The voice, or whoever was employing the knife, slipped in the blood puddled around the chair. As a result, the knife did not land as planned. The third finger was detached cleanly, but the index finger was not. Instead of hitting the joint, the sharp edged steel lodged in the bone between the hand and the first knuckle.

Metacarpal, thought Johnson as he screamed. The tunnel vision returned.

Someone threw a towel at the man in the chair. The blue gloved hand shoved it onto the wound with a savage thrust. The pain cleared Johnson's mind.

"You got lucky, that time." The voice sounded ragged. The labored breathing could have been caused by anger or exertion.

"Lucky!" Johnson shrieked. He meant it to sound sarcastic, but the accompanying laugh held a tinge of mania.

"Yes, lucky. Your IP information is on record. You visited the site for the first time just under a year and a half ago. You watched one portion of one video, then signed up. You provided false information, but a correct credit card number. You spent over an hour on the site that same day.

"That was a deliberate lie and a lie of omission. That should have cost you two fingers."

"Fuck you."

"I didn't think I was your type. However, while we are on the subject—what is your type, Mr. Johnson? What was that first video that enticed you to join the website?"

"No type."

"Pardon?"

"No type, no video, no answer."

"Defiance? This late in the game? And you are so close to the lightening round."

Johnson tracked the voice. Although he was barely able to hold his head up, he shifted his eyes to the left. He was certain that was where the knife wielding maniac was standing.

Which was why he was shocked when someone grabbed his right arm. The top of a big, bald head filled his vision. Johnson lashed out, trying to butt heads, but his assailant was just out of his reach.

Strong hands gripped his forearm. They were rough, calloused, bare. These were not the hands which held the knife, but they could have been belonged to whoever had hit him last.

One of the hands remained on his forearm while the other gripped the sodden towel. There was a moment of probing then the grip tightened around his remaining finger. The hand twisted and pulled. There was a snap, then the feeling of something tearing. The towel dropped to the floor with a wet plop. It was the last sound the man in the chair heard for quite a while.

***

Like a swimmer rising to the surface, Johnson slowly regained consciousness. Something had changed. The quality of the light was different. How long had he been out this time?

A pain, which lanced through his right arm, all but drowned out the steady throb of his left arm. Still, around it all, he felt a different kind of discomfort. He looked down and saw tubing running from a needle in his arm and disappearing somewhere behind his head. A yellowish fluid was being pumped into his vein.

His right arm was no longer strapped to the arm rest of the chair. A plank of wood was affixed to the chair, creating a second arm rest on that side. This one rose up at a 60 degree angle. His right arm was suspended from it. The hand was completely wrapped in gauze stained pink with his blood. All except for the thumb, it sat naked and alone on the wood.

Despite being raised above the level of his heart, blood continued to leak from the mutilated hand. As he watched, a fat drop collected at the end of the board and dropped to the ground. From the sound it made, Johnson could tell that it landed in a substantial puddle.

The voice returned.

"Ah, you are awake again. We had to intervene after that last incorrect answer."

The man in the chair could not tell where the voice was coming from. It seemed to be all around him.

"Now then, we are growing short on time and you are running short of fingers. How about we work through these last few questions quickly?"

He nodded.

"Good. What was that first video?"

Although his mind screamed for him to remain silent, his lips began moving immediately.

"A little girl, blonde. She was tied face down over a table or a bench or something."

"Did that arouse you?"

"No—yes." He steeled himself for the knife. When it did not come, he continued. "I was aroused, but not sexually. Something stirred in me. I liked that she was under someone else's control. I wanted to be the person in control."

"Is that why you joined the site?"

"Not really," he hurried on before he could be punished for the non-answer. "It wasn't just the video, it was the contest. I joined the website, then paid the extra fee to enter the contest."

He sighed. The numb feeling in his head was isolating him from the pain. His wounded limbs felt very far away.

"Every month there was a new video. Every month it was different."

Somehow Johnson thought the owner of the voice already knew all of this. His mind was working furiously. There was something, a revelation, just out of his reach. Meanwhile, he kept talking.

"Some months it was just someone begging, crying, pleading. Other months it was torture. The good months were when there was both."

Pacing, just outside of the reach of the lightbulb.

"Every month there was that little box. 'Enter here for a chance to be the star of next month's video.' I was surprised to find that there was a fee."

"But you paid every month, didn't you?"

"Yes, fifty dollars, every month. I wanted to win. I wanted to be the one in control. I wanted to be the star..."

His words trailed off. His mind finally made the leap.

"Oh."

It was all that he could say. The silence stretched for an eternity marked only by the dripping of his blood.

"You understand now?" The voice asked.

Statement, not a question, but it still seemed to require an answer.

"Yes, I understand. I won."

"Yes. Yes, you did."

"So what happens now?"

"The game is almost over. Only a few more questions. Do you think you can go on?"

The note of concern in the voice startled the man in the chair.

126

He thought about the question for a moment, then nodded.

"Good. Thank you. Now, what, would you say, is your type? What are you attracted to?"

That question again. Johnson mumbled his answer. "No type, no age, just the scenario."

"What is the scenario?"

"Helpless."

A moment of silence followed. The word seemed to fly around the room, hiding in the dark corners.

"Explain."

"Helpless. At my mercy. Bound, weak, scared, unable to..." Johnson trailed off. "Like me," he said finally.

"How like you?"

"Not like how I am right now, at this moment. Although, yes, like me right now, all tied up. But also like I am outside here. Caught up in everything, trapped by life."

Johnson looked up and saw the owner of the voice step into the pale circle of light. He was a very plain man. He was short, pale. He had a trim mustache and small eyes. A bit of black hair poked out from beneath the plastic poncho he wore. The poncho was splattered with clotting blood.

Johnson's blood.

The blue surgical gloves covered his hands. The right hand held the knife. It looked smaller now, less important.

"Last question, Mr. Johnson."

The man in the chair closed his eyes.

"You have answered a lot of questions tonight. You have divulged a lot about yourself, perhaps things you did not even know until you said them."

Johnson nodded, eyes still closed. He sobbed once, quietly.

"Given all that you have learned, all that you know about yourself now, and considering all that happened tonight, do you want to return to that life? Do you want to continue to be, how did you put it, trapped by life?"

Johnson's eyes remained closed. A tear traced its way down his cheek. As with many of the questions which had come before, the answer to this one was too horrible to contemplate.

The last question is always the hardest to answer.

"No," he said in the strongest voice he could muster. "No, I do not."

There was movement again. The man had moved behind him.

Had he answered all twenty questions? It seemed like more, but then there had been some repetitions, some which had surely not counted. First he had won the website prize, now he had won again.

Winning was a strange thing.

Johnson sighed again, eyes still closed, and let his head fall back against the back of the chair. He raised his chin towards the ceiling, and claimed his prize.

The knife entered the light one last time, one final arc. It bit deep, moving left to right, along the neck of the man in the chair. It severed both jugular veins and both carotids. It sawed into the trachea. Blood splashed, spurted. Air from the damaged trachea turned the vital fluid into a fine red mist. The owner of the voice stepped back.

The man in the chair thrashed once, twice, then finally fell still.

There was a moment of silence. Then the lights flickered on. Fluorescent tubes cast a harsh glow upon the body in the chair. They also revealed the rest of the room—a large concrete box. Positioned outside the area which had been illuminated by the overhead light-bulb were three cameras on tripods. One sat directly in front of the chair, one on either side. Another two cameras were suspended from the ceiling.

A large man with a bald head stepped over to the chair. He wore long gloves which encased his arms to the elbow in black rubber. He began picking up the towels which littered the floor and dumping them in the lap of the body on the chair. He pulled out the IV with one tug and dropped the bag onto the towels

The overhead cameras were lowered. A slight man in jeans and flannel collected the small cassette tapes from each of the cameras and placed them in a leather satchel. Then he began breaking down the cameras and tripods.

The man with the voice walked over to him. He had discarded the poncho and gloves. The knife was nowhere to be seen.

"How long before it's ready?" he asked.

"Give me a few hours to run through all of the footage. Another few to cut it together. I should have the rough copies for you tomorrow night, the next morning at the latest. Do you want audio?"

The big man had finished examining the floor. He placed a

finger into a Tupperware bowel. He looked puzzled. His eyes squinted, then opened wide. He walked over to the chair, picked up the towels and began to shake them open. An index finger fell from one. The big man smiled.

"Yes," the voice answered. "But remember, we need all audio regarding the website and contest removed."

"Of course, I will need a little more time to distort your voice. We should be ready to upload the new video in a few days."

"Then we can pick another lucky contestant."

Sisters

Chris Reed

Tony was standing outside the liquor store, drinking with his homeboys and trading the usual stories about pimping hoes, selling drugs and running from the cops, when he saw Lakiesha walk by. Her gold hoop earrings blinked in the summer sunlight and her size 36 double-D breasts jiggled inside her black sports bra—but it was her ass that demanded the most attention. It stuck out like a gorilla's, each cheek round and firm.

"*Daaaamn*!" Tony said, as his gaze locked onto her massive buns. "I *gots* to git some of *that*! Hey, baby!"

The girl looked, but kept her stride.

Undeterred, Tony capped his forty-ounce bottle of St. Ides and gave chase.

"Hey!" he called after her as he trotted down the sidewalk.

This time she stopped and turned around, crossed her arms in front of her chest and fixed him with an impatient stare.

Tony knew he had to drop his game quickly, so he flashed his gold-tooth smile and said, "What's your name, baby?"

"Lakiesha," she said. "What's yours?"

"Tony. Why don't you come on over to my crib and have some drinks with me?"

"I don't think so," she said. "Alcohol's bad for you. Did you know it causes birth defects?"

Tony's smile faded. "So what you saying, you pregnant?"

Lakiesha shook her head. "No, but—"

"Then what you worried about?"

"When I see someone drinking, it reminds me of my sisters."

"How many sisters you got?"

"Two," Lakiesha said. "We're triplets."

Tony's eyes got big. "For real?"

"Yeah, but we don't look the same," she said sadly. "My mama drank a lot and my sisters didn't turn out right."

"Oh," Tony said, his fantasy of getting busy with three fine women dissolving as quickly as it had appeared. But then he returned his attention to the fine-looking woman in front of him and said, "Looks like *you* turned out all right."

Lakiesha giggled, and that's when Tony knew he was getting that ass.

"So what do you say?" he said. "Come on back to my crib. We ain't gotta drink, we can just chill."

"It sounds like fun, but I should ask my sisters first."

"Why?" Tony said.

"Cause they might not think it's a good idea."

"Shit, who cares what they think? You're a grown woman, ain't ya?"

"Yeah," Lakiesha answered.

"Then you can do what you want, right?"

"I guess so."

"All right then," Tony smiled. "Quit worryin' about your sisters and let's go have some fun."

"But you don't understand," Lakiesha said. "Chandra and Quandra are different, they're—"

"Forget it," Tony snapped. "If you gonna be a baby, I got better things to do."

He turned to leave, but Lakiesha grabbed his arm. "Okay," she said. "I'll go with you on one condition."

Ten minutes later, Tony was butt naked and tied to a chair in his kitchen. Lakiesha's one condition had been that he let her restrain him. She explained that all her previous lovers had gotten cold feet and ran away when she got undressed, and she didn't want him to do the same. Of course Tony agreed. It had been a long time since he'd had a woman as fine as Lakiesha, and he didn't know what was wrong with those other fools, but he was definitely knockin' them boots.

Hip-hop music bumped from a boom box on the counter as Lakiesha danced for him. Tony had been to many strip clubs, seen many hoes working their bodies for cash, but he'd never seen anything quite like the woman in front of him. It was obvious she wasn't thinking about her sisters anymore. And even though the ropes on his wrist and ankles were so tight it felt like they were cutting off his circulation, Tony found it hard to stop grinning.

"Why don't you come over here and show me a little somethin'-somethin'," he said.

"You horny, baby?" she asked.

"Hell yeah."

Lakiesha took off her sports bra and flung it to the floor, unleashing two plump, black-nippled breasts. She smashed her huge tits into Tony's face who in return licked hungrily at them. Yet as much as he was enjoying sucking on those big brown monsters, he knew the ultimate rush would be the moment she wiggled out of her shorts and stuck that beautiful black booty in his face.

He let her nipple fall from his mouth and said, "Why don't you take the rest of your clothes off."

"I want to do a little something for you first," she said.

"Oh? What's that?"

She dropped to her knees and took his hard cock in her mouth.

Tony watched with delight as her thick, black lips slid up and down the shaft of his swollen rod. The head was superb, and he quickly found himself on the verge of orgasm, but each time he was about to come, she removed her mouth from his cock and sucked his balls instead. She repeated this, back and forth from cock to balls, until he was hard as black steel.

"You like that, baby?" she asked, her nose buried in the wrinkles of his sweaty scrotum.

All Tony could do was groan and nod.

"Good, baby," she cooed, giving his cock one final tight-lipped tug. "'Cause you *really* gonna like what I got for you next."

She stood up and unbuttoned her shorts... and the horror began.

She turned around, pushed the tight denim shorts down, and Tony's dick went instantly limp. What he saw was not the juicy ass he'd expected, but two human heads—a deformed face nestled in the meat of each ass cheek.

"WHAT THE FUCK?" Tony screamed.

"Meet my sisters, Chandra and Quandra," Lakiesha said, as she backed up to him with her ass sticking out.

Now that he was face-to-face with the sisters, he could see how truly horrible they were. Chandra—the left head—had only one eye, which was halfway concealed by a flap of flesh that stretched across the left part of the socket. Inside, her eyeball rolled around uncontrollably. Where her nose should have been were two small holes crusted with dark green snot. Below these rudimentary nostrils was Chandra's mouth, a small horizontal slit with just the slightest hint of lips.

Quandra was far more developed. She had two eyes, which were extremely close together, so close they almost touched each other. Her nose was large and flat, and her upper lip was slightly more prominent than her sister's. As different as each face was in appearance, the siblings shared a common characteristic—they were both covered from forehead to chin with terrible, pus-filled acne.

"Let me the fuck out of here!" Tony screamed as he thrashed in the chair.

"Oh baby," Lakiesha said as she straddled him. "Don't be like that. I thought you wanted to have some fun?"

She tried to put Tony's cock into her pussy, but it was soft as a wet noodle. So she stood up, turned around and said, "I got just the thing for you."

Tony watched, paralyzed in horror, as Lakiesha guided her ass down to his crotch. Chandra's mouth-slit opened and took his flaccid cock inside. "Oh, yeeaaaahhh," Lakiesha moaned. "You like that, baby?"

Tony was too mesmerized to respond; all he could do was watch as the freakish ass cheek slurped on his cock. Amazingly, within minutes, he was fully erect again.

As Quandra watched her sister feast on Tony's meat, she let out an angry, pig-like squeal, *"ERRRRRRIIIIIIIIEEEEEEEE*!!!"

Lakiesha rose up and Tony's cock slipped out of Chandra's mouth. She let out a shriek of protest and Lakiesha scolded her, "Oh, stop it! You know you have to share." Then she put her right cheek to Tony's crotch, and Quandra took over. She sucked him greed-ily—as if trying to outdo her sister—squeezing her mouth-slit tight around his shaft, pumping her mutant head up and down in a cock-hungry frenzy.

"OOOOHHH SHIIIIIIIIT!" Tony moaned, his cock about to burst.

"My turn!" Lakiesha said as she pulled her ass away, allow-ing Tony's dick to slide out of Chandra's mouth. She took the throb-bing member in her hand and guided it into her dripping wet pussy. She brought her ass down hard and fast, over and over, slamming her sister's faces into his crotch. She fucked him so hard the chair broke, and they collapsed to the floor in a heap. Lakiesha landed on top of him and continued to fuck him, hammering her black hole against his swollen cock. Tony wanted to come—needed to—but he didn't dare. He wasn't wearing a condom, and he didn't even want to think about what might happen if he got this crazy bitch pregnant.

So he warned her. "Get the fuck off me, bitch!"

"Why, baby?" she moaned as she ground her crotch on him. "Don't you like it?"

"I said, GET OFF!"

But Lakiesha and her sisters continued to gang rape him.

The collision with the floor had loosened the ropes on his wrists, and he managed to get his hand free. He reached behind his back where his pants lay on the floor, dug into the pocket and took out his chrome-plated .38 semi-automatic pistol. He put the gun to Lakiesha's temple and pulled the trigger. There was a loud *POP* and Lakiesha's brains sprayed out the other side of her head. Her body relaxed and Tony crawled out from under her.

Chandra and Quandra watched him as he stood, their eyes glued to his raging hard-on. He'd never been so horny in his life! Even the sight of this half-dead monstrosity on the floor could not quell his sex drive. He grabbed his cock and said, "You freaky bitches want some more of this?"

Both sisters groaned, their tongues slithering out of their slimy mouths, the sides of their faces caked with wet shit from where Lakiesha had voided.

Tony dropped to his knees, scooped up Lakiesha's butt cheeks, and proceeded to feed her mutant siblings. He fucked both mouths, ramming his pelvis into their meaty faces so hard that he broke Quandra's nose and popped Chandra's zits. Lakiesha's pussy was still sopping wet, and he fucked that, too, pounding her ebony slit, as her sisters' tongues flicked at his balls. When he finished with her cunt, he stuck his dick in her ass and banged away until he was on the verge of orgasm.

Unable to hold it back any longer, he pulled out and jacked himself off, shooting a thick stream of hot, white jizz all over the sisters' faces. When he was finished, he watched with disgust as the deformed twins licked each other clean. Then he picked up his .32 and put the barrel to Chandra's forehead. Her tongue slithered out and licked his knuckles, but now that he'd blown his load, what would have turned him on moments ago only made him nauseous. He pulled the trigger and the gun went off with a fire-cracker pop, putting a dime-sized hole in the thing's skull. Chandra's lone eye rolled back in her head, her tongue wiggled once, then went limp.

As Quandra watched her sister die, she let out an ear-splitting shriek. "*RRIIIIIEEEEEEEEEEEEEEEEE!*" Then, hoping to avoid the same fate, the panicked ass cheek strained to get away, to tear itself away from Lakeisha's corpse, to run and hide from the man with the gun. Tony watched, half sickened, half amused as Quandra actually managed to drag the body a few inches across the floor.

"You are one crazy bitch," he said.

"*RRRIIIIIEEEEEEEEEEEE!*" she squealed.

Tony put his gun to the side of her head.

"*RRIIIIIEEEEEEEEEEEEEEEEEEEEEE—*"

POP!

Tony looked down at himself, his naked body covered from the waist-down in a gooey froth of blood, cum, brains, and shit. He got into the shower, hoping that his homeboys were still at the liquor store. This time he had a story they wouldn't believe.

My Dark Lover

Stacy Bolli

I was the tender age of twelve years when I was forced to do the unthinkable, a task that nearly destroyed me.

I looked at the gleaming silver coffin, adorned with ornately carved silver handles, as six solemn pall-bearers prepared to lower it into the hard, frozen ground. A small intimate audience gathered and wept over the tragic loss of such a young and promising life. A life that just one year ago was at its prime, flawless in personality and pristine in beauty. A life that I watched slowly dissolve before me until that vibrant spark in her wonderful sky blue eyes had become completely extinguished, leaving nothing but a once beautiful shell.

I felt a burning sensation under my eyelids as the tears began to well. I wrenched my hand free of my father's firm hold and pulled away from the small, somber crowd. I ran to the casket and draped my upper torso over the glossy lid and openly sobbed over the injustice of it all. I offered one more good-bye kiss to the woman who was once my entire world. I felt my father's arms embrace me and pull me back as they lowered the coffin into the freshly dug grave—the final resting place of my mother. I watched as the Earth absorbed Mom's remains and all I could do to gather strength was to renounce my God.

The day I rejected God, *He* found his way into my vulnerable heart and took up residence. It began innocently enough as He initially appeared to me as a dark, featureless child. My father was so overwhelmed with his own grief that I felt utterly alone in the world, and so I eagerly embraced his dark innocuous presence. He never told me his name, I asked him once, shyly, to share it with me but He said it was his most intimate possession and must remain unspoken until the day of my death—to him death marked the sacred union of our souls. He was always present, a reliable force behind me, offering me comfort and companionship as we grew up and faced the harsh world together.

We entered puberty together and explored these newfound sexual sensations with an excitement beyond description. I would lay in bed, naked and trembling, as I felt his cold, hardness snake up and touch the tingling, magical folds between my legs. His ice cold pressure sent squeals of delight into my throat as my legs would wrap tightly around His dark and slender hips; hips meant only for me.

We would often come together in my pink princess bed and the molten flow he released would blazon its paths under my skin with the fury of Pele herself. I would often lie upon Him after the explosive orgasm and our bodies seemed to meld into one; I could feel his touch reach into my heaving chest and cradle my warm, beating heart. We played these games nightly and soon He became the sole reason for my existence.

The only thing he asked of me in return for his devotion was that I excel in school. I agreed; I had no other social life and I dedicated every waking moment to him and my studies. I graduated Valedictorian of my class when I was just sixteen-years-old. My father clapped proudly at the graduation as I accepted my diploma—this was one of those rare times when I gained his approval. I walked down the stage clutching my diploma in one hand and feeling His dark chill enveloping the other.

I was accepted into college and decided to attend Medical School after graduation from the University, all the while He stood beside me whispering answers and words of encouragement into my ears during exams and rotations—with him by my side I never failed.

When it came time to choose what field of medicine I would practice, he made the decision for me. "Vanity is humanity's most profitable sin; we will leave our mark on this world through vanity!"

After Medical School was completed I opened my own practice as a plastic surgeon. I soon became recognized for my incredible creations in rhinoplasty and breast augmentations. I viewed my surgeries as artwork and took immense pride in my masterpieces. The name Dr. Lindsay Davidson, became world renowned and respected.

While running my very successful practice, in the most superficial state of California, I became pregnant. My heart seized with terror as I came into the realization of my state.

How could he impregnate me? I desperately argued with myself. I was never with another man so it had to be his child growing within my womb.

The night I told Him of my condition and He appeared to be overjoyed. I felt his cool arms wrap around my belly that night as I drifted to sleep. I heard him singing words of a strange tongue to the dark embryo nested in my uterus.

Two days later my body rejected the embryo.

I was standing naked in my bathroom after a long, hot shower toweling my hair and looking into the mirror. I wiped the steam off the surface of the mirror and stared at my withered features in dismay. I looked positively spent and exhausted. As I pulled down the hair dryer from the closet a sharp pain sliced through my abdomen. I dropped the hair dryer and grabbed my tender stomach in panic. The vicious pain continued to pummel through me like the lethal waves of a tsunami. I cried out to Him for help as I felt a searing, hot fluid begin to trickle down the inside of my legs. I screamed against the fresh wave of pain and fell naked to the floor. I spread my legs wide so they would not come into contact with the molten fluid that poured from me. I watched in horror as the steaming clear liquid pooled around me and then I felt an enormous urge to vacate my bowels. I pushed against the pressure and three black capsules escaped from between my legs. The capsules were shiny and hard; covered in an intricate cobweb of thin red vessels that pulsated with flowing life. I cried out in fear and pain as the skin inside my legs burned with an invisible fire caused by the splash of acidic amniotic fluid.

As I lay weeping on the cold tile he emerged from my linen closet. He did not say a word as he crouched down to gather the results of his unsuccessful attempt of procreation. He held the rejected embryos to his chest and I watched a single tear drop from his eye. He bent his head to kiss his failed spawn and retreated out of the bathroom without uttering a single word to me. My heart was heavy with his disappointment as I mopped up the acidic amniotic fluid.

Three months later I learned I was pregnant again and one week later that pregnancy ended in a natural abortion. Again, He was there to gather his progeny and silently walk back to whatever lair He called home.

A couple of hours later he appeared to me; his form was slumped and he had a defeated tone to his voice.

"The only way I can bring my children into this world is through a willing female. It is obvious the usual method of carrying a pregnancy will not work in our case. We will not try it the normal way again, for I can't bear the disappointing results one more time. I have another plan."

"Oh, does it involve my body?" I silently pleaded that it would not; it was immense torture on my mental and physical being as well.

"No, but I do need your help," and he recited a list of his demands to me.

I frowned, "I can get this for you, but why?"

"You will find out when the time comes; trust my love," he gave me a small nod with his dark head.

That week I gathered his required supplies and assembled them neatly into a box. He accepted the box from me and left me to start on his project.

Days passed before I heard from Him again. I was beginning to worry if he would never return to me; he never stayed away for such a long length of time. My world would crumble if He should never return; I desperately needed Him to live. Much to my relief he appeared to me late that night cradling a box lined with an electric blanket.

He handed me the warm box and instructed me on what he needed next. "I need you to lure in the women. We need at least ten willing females; they must be certain and eager for the procedure. Announce an irresistible special on breast implants; bring these eager women to us and under your knife."

I nodded to him and walked into my bedroom to plug in the makeshift incubator.

That week I announced a 'Bogo' special for boobs. The deal was tempting, and many fish took the bait. My office was jam packed by the end of the week and my first procedure was scheduled for the following Monday. He seemed very pleased with my efforts and he rewarded me with a sweet and spicy kiss that left my lips burning.

When the day of the first surgery arrived and my patient was safely under anesthesia I took my first look at the impregnated saline breast implants. They seemed quite innocuous at first, only the saline seemed slightly cloudy. Upon further scrutiny I could catch flashes of darkness slithering through the cloudy, warm liquid. With a deep breath and a minuscule pang of guilt I placed the implant into the woman's open chest cavity and performed my magic. When she was all stitched up I stepped back to admire my work—her boobs jiggled slightly with the new life growing within them.

At the end of the very busy surgical week I reluctantly prepped my last patient, my next door neighbor. She was a very sweet woman and wanted these new breasts to please her husband.

"Are you sure you want to do this for him? It has to be for you, I suggest you put more thought into your decision, Laurie," I desperately tried to change her mind in my office before the procedure.

"No, I am doing this for the both of us and you are the best. I am sure I want this, book the surgery," Laurie was adamant.

I nodded with a heavy heart, agreeing to do this only for Him. I knew he would be pleased to have one of his children born close to home. I would do anything for him, including killing thy neighbor.

After the last surgery was completed He emerged to me and celebrated. As we explored each other's bodies, I noticed He was becoming more defined, as if his existence was becoming more of a permanent fixture in the world. I could make out the lines of his strong cheekbones and even the cleft in his large chin; he was becoming more handsome by the minute and I loved and sucked him even harder that night.

As the weeks passed my neighbor, Laurie, had become more active. She seemed to love her new breasts and flaunted them in tiny white tank tops as she planted and pruned the roses that lined the front of her house. She would always wave and shake her new assets for me to admire when we crossed paths outside. I could swear they seemed to be getting larger and on one occasion as we spoke; I could see the breast on the left shift under her the thin white fabric of her shirt.

One month later I found Him sitting on my couch when I returned from work. He had never looked more solid and inviting. His dark, ebony curls wisped softly around his beautiful black skin. His bare chest had become sculpted and the soft pink of his nipples created a sharp contrast with his surrounding black flesh. The feature that stood out most was his large member; the head stood proudly on top of his erect shaft and glistened like the highest quality of polished obsidian.

"Something wonderful is going to happen today, my love," he whispered to me and drew me on top of his throbbing lap. I smiled and enjoyed the waves of heat he created between my legs. I bent

140

down to taste those rose pink nipples when I heard frantic banging on my front door.

"Go get the door, my love," he pushed my rump up with his two large hands.

I groaned with frustration but complied with his wishes. I opened the door to a bloody and hysterical Laurie.

"Laurie, what happened?" I gasped

Laurie fell to the ground, wrapped her bloody arms around my legs, and let out a horrendous howl. I immediately felt the cool air of Him standing behind me and Laurie's eyes widened in terror as she beheld Him in his full-bloomed darkened glory. He reached down and pushed Laurie onto her back.

"Who is this, Dr. Davidson? What is going on?" she yelled, "You have to help me! My breasts are burning, they're *infected*! There's something alive, something scratching from the inside!" Laurie pulled her blouse open and her swollen breasts popped free into the open air. Blood tinged with a black tar like paste was oozing from the center of each aureole.

I also saw that each breast was beginning to crack. Scarlet fissures radiated out from each oozing nipple, the whole effect was that of a splendid red carnation.

"It's happening," I heard him crow triumphantly. He bent down and sat on Laurie's torso.

Laurie bucked and screamed under the assault of his massive weight and a new wave of pain seized her already contorted features. He bent down and delivered a sharp slap to Laurie's blood-streaked cheek.

"Be still, bitch. If you are still it makes it happen much faster."

Laurie wept her surrender as He reached down and cupped each breast.

I watched his blue eyes close and He whispered, "I can feel them move. I can feel my children! They're alive!" With renewed fervor he ripped opened one of the fissures in Laurie's breast. She whimpered as her white flesh tore, then mercifully fell unconscious.

I watched in fascination as a tiny black limb appeared from the tear—a black arm tipped in razor sharp, silver talons. Soon the entire child was delivered from his nurturing flesh prison and he scampered to his father's side. He beamed with joy and eagerly ripped open the other breast like a child opening a gift on Christmas morning. The second child emerged, a female, with long dark curls and smooth black skin. She yawned and stretched, embracing her new found freedom.

"My babies are here, free to roam and rule Earth with their father! A new era of darkness has been born!" He opened his arms and the children eagerly jumped into their father's embrace. He hugged them close to his wide chest and looked at me.

"Get rid of the body, she has served her purpose"

"You will protect me, right? You promised you will protect me forever!" I wailed pathetically, now suddenly fearing the legal and criminal repercussions of my actions.

"Don't you worry; I have secured a special place in Hell for you. You will sit by my side and we shall burn together for eternity." He continued, "Now, take this shovel, finish off the bitch-carrier and bury the body in the back yard. Then you can join me and our children in the living room."

I nodded and delivered the final blow to Laurie's head. I dragged the torn and bloody remnants through the house leaving a crimson trail behind me.

After the task was completed I returned filthy and bloody to my new family sitting in the darkened living room. All three were sitting still and silent as if waiting for something.

"The other children, how will they know where to go?" I asked.

He smiled, showing his now visible row of pearly white teeth, and flipped a dark curl from his blue eye. "They know the way home; sit beside me, love, and wait for our children to come."

His two newborns perched on the arms of the love seat gazing out the window with clear blue eyes, each no larger than six inches tall with skin just as sleek and luminescent as their pitch black father. They sat motionless as they waited for their siblings.

"Lindsay," I heard Him whisper.

"Yes?"

The next thing I knew his dark face loomed above my head showering me in the intense heat of his breath and searing the top of my scalp.

"My name is Chernobog."

A Laxative for Writer's Block

Forrest Ingle

Writer's block is a bitch, a pain in the ass, a goddamn hemorrhoid. It's one of those annoying ass bill-collectors that call you every night at dinner. One of those nasty rashes that won't go away. All writers suffer through it at some point or another. You try to write but you just shoot blanks. Every word's a struggle. It's like trying to shit but somebody's sewn your goddamn asshole shut. And what sucks the most is that there is no cure. No fucking laxative. You just gotta sit and wait until it eventually goes away, even though you know it's gonna come back like some horrible case of herpes.

But what if I told you that I've found a prescription for that bulging bastard? What if I told you that, right here in my hand, I'm holding a box of suppositories, ready and willing to jam every single one of them deep into your rectum? Go ahead, my friend, kiss your hemorrhoids goodbye. Despite everything you've ever been told, there is a way to defeat the dreaded writer's block.

See, the problem lies in the pussyfooted *waiting* that we writers do. The whole time we're infected, we just sit and stare at the monitor like brain-washed apes, thinking that any minute our Muse will return from her smoke break and fuck us into an orgasm of inspiration. But it never happens. She just stands outside the door, sucking on her cigarette while shooting us The Bird.

What we've gotta do is, we've gotta stop being so goddamn passive and fucking take control. We've gotta go out there and *find* her goddamn ass. Grab her by the wrists and fucking *force* her. Throw her whore ass on the ground and *rape* the inspiration out of her glorified puss. No more goddamn smoke breaks. You take that cigarette and put it out on her fucking eyeball if you have to.

Which is exactly what I did earlier: I was sitting right here, watching the cursor blink back and forth, taunting me, when suddenly I caught a glimpse of something in my monitor. I turned around and there it was—The Cure, The Laxative, The Oh-So-Glorious Nicotine Patch—playing on the playground across the street.

It was a *she*. A little girl, no more than eight or nine. Prepubes. Nice and smooth.

She swung on a swing, slid on a slide, and as I stood in my window watching her, I felt the staples in my ass loosen and fall. I had a fucking hard-on, both mind and body, head on my shoulders and head in my pants. No more shooting blanks. I was *cumming* creativity.

But it wasn't enough. Not yet. The Muse was flashing her bush, and I could've probably written a decent story just based on the visual—but no, I'm more ambitious than that. I wanted to reach a little higher, try to brush my fingertips against *greatness*. But to do so I needed to get up close and personal with that shit. Needed to stick my nose in it and nibble the clit. Floss with her pubes and chew on her tits.

Only problem was, the little bitch's mom was with her. So I paced back and forth and I watched them, trying to devise a plan inside my mind. Turned out I didn't need one because the mother did it for me. She just kissed her daughter on the cheek, hopped in her van and drove away.

I didn't think much of it at first. Just figured the mom had gone to get them both a drink or something at the local convenience store. These parts are known for being pretty safe. Guess she figured her daughter would be alright for a few short minutes. Irresponsible bitch might as well have dropped her daughter on my doorstep, though. Could've made a sign pointing to the little girl's crotch: *Free Admission.*

When the van disappeared, I hurried outside and across the road. Wasn't a sign of life anywhere around except for the little girl, now sitting on her idling swing, watching me approach.

When I walked up to her, I smiled, all Joker-like and shit, and said, "Hey, princess, what's your name?"

No response. Mum for anyone but mom, I guess.

"Well," I said, "I just got a call from this lady. Said she had a flat tire and wouldn't be back for quite some time. She asked me if I'd take care of her little girl on the playground until she got back."

Thank God the little girl was dumb as a rock. Her little lips started quivering. "B-but M-Mommy said she be right b-b-back!"

It took several minutes to get the girl to drop her guard. I was sweating like a goddamn nigger, too, partially because of the sun but mostly out of nervousness. I almost shit myself every time I heard a vehicle. The girl and I joked around for a few short minutes while playing on the jungle gym. I promised her an ice-cream sandwich if she could beat me in a race across the street. She won, by the way, but only because I let her. Her mouth was so goddamn cold I think it gave my dick frostbite.

Don't worry, though, I'll spare you the grisly details. That isn't what this thing's about.

Let's just say, after I...um, *directed* her to give me oral pleasure, and then—*lightly* tossed her onto the floor and massaged her neck while...you know, teaching her about the birds and the bees and all, I immediately felt an urge to sit down at my desk and finger the hell out of my goddamn keyboard. Finally, after three long weeks of constipated grunting, I had my laxative. The muse was back. This time with crotchless spandex and a ten-inch dildo. Lubrication required.

Now, before you freak out and stop reading and call me a monster or a horrible, terrible, evil human being, understand that what I did was because of Love. That's right, Love. I did what I did because I care about my craft. And like any artist, I'm willing to do whatever it takes to be the best at what I do. It's called Determination with a capital D. The little girl, well, she was simply a necessary sacrifice. But don't hang your head and weep, because she died for a worthy cause. In many ways, I gave her life, gave her purpose. Rejoice. Celebrate. She'll now live on forever through my writing.

Still don't understand what the hell I'm talking about? Well, it all boils down to that old cliché, the one that every bearded forty-something creative writing teacher preaches at your local community college: *write what you know; write from experience.* But if you've ever really stopped to think about it, you'd see that all we writers fucking do is sit and daydream. We fucking *fantasize.* Look at all the horror writers who write stories about crazy psychopath serial killers. Yet how many of them actually know what it's like to stab, rape, or chop another motherfucker's head off? Hell, half of all erotica is written by disgusting ass bitches who couldn't even pay an overweight blind man to have sex with them.

Now, I have no idea how many stories require the knowledge of what it's like to kill and rape a little girl, but that's beside the point. At least now I know what it feels like to take somebody's life. I know firsthand that rush of adrenaline. That crazy surge of power. I know the panic, the fear, the paranoia. From now on when I'm writing I won't have to fucking daydream. What more experience could

I possibly need? I just graduated with a Ph.D. in Psycho Shit.

And to answer your question, no, I'm not delusional. I know I can't get away with this forever. That isn't even my intention. I want to get caught. Only then will my writing receive the attention it deserves. Everyone's gonna be intrigued, wanting to look inside the mind of a murderous pedophile with a fetish for necrophilia. I bet even English scholars will try to analyze my shit (*Is the broken vase in the bathroom a symbol of the deflowered little girl?*).

I'll become as famous as Mr. Charles Manson. Not to mention a literary genius. Kind of an Edgar Allan Poe of the new millennium. I'm living the story now. I am the narrator. And it's all thanks to...shit, what did that girl say her name was?

In the Make-Out Room

Matthew Keville

A slow song was playing, and the crowd on the dance floor had thinned out a little. The lights were low, the strobes had gone still, and it was easy for Kristen Norton to pretend that she and Adam Delaney were in a private little world, a soft warm place made of music and two swaying bodies...

Instead of in the gym at Carver High School...which was where the couple actually was.

They'd gone to the Horseshoe Inn for a real dinner out—the early-bird special, of course—and they'd probably stop by Gino's for a slice before they went home, but right now they were dancing, and that was the part that made Kristen feel that they were not just dating but *together*.

The funny thing was that they were actually quite a bit *apart*. Adam was holding his pelvis back and away from her, probably to hide a hard-on. If only he knew. She pulled him a little closer, enjoying the secret thrill of her breasts pressing against his chest. Perhaps taking his cue from this, he relaxed a bit, and let their lower bodies touch.

Yep. Hard-on.

A new, deeper thrill raced through Kristen as she felt it. She took a deep, shuddering breath as—

The slow song ended, replaced by a garish dance beat, and their fellow students rushed back onto the floor. It was like getting dashed with ice water.

Adam started to pull away, but she didn't let him go just yet. Starting the evening, she hadn't been sure that she was ready for this, but now there wasn't a doubt in her mind.

She pulled him closer, like she wanted one last hug to finish off the slow dance—which was, in fact, true—and murmured, "Adam?"

"Yeah?" he asked, hugging her back.

"Do you want to go to the make-out room?"

His eyes widened—just a little bit—but the rest of his face

stayed very carefully composed. It wouldn't do to announce to everyone around what was going on. "Sure," he said casually. "That sounds like a great idea."

With that, he led her off the dance floor, doing his best to hide his haste as she smiled secretly to herself.

It took a few minutes for them to find a weak point in the dance's adult supervision, but as soon as they did, they made a dash for it. Around the corner, into the shadows and they were gone. Once they made it to the Lost Hallway, they were safe.

Back in the Fifties, Carver High School had converted one of its sub-basements into a secondary gym. Kristen had heard that the 'underground' gym was never intended to be permanent, but it was still in use forty years later when a kid died in there in some kind of accident in the early nineties. Kristen had never been able to get the details of the accident—or rather, she'd gotten too many different versions of them—and it was finally closed down, abandoned. Now, all that remained was the Lost Hallway, a forsaken stretch of gray-painted concrete that led down into the darkness where the 'underground' gym had been, ending in a double door that was always locked. A deserted place where the dim flickering fluorescents were never replaced and almost never turned on.

What was behind that door now that the gym was deserted? No one knew. Sure, whenever anyone wanted to be *sensible*, they admitted that it was probably just more storage space. But who wanted to be sensible and ruin such an intriguing mystery?

Of course, none of that mattered right now to Adam or Kristen. The only thing that did—the only thing *useful* about the Lost Hallway—was the Make-Out Room.

The Make-Out Room was a big storage room inside the hallway with a ratty old couch. It was the perfect trysting-place—the door even locked from the inside—the teachers *had* to know about it, but no one did anything. Unless there was somebody already inside, you could always get in.

There was nobody in there when Kristen and Adam arrived.

Adam closed the door—quietly, carefully—and locked it. Then he hurried across the room to the couch, where Kristen was already waiting with a smile on her face and her arms held out.

The next few minutes were lost in eagerness, awkwardness,

148

anxiety and pleasure. They pressed close to each other, trying to find room for this arm or that leg. Their tongues wrestled, slipping into one mouth first, then the other. Adam tentatively slipped a hand up under Kristen's shirt, and she urged him on with a whispered, "Go ahead."

His hand was hot, heavy and trembling on her breast, and his attempts at caresses were a lot clumsier than her own, yet there was something about having someone *else's* hands on her and she gasped—

They both froze.

"What was that?" She whispered.

He shook his head as they both held still, listening.

The sound that had startled them had been a long, loud creak. Now, instead, they heard strange tapping noises all up and down the hallway outside. It was like giant crabs were walking around.

Adam made a face that Kristen just barely saw in the dimness.

"What is it?" She asked.

"Someone must've seen us come back here," he said. "Now they're trying to spook us."

Kristen was instantly relieved. Students weren't supposed to be back here—and so couldn't report them—and teachers wouldn't be tapping on the walls so much as pounding on the door. Anything else, by definition, didn't matter.

"So," she said, grinning up at him. "Are you spooked?"

He looked down at her, seeing her grin as a dull gleam of teeth in the darkness, and realized that his hand hadn't left her breast the whole time.

"No."

"Good."

Adam had just unzipped her jeans, Kristen's hips were arching up to meet his hand as it slipped into her panties to cup the damp curls of her sex, and she was all but dislocating her wrist to get her hand under his belt to stroke the soft skin of his hard-on when someone began rattling at the doorknob.

They sprang to opposite ends of the couch, pulling their clothes back into place. In the time it took them to do that—and to remember that the door was locked—the person on the other side gave up on rattling and started knocking. Knocking softly. Whoever

149

it was didn't want to be heard.

After a second, a whisper replaced the knock, "Hey! Hey, who's in there?"

Kristen and Adam both stifled groans. Randy Orsen. If there was one classmate who was *guaranteed* to have the story of catching them in the Make-Out Room—complete with leather, whipped cream and farm animals, no doubt—all over the school by Monday, it was Randy Orsen.

"Room's occupied, Randy," Adam said, hoping he was loud enough to be heard by Randy, but too quiet to be heard by anyone else. "Come back later."

"You gotta let me in, man," Randy said, starting to twist at the knob again. "You gotta let me in!"

"I said piss off!"

Instead, Randy started pulling and pounding at the door. "I don't care what you're doing in there," he said, his voice rising. "Please, you gotta let me in!"

Adam sprung up off the couch. Kristen hoped that he *would* open the door, and then bust Randy in the nose. Randy was the kind of guy who snapped bras, flipped skirts, depantsed ninth-graders—of both sexes—and generally molested people as much as he could get away with because he thought it was funny.

"Shut up, Randy," Adam hissed. "You're gonna get Mrs. Boyanksi over here!"

"You don't understand!" Randy shrieked, yanking and hammering at the door so hard the jamb creaked. "There's something out here and it's coming and you've gotta let me in. Y*ou've gotta let me in—*"

Adam was across the room and reaching for the doorknob when something hit the door, rattling it in its frame, and Randy's scream cut off.

Adam froze.

"Randy?"

Outside the door, there was a strange sort of gurgling noise, then the same rattle-tap-scrabble they'd heard before.

"Randy?"

Adam started for the door again when Kristen heard the *squip* of his shoe slipping, and saw the shadow of his shape in the darkness crash to the floor.

She was across the room in a second, kneeling at his side.

"Are you okay?" She whispered.

"Yeah. Yeah, I guess so," he muttered. "I just slipped on something."

"Still got that mini-flashlight on your keychain?" She asked.

"I didn't land on it, if that's what you mean."

"Here," she said, holding out her hand. "Let me see it."

He obliged, handing it to her as he pulled himself up into a sitting position. She, in turn, clicked it on and turned it toward the door.

What she saw turned her blood to icy slush in her veins. "Oh, God."

"What? What is it? Oh, fuck!" Adam screamed, scrambling backward and away as he saw what his foot had slipped in. A pool of blood, almost certainly Randy's, had seeped under the door and was still spreading.

Suddenly a piercing roar came from the direction of the gym. Both their faces went white. And that was when the screaming began.

***

Kristen didn't know how long she and Adam sat there on the couch, clinging to each other. The other students' screams didn't last long. No one else tried to get into the Make-Out room with them. She was glad about that. They'd hate themselves later for Randy, she knew, but they could at least tell themselves that there was no way they could have known. If anyone else had come knocking at the door afterwards, she didn't think she'd have been able to open it for them.

Horribly, the music kept playing long after the screams stopped, but then there was a crash and an ear-piercing squeal of static, and that went silent, too.

"Is it over?" Adam asked.

"I don't know, and I'm not going out there to find out," Kristen answered.

"We can't stay in here forever."

"We can wait a *little* longer."

"*How* long? We can't just sit here all night!"

"Sure we can."

Kristen could hear the frustration rising in Adam's voice. She didn't know if it was courage or panic, but he wanted to move. To do something. The problem was, that meant opening the door to whatever was out there.

"How will we even know when it's morning?" His last-ditch effort.

"We've both got watches." *Her* last-ditch effort. She wasn't handling this very well.

"Well, you can just sit here if you want to," he snapped, "I'm not—"

"Wait!" She said, grabbing his arm. "We're both being very stupid." She pulled out her cell phone and flipped it open. Bathed in its blue light, his face looked rather sheepish. Then he frowned, pulled out his own, looked at it, scowled, and turned it toward her.

No bars.

"We're sitting at the bottom of a giant cinderblock," he said. "Guess it's not very good for reception. So much for that idea." With that, he turned back toward the door.

At the exact same moment the tapping-tacking-scrabbling sound came down the hall again, accompanied by a slithery bumping sound. Then silence.

Adam quickly returned to the couch.

Kristen didn't know how much longer they sat there this time, clutching each other's hands, eyes useless in the dark room, ears straining for the slightest sound. It could have been minutes or hours. She didn't check her watch, because she knew that minutes were more likely, and checking would only make time pass even slower.

So she wasn't sure how much later it was when Adam finally spoke up again. "You know, I was having a good time...you know, on the date."

She was glad about that, and she smiled, but she also snorted. "Of course you were," she said. "You got at least partway into my panties."

She expected him to get all gallant, say something like: '*It wasn't just that,*' but he surprised her. "Well, yeah," he said. "That's the thing. I thought that if we did anything, it would be you *letting* me do stuff, you know? Would you let me touch your tits, would you let me get to third base. But you were...really into it. You were actually *participating*. There are times I wonder if girls even *get* horny; but you were right in there like a guy, and I think that's really cool."

She smiled again, more genuine this time. "There's a lot you don't know about girls," she said. "We're just as horny as guys, but it's easier to hide it...and a lot riskier to let anybody know. Being called a slut sucks, you know? Especially by a guy who said he liked you on Friday night. But I trust you not to do that."

"Why?" He asked. "I mean, I'm honored, but why?"

"Because I've known you a long time and I know you're not like that," she answered. "I mean yeah, you're my friend, but even if you hated me, you're a stand-up guy. As much as you hate Lindsey, you don't help spread those rumors about her having a gangbang with the football team, or her having a night job as a stripper, or her being knocked-up. You don't use the fact that she has a pussy against her, you know? And if you don't do it to her, you won't do it to me."

"Oh. I guess that makes sense."

They were left in silence again. But this time, the silence seemed to have a different charge. She noticed Adam was huddled closer to her than ever before. Maybe he felt it, too.

"Adam?"

"Yeah?"

"Do you want to fuck?" Kristen asked.

"What?"

She could feel him staring at her incredulously in the darkness. "It's only our second date, so I don't think I can really call it making love, but we could die any second and we don't have anything else to do so would you please just fuck me?"

"I...uh...wasn't expecting...I don't have any—"

"If we live through this, I'll get some Plan B! Now come on! *Please!*" Her voice broke on the last word. She hadn't realized how desperate she was.

"Okay."

While Adam fumbled to open his pants, Kristen simply shoved everything below her waist to her ankles, then kicked it off and straddled him.

He was hard. Very. She grabbed his hardness, pointed it upward, fit tip to lips, and slammed down.

It hurt. A stab, tearing, then burning. She should have been more gentle with herself, but she couldn't, any more than she could stop now. She rode him hard, and in a minute the burning started to fade, replaced by heat. A minute later, she felt the familiar pressure starting to build in her belly. She'd never come this fast, and probably never would again; she was in a primal fury of terror and need, riding wild, and—

"Kr-Kris...I can't...can't! Can't hold it anymore!"

"It's okay, go ahead, just don't stop, don't stop"

He didn't. She felt the hot, tight, rubbing, stretching, burning feeling between her legs turn into a hot, wet, slippery feeling, spurt by spurt as Adam groaned beneath her. And that was okay. That was good. It soothed the burning and he kept thrusting and she could feel the pressure in her belly, in her womb, building and coiling, bigger and tighter than it had ever been before. Bigger than she'd ever imagined it could be until it finally burst and she screamed out into Adam's mouth.

***

"Kris...Kris, wake up."

Kristen blinked and opened her eyes into darkness. Adam was shaking her shoulder. Somehow she'd fallen asleep. Her hip joints ached, her vagina felt like someone had shoved a log up it, bark and all, and her panties were damp and uncomfortable. Never mind the fact that there was something prowling out in the dark.

"What time is it?" She asked.

"It's two o' clock. We've been asleep for hours," he said. "I think I should go check it out."

She stared at him—not that he could see it, or that she could actually see him. It was too dark for that.

"No, you shouldn't."

"I've been awake for longer than you have," Adam insisted. "It's been quiet the whole time."

"So what?" She retorted. "Don't you know how this story ends? You go out there, you never come back, and when the cops show up tomorrow, they tell me to come out without looking back because your body is hanging over the door!"

"The police? We don't know if anybody's coming!"

"This isn't Gilligan's Island," She snapped back. "It's a High School dance! When they notice nobody came home, they'll send some help! If they run into trouble, they'll send some armed help. How does you getting killed before they do that help?"

A long moment of silence. When Adam's voice came out of the darkness again, it was conciliatory. "It doesn't, you're right," he said. "But it really has been quiet for a long time. I think it...they... whatever was out there...is gone. We could get out, get to somewhere our phones work—"

154

She was about to interrupt him, argue some more, say those things weren't worth his life when all they had to do was wait, but the next thing he said brought her up short.

"—see if anybody's still alive out there. What if there is someone out there that we can help? Or someone who might live if we called for help right away, but might die if we wait for people to figure out they need to *send* help? I don't think I could live with myself."

Kristen wanted to say, '*You might not live at all*,' but she didn't. She was thinking about Randy. He'd been seven different kinds of asshole, but he didn't deserve whatever had happened to him out there. Did she want any more screams for help haunting her dreams for the rest of her life? She didn't think so.

"Me neither," she admitted. "Okay, fine. But I'm going, too."

Adam opened the door, slowly, but it still creaked and scraped. Kristen winced at the sound. With the music pounding out in the gym earlier, the door's noises had been nothing. Now, the Lost Hallway had been turned into a silent echo chamber, and any noise could bring attention from whatever was responsible for the screams.

She squinted against the light, and she could tell that Adam was doing much the same as he raised a hand to shade his eyes. It said something about how long they'd been locked in the darkness of the Make-Out Room, and how nearly total that darkness had been, that even the dim, flickering, damaged fluorescents of the hallway hurt their eyes.

At the same time she was struggling to regain her vision, she was also fighting a desperate battle with her stomach, one that she only won because she was terrified that puking would make too much noise. The hallway smelled of raw meat, shit, and most of all, the coppery scent of blood. It was everywhere. The floors, the walls, and even the ceiling were painted with dripping crimson. Was it possible that this had all come from Randy? Did a single body even hold this much blood? Heck, it was impossible to tell if the random chunks of meat and bone strewn about the hallway had come from one body or several.

Even as her eyes recovered, Kristen was looking up and down the hallway, scanning to see if she should jump back into The Make-Out Room and drag her stupidly brave lover back in by the hair.

Adam was directing his attention upward to the gym, while Kristen was looking to the back end of the Lost Hallway.

What she saw terrified her. It wasn't the gore—although that was plenty bad enough. No, whatever had come through here had scratched and cracked the bare concrete floors and gouged the cinderblock walls. But even that wasn't the worst of it.

The double doors were standing open. And beyond them lay a deep black that made the Make-Out Room look like a sunroom at noonday.

"Come on," Adam said. "I don't see anything coming. This could be our chance."

Kristen didn't want to. Didn't want to step out into the hall, away from the shelter of the Make-Out Room...in front of those doors. But Adam was right, and he'd been right in the room too. If it was just about them, they could sit on the couch and wait. But if there were people still alive out in the gym, they had to try.

Adam went first, she followed. They moved like escaped convicts in a movie, hugging the wall. It was only twenty feet or so to the junction to the gym, but to Kristen it seemed like her senses suffered a new assault with each step.

Blood and viscera coated the walls with a red spackle and their shoes squelched and stuck with each step.

Blue-white flashes came from around the corner. Were live wires sparking?

And the smell...growing stronger the closer they got...human death mixed with something else. Something dry and sharp and... alien.

"Adam, I don't think—"

"Shh," he said, putting a finger to his lips as they reached the corner. "I'll go first."

He was being the Macho Man again, and that was bad. He wasn't paying as much attention, wasn't getting the same warnings she was. She had to—

Too late. While she'd been thinking, he'd taken a quick, careful peek around the corner. Now he turned back to her and bent for a quick peck on the lips.

"I'll be right back. Promise."

"Adam!"

But he was already gone. She could hear his footsteps be-

156

yond the corner. One step. Two. Three. Silence.

Then she heard those same three steps coming back toward her. *Sprinting*.

"Run!" he shrieked as he came flying around the corner. "Ruuunnn!"

She did and recognized the tap-tick-scrabbling-scratches. Something was coming.

It was only twenty feet down the hall to the Make-Out Room. Five running strides and a dive, and Kristen was in.

Adam tried to make the same dive, but something hit him, knocking him down. He screamed once in shock, then he began to scream in terror.

Kristen spun to see him, scrabbling desperately at the blood-slicked floor as something dragged him away. She caught only the barest glimpse of chitinous plates and a spike-pointed limb in the flickering light before focusing all of her attention on Adam. If she looked, she wouldn't be able to go on.

She grabbed Adam's hands and was promptly dragged forward herself. Whatever it was, it was impossibly strong. Her feet slipped out from under her slamming her ass hard against the concrete floor. Ignoring the pain, she braced her feet against the door-frame.

Adam's screams rose to high, sexless shrieks of animal agony and fear. And still Kristen focused on his face, not daring to look at her opponent for even a second.

Then—impossible, but she felt it—she started to gain ground. Adam's screams rose even higher, and she could understand why, it felt like every ligament in her arms and shoulders was about to tear loose, but still she held on.

And then Adam was free, in the Make-Out Room, falling in on top of her, and with the last of her strength, the end of her conscious thought, she kicked the door closed, and the last sound she heard before she fell down into darkness was the satisfying sound of the lock clicking into place.

***

The rescue workers finished cutting around the doorknob—big job, too, damn thing was a big metal fire door. Otherwise, it probably would have just been smashed in during the attack like the one on the coach's office—and pushed the door open.

"Hello?" One of them called as they played their flashlights around the room. "Anybody here?"

Then they froze.

They'd known there was someone in the room. They wouldn't have cut the door open if they hadn't; they never would have thought to look for survivors in an out-of-the-way storeroom so close to the source of the attack if they hadn't heard someone talking in here. But why, more than one of them had asked as they were cutting the door open, wouldn't those survivors let them in or at least respond to them?

Now they understood.

There was a survivor, all right. A girl. And she was definitely talking. But they could see why she wasn't responding to them.

She was right in the middle of an animated conversation with a boy who'd been bitten in half.

"Miss?" the workers tried again.

"Oh, hello," she said, finally noticing them. "Are we glad to see you. Come on, Adam," she said, nudging the half-boy in front of her. "They're here. We're getting out." Ignoring his utter lack of reaction, she got to her feet and brushed the dirt off the seat of her pants with bloody hands.

"Could one of you guys take me to the pharmacy? I need to get some Plan B!"

Sickened

Tonia Brown

Pressing his face against the cool porcelain, Clemet wondered what had his stomach so upset. He supposed he might have eaten too much of the widow Baxter's pecan pie from the night before, but he never had a problem with eating in the past, excessive or otherwise. Besides, it was a very good pie, all gooey and sweet, which was why he had two slices. Thinking about the pie got his stomach rolling again, triggering his gag reflex, which sent him into another bout of puking.

After six or seven heaves he flushed the acidic yellow mess, lest it prompt him to vomit yet again. Not that there was anything left to vomit. The remnants of his only meal in the last twenty-four hours was long gone. A chunky, throaty mess of greasy fried chicken, biscuits, mashed potatoes, gravy, and at last the pecan pie, easily dispatched in his all day session of knee-bound toilet hugging. The physical act of vomiting was especially harsh on Clemet, being he was the kind of man who'd thrown up maybe twice in his life.

This being the second time.

He leaned against the bathroom cabinet, head back, praying for the moment to pass. "Dear God in heaven. I don't know if it's the flu or what, but please let it pass. I don't know what I done, or what I said to deserve this, but please just let me get better."

As if defying his request, or perhaps even to mock it, his stomach rolled, contracting in sputtering lurches, until Clemet was face first in the bowl again. Heave after heave, he pondered if this was indeed some form of punishment. It felt like God Himself had Clemet by the gut, squashing his intestines bottom up, like a tube of toothpaste, aiming to squeeze the sin right out of his mouth.

Sickness was just an outer show of inner sin, at least that's what momma used to say. According to her, every ache, pain, sneeze and sniffle Clemet suffered growing up was his own fault for being a bad boy. Yet when it came her time to be sick, it was just part of God's plan. Still, here he was on his knees, so maybe he did have something to hide. Sin knew all secrets, Clemet was well aware of that. Dealing with sin, after all, was his bread and butter. It paid his bills, put clothes on his back and food on his table.

That was to say when he wasn't eating his meal off someone's casket.

Clemet closed his eyes, taking mental stock of his offenses as he emptied his stomach. He settled on a few possible culprits, singling out a particularly nasty one. Looking to the ceiling, he said, "If this is about that movie I bought on the internet, the one with all them nekkid girls in it, I'm sore-fully sorry. I'll send it back or throw it away or whatever you want me to do." He paused to belch a belly full of acrid stench. "Please just make it stop."

Clemet belched once more then, miracles of miracles, his stomach fell still. With his head over the bowl, Clemet mumbled his thanks and praises. He flushed then leaned against the cabinet again, waiting a few minutes to see if it was safe to leave the sanctity of the bathroom. One calm minute passed, then two. Five full non-vomiting minutes later Clemet dared to stagger to his bedroom.

The few feet between the rooms stretched into miles. Clemet hobbled, one unsteady footstep at a time, all while he hugged his thin frame, praying for the cease fire to last long enough for him to get some sleep. Not bothering with the sheets, or his clothes, he collapsed on his bed with a heartfelt sigh of gratitude. Praising God once more for good measure, Clemet fell into a troubled sleep.

He didn't last an hour.

Nor did he make it to the toilet this time.

Clemet always hated his momma's sense of formality. Doilies on the chairs, runners on the carpets and placemats on the table had always been a special set of splinters under Clemet's skin. Yet after momma passed on, and he had eaten her sins away like a good son should, he found himself bound to her memory, deciding to leave things just as she had. For once, he was glad he did. Otherwise he would have never had a wastepaper basket beside his bed. He could almost hear his dead momma wailing in disgust as he hugged the bucket to his spastic body, filling it with a substance far flung from its intended purpose. Throwing up in the plastic bin was one thing, but the thought of having to clean that mess off the carpet later, well that was a whole different pile of puke.

Only when Clemet got a look at the inside of the bucket, it wasn't a pile of puke staring back at him. The crisp, white container was filled with a slimy, black mess. Clemet narrowed his eyes at the pool of black, wondering what on earth the widow Baxter put in that darned pie, when a trace of red caught his eye. It was the shape of a single fingerprint, on the rim of the plastic, from the hand that Clemet had just wiped his own mouth with. He held his hand up to his face, and sure enough, a thin sheen of dark crimson coated the inside of his palm. Clemet pulled on the corner of his well-tucked sheet to daub his mouth.

It came away in a mix of black and red.

Clemet had only seen blackened blood once before in his young life, when Grandpa Jones was dying and the doctors said his bowels bled from the inside out. Before it was done, the man vomited what looked like a quarter ton of wet coffee grounds all over the living room carpet before he fell eternally still. They had to hold his wake in a neighbor's house because the stench wouldn't come out of the rug. Clemet never forgot that reek— it was the same smell that wafted from the wastepaper basket between his trembling hands.

Clemet fumbled with the phone, his blood soaked fingers slipping over the keys as his hands shook from dread. He wondered if it was too late to call Doc Pearson at home, or how long it would take an ambulance from the city to come all the way out to the boonies to rescue him. After a few misdials, he tossed the phone to the floor, scrambled to his feet, grabbed his keys and headed out the door with trashcan in hand.

The drive into the city was a fifty-mile nightmare of staggered gear shifts between spastic spewing. By the time he arrived at the hospital the right side of his truck was crimson coated from tipping the full bin out the window every few miles.

A cute little receptionist greeted Clemet at the front desk, explained there would be an hour's wait, then stuck a passel of forms under his nose, which he promptly smothered in blood.

He went straight to an examining room after that, where the baffled medical staff fussed and mussed, prodded and poked, squawked and squealed for hours trying to discover the mysterious source of Clemet's bloody vomiting. Some bright intern called Clemet's home doctor, in hopes there was some past medical history involved that Clemet didn't know enough about to share.

"What's going on with you, Clem?" Doc Pearson asked. "Dragging an old man all the way out here in the middle of the night."

Clemet pulled at the paper-thin gown, ensuring his privates weren't being made public. "Nothing. Just not feeling good, is all."

Doc Pearson flipped through Clemet's chart before he spoke again. "Not feeling good? You call vomiting nearly five quarts of blood in the last hour alone just plain old not feeling good? Son, if this is your idea of not feeling good, I'd love to see your idea of feeling sick."

"What's wrong with me Doc? Is it like Gramp Jones?"

Doc Pearson shook his graying head at Clemet. "Nothing so simple."

Clemet swallowed hard as his stomach lurched again. "Is it like momma?"

"No, son. It's not cancer." The doctor eyed Clemet's chart again. "In fact, I never thought I'd say these words, but I kind of wished it was. Then at least we would know what we were dealing with."

"Then what is it?"

"We don't know."

"But you're my doctor."

"And that's why I'm here at three o'clock in the morning, because I'm your doctor, Clem. I just don't know what's going on with you."

Clemet's nostrils flared. "You guys poked more holes in me than a moth eaten curtain and took enough stuff from me to make a whole new man from. You took all manners of pictures of my insides with that x-ray machine. Then you ran that camera up both ends of me to get some colored photos, and after all that, you still don't know?"

Doc Pearson shrugged.

Clemet winced as his stomach roiled. Doc Pearson pushed the tall, red trashcan marked "Bio-hazard" toward Clemet. The idea of using a normal basin was abandoned after he filled the first one in a few heaves.

As Clemet hovered over the can, readying himself for the next onslaught, Pearson said, "It just doesn't make any sense. You show no signs of internal bleeding, no drop in hemoglobin or other blood levels. In fact all of your labs are perfect. If it weren't for the vomiting, I'd say you were in the best shape of your life."

"Doc," Clemet said between heaves. "You gotta help me. I can't live like this." He pitched forward against the can as God squeezed his insides some more. "Surely I must be dying."

"That's the thing, Clem. You're not. Whatever is happening, it's not killing you. Sure, you can't eat, but we can intravenously feed you if need be. But this blood, it isn't coming from you. God only knows where it's coming from, but you aren't the source. At least that's what science says."

With nothing but his eyes, Clemet pleaded for help as a steady stream of black goop poured from his mouth into the can.

"I know," Doc Pearson said. "I know, son, and I wished like hell I could help. But we really don't know what to do for you. You aren't responding to any of the usual anti-emetic treatments, neither the shots nor the suppositories."

Clemet grunted at the memory. "And it'll be a cold day in hell before I put anything up there again. After those darned things and that camera, I'd be surprised if I even make a noise when I fart."

Doc Pearson laughed, clapping Clemet on the back. "I can sympathize, son. Wait till you get my age. You won't believe the stuff they want you to do."

Rolling away from the can, Clemet grinned as best he could. He knew the doctor meant well.

"Let's talk about your diet," Doc Pearson said.

"I ain't on a diet," Clemet said.

"I mean your eating habits. What did you have for supper last night?"

"Nothing. I couldn't stop puking."

"The night before?"

Clemet turned away, unable to meet the doctor's gaze after such an awkward question. "You know. The usual stuff."

"Such as?"

Clemet narrowed his eyes at the doctor. "Don't you recall? It was Paul Baxter's wake."

The doctor dropped his pen and his smile. "I'm sorry, Clem. I nearly forgot about that."

The men fell quiet for a few moments, a silence punctuated by the occasional belch from Clemet's ever rumbling belly.

At length, Pearson asked, "Does this mean you're still eating folk's sins?"

Clemet winced, this time from weight of the doctor's question. Everyone knew what Clemet did, who he was, but Doc Pearson was one of the few people in the small mountain community who didn't subscribe to the age old practice of sin eating. He was also one of the few folks who would look Clemet straight in the eye, not to mention calling him by name.

"We shouldn't talk about that," Clemet whispered.

"You're sick, Clem. Maybe something you ate at the Baxter's has something to do with all of this."

"I told you, it was the same old, same old. Chicken and biscuits. Pie. Lots of pie." Clemet burped again with the thought of all that pie.

"Clemet, I'm not talking about the chicken, or the pie."

Lost in confusion, Clemet furrowed his brow.

Pearson heaved a tired sigh. "Look, you know I don't get into all of this backwoods mumbo-jumbo, so far be it from me to try and piece it together for you. But as I understand it, after the wake these people leave out food on the casket in hopes that it soaks up whatever sins the recently deceased person had lingering about, right?"

"Sounds right," Clemet said.

"Then the eater—that's you—comes up in the night, sight unseen, and eats as much of it as he can, in the family's hopes that you'll consume these left over sins." Raising an eyebrow, the doctor looked over his glasses at Clemet.

Clemet nodded.

Exhaling another long sigh, Pearson finished with, "Then you take the rest of the food, along with as much cash as the family can spare, in payment for your kind deed. Is that all?"

The way Doc Pearson put it made Clemet feel sort of foolish. There was so much more to it than that. Like the pressure put on him to follow in his father's footsteps. Or the way he spent his whole life being treated like a leper by the very same folks who depended on him to save their immortal souls. Not to mention the hours upon hours Clemet spent in prayer after each sin eating session.

He held his rumbling belly as he hung his head. "Yeah. That's all."

"And nothing about that seems remotely connected to this?" The doctor waved a hand at the nearly full trashcan.

"I thought you didn't believe in backwoods voodoo."

"I don't. And I didn't call it voodoo."

"Then what are you getting at?"

"If the problem isn't physical, and it isn't, then what's left?"

164

Clemet narrowed his eyes at Doc Pearson. "You saying I'm crazy?"

"No. I'm saying it's awfully coincidental that the night after you think you've eaten the mistakes of a dead man, you start vomiting blood as black as sin itself."

Clemet never claimed to be smart. He knew his limits better than most, and tried to live his life accordingly. Yet no sooner had the last word left the doctor's mouth, Clemet made a connection that would have left his mother proud. The vomiting began after he ate Paul Baxter's sins. Not just the widow's food, because that wasn't what was on the casket by the time Clemet arrived. No. Clemet consumed the man's actual sins. There was only one question left. What in God's name had he eaten? Clemet eyed the bloody black insides of the trashcan, trying to imagine what kind of trouble an old fart like Paul Baxter could have possibly gotten up to.

"Clemet," the doctor said. "I'm gonna get a specialist to come talk to you."

"You mean like a gut doctor?"

Doc Pearson shook his head, then tapped his temple with one finger.

"I ain't crazy," Clemet said, before he leaned over the can to vomit again.

"I'm not saying you are. But we have to rule out every possible problem, and as much as I hate to say it, this is looking more psychosomatic with each full can."

Clemet could see there was no use arguing. Wiping a trail of dark red from his chin, he said, "Go get your psycho doctor then. Let's do this."

The doctor left the room.

Clemet left shortly after.

It didn't take near as long to get to the Baxter farm once Clemet got the hang of shifting between heaves. He climbed out of the truck, empting his plastic bin along the drive as he approached the house, not wanting to carry the filthy thing at all, much less full of puke. Clemet took his time approaching the house, working out how to ask a widow for her dead husband's deepest secrets.

As he set foot on the first step, the porch lit up and the door flew open. A frail, elderly woman stood in the doorway, staring down the length of the steps in surprise.

165

"You?" Mrs. Baxter asked. Once she realized who he was, she dropped her head, refusing to look up at him again. "What are you doing back here?"

"I hate to bother you ma'am," he said. "I just need to ask you about a few things."

"I'm afraid I don't understand."

As Clemet reached the porch proper, he got a good look at the widow Baxter. She was in an awful state, as nearly ragged as her old, worn gown. Her eyes were swollen with grief, huge and red, probably from hours of crying.

"I'm sorry," Clemet said, backing away. "I think I made a mistake. I'm sorry for troubling you."

"I still don't—oh, my! Are you all right?"

Clemet was far from all right. He doubled over his bucket again, vomiting up what he swore was his own intestines this time. Slick chucks of black tar slid from his mouth, filling the pail in wet slops.

To Clemet's surprise, the widow grabbed him by the elbow, guiding him into the house. "Come on, you shouldn't be out in this kind of state."

Clemet could only nod in agreement. She led him to the living room, sitting him on the edge of a plastic covered couch, while she dashed away into what he assumed was the kitchen.

"I'll just get you a glass of water and a towel," she said as she left the room.

Holding his bucket between his legs, Clemet looked around the room to distract himself from his seizing guts. Although he had been here only last night, it was by the backdoor to the parlor, where the body and his meal waited for him. The whole affair lasted a meager twenty minutes. Eat and run, that was his dad's motto. Now it was Clemet's.

A roaring fireplace gave the room a warm glow, almost too warm as far as Clemet was concerned. He stood to move to the far end of the couch, when he caught a distinct smell in the air overpowering the pungent odor of his bloody bucket—the char of burning paper. A foot or so in front of the open fireplace laid a thick photo album. A few sparks from the crackling fire had leapt to the cover of the album, setting it to a slow burn. His nausea forgotten, Clemet dropped his bucket to the floor, kicked the album away from the flames, then stomped on the smoldering cover until it was out. He

166

picked up the hefty album in time to hear the widow return.

"I thought you might like some tea instead—" she started, but paused when she spied the album. "Where did you find that?"

"Near the fire," Clemet said. "It was almost in flames."

"Put it back."

"What?"

"Put it back," the widow said as she placed her tray on the coffee table. "It's full of bad memories. Please, just toss it on the fire."

Clemet understood where she was coming from. When his momma died, Clemet nearly sold the house, stopping only when he realized it was all he had left of her. "Mrs. Baxter, I know this ain't my place to say, but you don't want to burn up all your memories of Mr. Baxter. You'll even miss the bad ones one day."

Mrs. Baxter pursed her thin lips as she shook her head. "Burn it, Clemet."

Clemet started at the sound. He hadn't heard his own name from a local woman's mouth since before momma passed on. He couldn't imagine what had the woman so fired up about the picture book that she would let her just push a lifetime of traditions aside like that.

Clemet cracked the album open, in hopes of showing her some photo that might lure her into reason. "But why would you want to burn..." was all he could say before he laid eyes on the pages of the book and the nausea took him again.

While the photographs featured Mr. Baxter, they didn't include his widow.

"Give it to me!" the widow shouted as she lunged forward, attempting to snatch the photos away.

At least a foot taller than the elderly woman, Clemet held the album at arms length while he flipped from page to page. The first picture was in black and white, showing a young Mr. Baxter, and an even younger girl, perhaps seven or so. But the thing Mr. Baxter was doing to the child was something God never intended to be done.

Maybe not even between consenting adults.

The next photo showed a naked young boy on his knees in front of Mr. Baxter. The older man in the photo was wearing nothing but a wicked smile, frozen in a moment of twisted pleasure. The next picture was much the same, as was the next. Only two things changed as the pages progressed, the quality of the photographs, and the age the leading man. With every new picture, Clemet's stomach pitched against his esophagus, as if it were desperately trying to flee his body.

Unable to tear himself away from the photographic horror, he asked, "What is this?"

"I don't know," the widow said from the couch. She had long given up trying to wrestle the thick book away from Clemet.

"How could he do that?"

"I didn't know," she repeated before she buried her head in her hands. Her weeping finally broke the spell of the cursed photos, grabbing Clemet's attention long enough to let him shut the album. "Please, just throw it away."

Clemet cowered in the corner of the room, staring at the weeping widow for what felt like an eternity, not knowing what to do. He prayed in silence, asking the heavens for the strength to deal with this mess.

As if sensing his hesitation, the widow glanced up to him, looking him dead in the eye.

Clemet's skin crawled.

"Please," she begged as she stood, taking a few tentative steps forward. "Paul was a good man and a good citizen to this town. He just made a few mistakes.

"A few mistakes?" Clemet asked. Nausea washed over him, but this time it was a pure and simple sickness, not the same gut wrenching from before. "They were just kids. How could he do stuff like that to them?"

"Please don't let him die like this. Be remembered like this. Please, just burn it."

"How could he?"

The widow clenched her fists on either side of her head and screamed, "He didn't know what he was doing!"

Clemet found that hard to believe. "How could he not know? With that satisfied smile and his...his..." Clemet choked, unable to speak the words. The idea of what Mr. Baxter had done, had been doing to those kids right up to the very last photo, gripped Clemet in a righteous anger. Full of fury and fire and a rage that he had never felt before, he shook the album in one clutched fist at the widow. "Good God woman, he's posing in every picture! How could he have not known?"

The widow collapsed at Clemet's feet in a howling heap.

168

"I'm so sorry. God help me I am so sorry."

Clemet's anger stalled in its tracks. All of the fight went out of him when he looked down on her shuddering form. He rested a hand on her shaking shoulder. "Mrs. Baxter, it's not your fault."

The widow didn't seem to listen to him. Instead she mumbled, "Merciful God in heaven please forgive me. I'm so sorry. I'm so very, very sorry."

"Peggy," Clemet said, risking all propriety by speaking her first name. "Peggy please, it's not your fault. Don't take this into you. Just because you were man and wife don't mean you share this sin."

At the sound of his own words, Clemet finally understood what had been happening all along. He had supped on the horrible lifelong secret of a sick and twisted man. He had eaten it, absorbed it, and his body rebelled against it in the only way it knew how.

Clemet looked down at the album he held, the proof of Paul Baxter's sin, knowing what had to be done. He had to right this wrong. It was the only way to set his troubled body at ease. The nausea was already passing just with the idea of it.

"What's done is done," Clemet said. "We'll turn this album over to the police, and I'm sure they'll handle it as quietly as they can. After all and I do hate to put it like this, they can't arrest a dead man." He almost smiled, but thought better of it.

The widow, quiet now, raised her face to him. In her eyes lay an anguish Clemet hoped to never see again. "You don't understand."

"Mrs. Baxter?"

"I can't let you turn that album over."

"I have to. I need to do the right thing by those kids."

"I need you to destroy it." Quick as lightening, Mrs. Baxter was on her feet again, clawing for the book. Clemet tried to pull away, but it was too late. The woman had it in her hands one moment, the next it was ablaze. She stood guard in front of the fireplace, as if Clemet would reach into the flames to retrieve the burning album.

Clemet had other things to worry about. As soon as the picture book hit the flames his nausea returned. While the proof of Paul Baxter's sin burned merrily away, Clemet Jones's stomach roiled.

Grasping his stomach, he stared down at the widow, and asked, "Why?"

In the shadows of the flickering firelight, her pale lips curved into an evil grin. "Who do you think took all those photographs?"

A swell of nausea struck Clemet again, driving him to his knees.

"I can't go to jail, Clem," she said as she stood over him. "I'm too old and too tired."

"You don't have to," Clemet gasped between groans. "No one has to know you took 'em." Even as he said it, his stomach disagreed by trying to leap up his throat.

"Not good enough. Paul gave everything to this town. He deserves to be remembered with respect. I won't let you just come in here and soil his good name. Not some sin eating, low life like you." After she made her grand speech, she snorted up a good sized loogie and spat it right in Clemet's face.

Clemet was doing his best not to vomit, but once that warm spittle oozed down his cheek, it was all over. His guts contracted, sending up a monster of a belch, at which the widow wrinkled her nose in distaste. Before she could verbally protest, the belch was followed by a flood of the blackest, thickest, slimiest blood Clemet had seen all night. It shot out of him with fire-hose force, knocking the widow off of her feet as it pummeled her. She fell to the wayside with a surprised shout, accompanied by the distinct crack of bone, probably a hip.

All Clemet could do was brace himself on his knees, keep his mouth open, and pray that when he was done some poor soul would have enough pity on him to eat his sins before they put him in the ground.

Clemet woke a few hours later, back in the hospital and the paper-thin gown. Only this time he was tied to the bed by his wrists and ankles. He tugged at the leather manacles, wondering what in the heck was going on.

"Welcome to the land of the living," Doc Pearson said.

Clemet looked over to find the doctor sitting at the bedside.

"What's going on?"

"How do you feel?"

"Why you got me chained up like some animal?"

Pearson leaned in close to Clemet. Between clenched teeth he said, "Because you only get to make a jackass out of me once, son. Now answer the damned question."

Clemet stared at the doctor with wide eyes. "Yes sir. I feel fine, sir." It was the truth too. In fact, he felt better than he had in years. He said as much.

Doc Pearson nodded before he stepped to the doorway. He shouted into the hallway, "Who do I have to sue to get my patient out of these restraints?"

"Doc? I don't understand what's going on."

The doctor turned back to Clemet with a shrug. "Neither do I."

"How did I end up here? What happened to the widow—"

"She called the cops on you."

"Me?"

"She claims you broke into her house. The police found you passed out in her parlor."

"The police?" Clemet swallowed hard. "But I didn't break in. Honest!"

"Don't worry about it, Clem. She's got bigger worries now."

"Like what?"

"Aside from a pair of broken hips?"

Clemet grimaced. He felt sort of guilty for that.

The doctor leaned in close again, whispering, "They found the photographs."

Clemet stared hard at the doctor.

"The album, with the kids..." The doctor's voice trailed off, as if he couldn't bring himself to finish the sentence. Which he probably couldn't.

"That thing was on fire last I saw it," Clemet said.

"From what I understand, they found it in the fireplace while collecting your bloody vomit as evidence. The book was a little charred around the edges. It was also a lot bloody. Which made it wet. As in put-out-a-fire kind of wet." The doctor raised his eyebrows and cocked his head at Clemet.

Clemet, for the second time that evening, made a grand leap of intelligence. He smiled at the warm feeling of it. "Wow. Sort of a blessing that I was so sick, huh?"

"A blessing? If that's a blessing I'd like to see your idea of what dammed is."

"No you wouldn't." Clemet closed his eyes for a moment, shuddering at the images forever burned into his mind. "I've done seen what dammed is like, Doc. You really don't want to see."

171

Doc Pearson grinned at Clemet. "I do believe I'll take your word for it."

A beautiful blonde nurse joined them, setting Clemet free from the awkward cuffs. Clemet got an eyeful of her tight behind before she slipped away from the room. He reeled back on the rising lust, tamping it down before it could flower into another sin, or worse, another bout of vomiting.

He had just about enough with outward shows of inward mistakes for one lifetime.

Glutton for Punishment

Robert Essig

Lights, like so many stars, lit the city against the dark night. It was a view from his fifty-first story penthouse that William Buckingham, president of Buckingham Enterprises, would never live to loath. At least that's what he thought.

He stood there in front of the floor to ceiling picture window—a wall of glass that looked out upon the bright lights and constant mayhem of New York City—contemplating his wealth, family and future.

Contemplating these things, all because of a nasty case of the clap he received from a twenty thousand dollar whore.

William sipped a single malt scotch as he thought about his life. *How the hell can I get the clap from a twenty grand hooker?*

Those kinds of prostitutes were suppose to be at the top of the heap, the cream of the crop. For twenty G's they sure should be, but this one...she was dirty on the inside. He could have paid a skanky tramp in Queens a twenty spot for the same thing.

But she was beautiful, thought Buckingham, a*nd that body...*

What the hell did that matter? A night with Venus and a lifetime with Mercury, as the saying goes.

But how could it happen?

William's mind came back to that thought, again and again. For twenty thousand dollars she should have been double checked for disease, but when he really thought about it, she was only one of many things he paid dearly for that weren't up to his standards.

Take the meal Mr. Buckingham had two weeks ago at Pravda, an exclusive new restaurant. He ordered a Kobe beef steak—a New York cut, which, in some circles is considered the absolute choicest steak in the world—and you know what? It was no better than filet mignon at a casual dining steakhouse; but the Kobe steak cost several hundred dollars.

And what about his new suit?

William crooked his head to look at the seam on the shoulder that had already split. This was the first time he wore the suit, it hadn't even been to the cleaners yet, and there was a split in the hem! He had it tailored at the best shop in town and this is what he got.

Should have gone to the Men's Warehouse.

What was the point of all this money if it was being wasted on superior products that were nothing more than inferior garbage?

It was eating Mr. Buckingham alive.

He looked out from his million-dollar view wondering what was wrong with *it*. Surely there was something amiss. Perhaps there was someone in another high-rise spying on him with a telescope. Something.

He sipped his single malt scotch suddenly aware of the taste it left in his mouth. He was very used to that sweet burning taste, but for all he knew it was nothing better than neutral grain spirits.

Nothing better than two-buck-chuck swill.

William Buckingham smiled as he looked across his penthouse suite to the mini bar. There stood two decanters, the one with the good stuff and the other one for guests filled with cheap store-brand liquor. He wasn't even sure it was scotch at all, probably bourbon.

William looked at his glass and thought of his family—his wife and youngest son, Charlie. He also thought of his other son, Daniel, the child from his first marriage, the heir to his enterprise.

He poured his drink out and replaced it with the cheap guest liquor—no rocks. After all, what was the best worth if it wasn't the best? What was a Gucci suit worth if the seams split before the first dry cleaning; what good is a Kobe steak that tastes like a steakhouse special?

He sipped the liquor feeling the burn as it coated his larynx on its way down—resting like a fire in his stomach.

To him, the single malt scotch was just as useless as a twenty thousand dollar whore.

William had a family out there somewhere. He knew where. He would leave his suite eventually, after he was half in the bag, to slip into bed beside his wife. In the morning he would see Charlie, smile a fake smile, and watch his boy leave for school.

That was about all he ever saw of Charlie lately.

He spent a lot of time in his fifty-first story suite these days.

Diana loathed him. He could swear she shuddered every time

he slipped into bed next to her. But there was a prenuptial agreement; she had to stay or she wouldn't get any of his fortune. Diana lamented over signing the prenup. She even hired a lawyer once to see if anything could be done to release her from the agreement and was told nothing could be done. If she divorced or left William, she wouldn't get a cent.

She married money and William knew it. Their wedding day kiss was reserved and frigid, no passion at all. He practically had to pay her to have sex with him that night and showered her with gifts all throughout their honeymoon just so she would put out.

He realized then that he had made a mistake in marrying her, but what could he do? He sure as hell didn't want to give her a chunk of his fortune, so he decided to buy the suite and let her fester on the side like a painful canker sore; he played the irritating tongue that never let it heal.

William picked up the phone and dialed his personal assistant. "Jennifer, I want you to take care of something for me, first thing in the morning. Call my lawyer. I want to file for divorce...no, it's nothing like that. It's just something I have to do. Why live with a twenty thousand dollar whore, right?" Jennifer didn't know what to say to that. "Yes, just make sure you do it first thing. Thank you."

Diana was a twenty thousand dollar whore that would soon become a multi-million dollar whore, but what was money when all it bought was the finest cheap liquor and the most expensive cheap suit, not to mention the most expensive diseased hooker in all of New York City.

Why stop there, William thought as an image came to him of a certain trampy slut he remembered from high school, Becky Tarantino.

Mr. Buckingham swallowed the last of his whisky deciding to sleep on the floor rather than on the bed with the four hundred thread count Egyptian cotton sheets. After all, they were probably no better than the sheets on clearance at Wal-Mart.

And why stop with gonorrhea, IIe thought, *my money could go so far. I bet Becky has it all, even full blow AIDS.*

As William lay down he wondered what it was all for: the huge corporation, the millions of dollars, the investments. Why so much when it could all be ruined so easily?

His body trembled as he looked around the darkness of the suite. Anything could happen. The building was supposed to be safe, surveyed twenty-four hours a day by security cameras and armed guards, but what was any of that *really* worth? Nothing else seemed to be worth its cost.

A crazy man could bust the door down and assassinate him, or perhaps take him and torture him until he handed over his fortune. Anything could happen.

Normally William would be going home to crawl beside the woman who despised him. He had only slept in the suite on rare occasions—like the other night with the twenty thousand dollar whore!

In the past he never worried about the security of the building any more than he questioned the quality of his scotch or the softness of his sheets. He never really questioned anything before, just took everything for face value, literally. Value was everything to William Buckingham. To him, life was only equal to the value of everything therein. He liked only the finest.

But what happens when the finest isn't so fine after all?

Sleep alluded him, leaving his mind to torment itself—he worried about his dental work, and he could swear he felt pain in the tooth he had a root canal in about six months ago. The dentist was supposed to be the best in Manhattan, but then again...

His paranoia gave way to relief when he thought about the divorce he would be pursuing in the morning. *To hell with it*!

He thought of Becky Tarantino again. He was going to have to make a call tomorrow, see what she was up to, see if she wanted to make a quick buck.

It wasn't that catching the clap was the end of his life—the disease was an easy fix—but something snapped in his brain and suddenly the world around him wasn't what he always thought it to be. Somehow he had been hoodwinked into believing that he really could live exclusively, but it wasn't true.

He was going to have to start living in reality.

The best of the worst that money could buy.

It wasn't hard to find Becky Tarantino. She hadn't married and her name was well known by those on skid row. There was a corner she frequented when she needed money for dope and that was where William found her. She hardly looked like a hooker—at least what he thought a hooker should look like—the way she was dressed in a tattered shirt and baggy sweat pants.

He suddenly realized that walking the streets in this part of town, regardless of how awful a woman looked, would have men pulling up to ask for a blowjob in broad daylight. It was just that kind of neighborhood.

William must have driven by ten times throughout the evening before he saw her. He promptly picked her up and told her he would pay grandly for her diseases. Even in her state of degradation she was offended by his comments; however, when he flashed a wad of cash as thick a hardcover novel, she smiled and stepped inside his Honda Civic (William Buckingham wouldn't have been caught dead in a Honda only a few days ago, but now that he knew the true lack of value in everything he traded his loaded Lexus for a low end Civic).

She picked at her skin in the most disgusting manner as William drove them to his suite. Once there, he did things to her he should be ashamed of in spite of who she was and her soiled reputation—but that was what he was going for. He wanted her disease, wanted to writhe in it until his flesh broke out in a rash of severe boils. He wanted to hurt, to feel pain that would take the place of the pain he felt at being so ignorant for so many years.

He threw her out of his suite; gave her far too much money, and told her to do society a favor and kill herself.

He wasn't sure why he added the last part, if nothing more than mere bitterness that she was fortunate enough not to see just how useless life really was. Here she was, happy over a couple thousand dollars she would undoubtedly waste on bad dope and cheap booze after which she would have to drag herself back to the corner where she would never sell her miserable body for near as much money ever again.

William decided against drinking liquor for he wanted to feel her disease infiltrating his body, flowing through him like venom, and to his disappointment, he felt nothing. There wasn't even the suspected irritation on his groin he had hoped for.

It isn't quick enough. I need something that will work faster.

That's when William found the razors in his medicine cabinet and decided to cut a grid on the bottom of his feet like bloody grill marks. The pain wasn't what he had hoped for, but he knew the wounds would become infected and scab up, at which point it would feel as if he were walking on broken glass at all times. That was the kind of punishment he was looking for, the kind of constant reminder of his incessant ignorance he needed.

Over the next month, William Buckingham was rarely seen in public. There were phone calls that filled his voice mail to which he never answered; at least a hundred messages on his phone at the office went unheard.

Strange business dealings were being approved as William sold pieces of his company for pennies on the dollar, in some cases giving whole factories to smaller unknown businesses that likely wouldn't be able to handle such a workload.

Though William was the CEO there were others, top shareholders in Buckingham Enterprises, who were concerned by his rash decisions, but they couldn't locate the man and those that used to be close to him—at this point nobody was close to him—weren't talking.

His soon-to-be ex-wife was off in the Bahamas having the time of her life without a care in the world to the state of Buckingham Enterprises. It wasn't until the shareholders spoke to William's older son, Daniel, that they came up with some answers.

Daniel was the heir to Buckingham Enterprises and no one was more concerned about his father's sudden decisions to sell off the company so quickly and for so little. He vowed to the shareholders that he would find his father and bring sense to him.

It was in one of the old abandoned warehouses where Daniel finally found William. He was a sorry sight, a man on the verge of death from sheer exhaustion, lack of nutrition and severe infection. It had been a while since Daniel had seen his father, and never had he seen him in such a state.

"What's happened to you, dad?"

William looked at his son, his face shrunken in, flesh hanging from his bones like a man so much older than himself. He had been standing in the middle of the warehouse amongst the racks of old product that had been stored there and forgotten. He looked so peculiar the way he stood silently as if there were people there waiting to yell 'surprise.'

"Son, you found me," William's voice hissed.

It was obvious William knew people were looking for him.

A gunshot rang out dropping Daniel to the floor. The bullet hit William in the right arm knocking him off balance though he somehow remained standing.

"Shit! Someone's shooting at us!" yelled Daniel looking for cover.

"At me, son. You don't have to worry."

Daniel looked from the ground at his father, his brow wrinkled in confusion. He didn't understand what his father was saying to him.

"Who's shooting at you? We've got to get out of here, you're wounded."

"I hired him, son. He's not the type of guy you would hire to kill a congressman, you couldn't trust a guy like that anyway. He's just a small time hood who could use the money. You see, he doesn't know how useless money really is."

"What do you mean you hired him?"

William looked around the warehouse at the rafters and storage area, accessible by ladders that went up three floors or more. "He's out there somewhere. I told him to shoot me periodically, in the arms and legs, nowhere fatal."

"What! Nowhere fatal; what the hell are you talking about?"

Another shot rang out causing Daniel to yelp and take cover. The bullet ricocheted off the concrete floor.

"I knew what I was getting, son. I knew he would miss once or twice. Can you imagine paying for a hit man that misses? It would be like getting the clap from a twenty thousand dollar whore."

Daniel didn't know what to say. His father stood there like some crazy martyr waiting for the next bullet. His arm was bleeding onto the floor where Daniel saw the state of his father's feet. He was without shoes, his skin puffy and red, infected with poorly scabbed wounds.

"It wasn't enough, son. I needed more."

"More what?" Daniel's concern for Buckingham Enterprises was completely replaced with shock.

"More punishment. The twenty thousand dollar whore, the Egyptian cotton pillows, the single malt scotch—all of it lies. All my life believing such lies, and now..."

"You've completely lost it, haven't you?"

"...Now I know what's real." William looked his son dead in the eyes as another bullet fired, echoing through the warehouse. This one hit true blasting a hole through William's left leg. The loss of balance brought him to the floor. He cried out and winced, but there was laughter as well, laughter that Daniel loathed. He didn't like the bullets either. It would be far too easy for one to mistakenly hit him.

"Why bring down Buckingham Enterprises with you, why do this to me? What have I done?"

Now William was on the floor, too weak to stand. His immune system was working overtime to deal with the influx of disease he had given himself: flus, various VD's—he had even located people with deadly skin diseases and persuaded those willing to allow him to touch their festering sores and rub the discharge over his body.

"You have made the same fatal mistake I have, son. You too have found superiority in things inferior. It's all cheap, son. We've been fooled into just giving our money away, and for what? A bottle of cheap scotch with a fancy label, an expensive hooker with gonorrhea? Nothing is what it seems."

Another bullet came out of nowhere, this time barely missing William's head. It ricocheted off the floor lodging itself into Daniel's leg. It felt like the sting from a very large bee with a quarter inch stinger.

"I'm getting out of here!" said Daniel. "I'm going to my lawyers to file that you are insane and unable to further handle your estate."

"Too late," said William, his voice almost too weak to speak. "As of this morning, I have no estate."

This stopped Daniel in his tracks, clutching his wounded leg. The question sounded more like a squeak. "What did you do?"

"I found truth, Daniel. I found what I had been looking for: reality. I lived such a miserable life and never knew reality, pain, or suffering. I was shielded, as you are now. I decided I could do something to save you from a miserable end as the one I am suffering; because if you continue to live like this, you too will want reality and punishment for a life wasted."

"What did you do?"

"The pen, son, is truly mightier than the sword. It has power no one can fool you with, truth that cannot be hidden behind a fancy label or a hefty price tag."

"What...did...you...do?"

"I took a pen this morning and signed away everything. You should be pleased with me, son. Now you won't have to make the same mistakes I had to."

Daniel rushed his father, kneeling before the man. He

180

grabbed his collar slamming his body into the floor.

"Why?" Daniel screamed. "Why did you do that?"

In his fury he took a swing, disgusted at the sight of his father, a man he never really knew, a man who had always been too caught up in his work to make time for his family. He took another swing and yet another, hitting his father so hard he fractured the older man's skull.

Behind him the door to the warehouse opened, a figure slipping out into the sunny day. It was the man who had been shooting at William.

Daniel jumped to his feet running to the door, but he was too late. The man was gone; he could have fled in any direction. On the floor was a piece of paper. Daniel picked it up and read:

You'll find me at the warehouse on 56th and Vine. Do as we discussed, shots to the arms and legs until my son attacks me. At that point you may leave with the money in this envelope. No strings attached.

Daniel looked at his father's body wondering if he was dead or alive. "You set me up to attack you?"

There was no answer. His father was dead, and he went out just as he had planned. He did hope this experience would teach his son something about the true value of life; he hoped Daniel wouldn't have to make the same mistakes, and felt certain that Daniel wouldn't have the opportunity now that he would have to find a job and live as a normal person on a modest income.

It was by the hands of his own son that he was dealt the final blow and what else could he have expected? A son isn't supposed to kill his father, but many times things aren't what they're supposed to be. Like the dirty whore, the one that was supposed to be clean, the bad scotch with the fancy label, and the Kobe beef that was no better than a sirloin.

And that's all it took to make William Buckingham of Buckingham Enterprises a glutton for punishment.

Guys

Eric Dimbleby

"Got some big ol' steaks," said Tommy. He pointed his tangled beard towards the kitchen, the smell of searing blood wafted through the doorway to the cluttered, musty den. "Onions and peppers and corn on the cob, too."

They grunted in response, their eyes transfixed on the television—a porno slapping around on a broken whirring VHS tape.

"Nachos. Jalapenos and ground beef. The Old Lady put 'em together before she left." They grunted again. Old Ladies were good about those sorts of things, and Tommy had himself a hum-dinger.

It was a 'Guy's Weekend,' as Tommy had labeled it. The Old Lady was visiting relatives for the weekend, several states away. Somebody was sick or getting married or having babies or putting on a fucking flute recital. Tommy wasn't quite sure as to the purpose of her evacuation, but he 'uh-huh-ed' her in idle agreement, to remove her from the house, from his eyesight, and from his grasp as quickly as possible.

"I'll just have a couple of the boys over," he had warned her. A couple of boys equated to exactly twelve buddies, from all over town, country, heaven and hell and back.

The Tall Guy. The Short Guy. The Drunkard. The Dog Trainer. The Mechanic. The Welfare Leech. The Other Welfare Leech. The Shop Owner. The Fisherman. The Factory Guy. The Ugly Guy. The Big Dick Guy. Just a couple of the boys.

Tommy had known many of them since childhood, had even gone to Sunday School with the Short Guy. Lost his virginity to the Fisherman's dullard sister with the fat tits. Beat up the Ugly Guy for 'being gay' when they were in high school shop class, only to find out later that he was straighter than a mid-western railroad track. The Big Dick didn't know the Dog Trainer's name. The Welfare Leech had never even exchanged words with the Other Welfare Leech, though they had so much in common, which always baffled Tommy.

"Let me check on them steaks," said Tommy, to which the

Drunkard grunted in response.

The steaks were delicious; slightly pink, but not raw, the perfect mix of moist and dry. The blood and seasoning had sunk deep into the fibers of the meat, intermingling with the onions and peppers. The nachos had satiated them as an appetizer, but the steaks were what put the asses in the seats. The Tall Guy had grunted, eyeballing the Factory Guy during their greedy consumption. They had nodded in concurrence, approving of the incendiary mélange of flavors that Tommy had provided them with, their palettes dizzy with sensations that could not be explained by mere vocabulary. The Dog Trainer had moaned in a very orgasmic tone upon slipping the first bite of meat between his rotting teeth.

As they poked at the gristle and fat remaining on the plates, their bodies accumulated around the television like a gestating virus (all while setting a new world record for the first group of men—or solo viewer, for that matter—to ever finish a pornographic film in its entirety). They made low guttural sounds of pleasure in unison, to display their gratitude towards their host for a great meal and an even better film choice.

"You boys look full," Tommy said in a tone that he often used with his German Shepard, wiping away a spot of seasoned blood from his beard. They grunted in response. Yes, they were full, satisfied to the core. "Let's drink some beers?"

And so they drank beers. Hundreds over the course of only two hours. Thirteen apostles of Budweiser, recounting with their eyes and facial gestures their troubled lives and bitchy wives, wishing aloud that they had committed to better choices in their histories. Tommy spoke to them in stories and maxims, and they listened quietly. They guzzled and laughed and nodded and said not a word. They eyed each other, each reveling in the fact that they were brothers on a unique mission. Some acquainted, others new to their bizarre brood, but all basking in the glory of being male and free of their mundane existences, if only for a single evening. "Shall we watch some more porn, boys?" Tommy queried his posse of men.

And so they finished the last of their beer, moving on to an unending supply of discount package store whiskey, gaping at a new porn film, *The More The Assier Part 4*, while they awaited Tommy's next command for delightful distraction. At the part where Bobby Javelin exploded upon Tina Tightlips' chest, they grunted in satisfaction. During the final sequence when Tina finally discovered that

Doctor Acula was indeed the reincarnated manifestation of Vlad the Impale-Her, the Big Dick and the Mechanic high-fived in a spontaneous but gratifying eruption.

"And how about that engine out back in the garage?" Tommy wondered aloud.

And so they stood in a loose circle, passing around a crush-proof pack of Camels, lighting and dragging on them deeply. By the time the pack made a full round, the first smoker had extinguished, and so it continued. When a pack ran out, Tommy would toss a fresh one to the next man in line, insisting, "Smoke, smoke, smoke. Our ball and chains would never allow any of this shit. Get it while the gettin' is hot."

They smoked until their lungs burned, for more than an hour non-stop, while Tommy professed his love for the new engine he had acquired at an auction in benefit of the local fire department.

"BMW engine, V8. Not sure where those fuckers picked this up around *here*. That's a rich man's vehicle right there. Not for folks like us. But look at that puppy," explained Tommy, running his index finger along the glistening surface, pausing for a moment at each cylinder, rubbing a bit of grime away from the timing assembly.

He pulled long and hard on his Camel, glancing at his audience for reaction. They were quite amused, he concluded.

"Scrubbed this sucker for two weeks before it was even recognizable. Looked like it had been through a fire, if I had to hazard a guess. Maybe that's where the fire chasers got it. Nothin' you can't get clean with WD-40, can I get an amen?" he said. They grunted. "I need to go in the backyard and light a fire. I've got some shrubs to burn. Please join me."

And so they stood in a half-moon about the raging fire, careful to move collectively when the wind changed to avoid smoke inhalation. Whenever they shifted, they lit another Camel. One smoke, it would appear to a casual onlooker, was more desirable than the other. The Tall Guy glared at the smoke, as though it were purposely trying to attack him when a breeze hit the wrought iron fire pit.

"Tore these shrubs out after I shot that woodchuck in the face. Didn't want to give his wife and kiddies anyplace to hide. Now when they decide they're going to walk across *my* land, it's at their own risk," Tommy informed his gang, throwing a fresh shrub on to the inferno. They grunted. "Took that ol' boy down with my new

Magnum. Would you boys like to look at my piece?"

And so they unloaded their weight at the kitchen table, some sitting and others standing, while Tommy dismantled his gun—a .44 Special with a shiny black body and a barrel that was nearly as long as his forearm.

"When I first bought this sweetie-pie the hammer was always getting stuck on me. Which is fine when I've got a close range situation. When I'm more than twenty yards away though, I always need extra shots, especially with varmints and foreigners on my land. I like to get off all six bullets whether I need to or not. Let the rest of them fence-jumping citrus salesmen and gophers know that I mean business. The hammer don't stick no more. Not sure what I did... just worked itself out, I guess."

The Ugly Guy and the Shop Owner exchanged a glance. They too had similar killing machines in their respective homes, and wished that they had brought their bright little killing machines along for the evening. But that went against all of Tommy's well-defined rules.

Rule One: no weapons. If you need a weapon, one will be provided to you.

Rule Two: keep it in the basement.

Rule Three: don't break any fucking rules.

Rule Four: enjoy.

Three knocks sounded at the front door.

"Let's take this party downstairs. The whores are here and right on schedule."

They grunted.

Whores.

The prostitutes danced for more than half an hour before they needed a breather. In the old unfinished basement of Tommy's home, the women worked their rhythmic magic and never scoffed at the musty odors or moistened floors. They never even questioned the reasoning behind their clandestine performance in the deep underbelly of Tommy's otherwise respectable home. The Blonde One assumed that it was to hide their visit from the nosy neighbors, who would surely snoop through the windows with their binoculars and report all of the miscreant activities to Tommy's wife. In towns like theirs, people took names and places down in secret little notebooks in secret drawers of secret rooms and whispered painful truths only

185

at the supermarket or library or church groups.

Several of the men started tearing off their shirts, which pleased the hookers. They would receive payment for each and every man they mounted sexually. They stood to inhale a windfall of cash by evening's end. The Ugly Guy groaned and shouted, waving his shirt helicopter-style above his head in celebration. The Mechanic growled and the Dog Trainer howled.

"Keep these whores dancing," Tommy whispered to Big Dick, who nodded and rubbed up against the Redhead Trick, and then moved in closer to the third of the trio, the One with the Nine-Year-Old Boy Haircut. When he brushed in close to them, cajoling his hips, they must have caught notice of his endowment through the fabric. The Boy Haircut smiled at him and made a decision right then and there that all the rules were meant to be broken on such an evening.

While the Big Dick, the Short Guy, and the Ugly Guy made their best attempts at free sex, Tommy and the Mechanic walked around the perimeter of the basement, clasping shut the squat basement windows, applying industrial tape to the cracks and positioning thick sticky brown paper over the panes. Tommy then offered a nod to the Shop Keeper, who grunted and rolled out a long tube of clear plastic on one side of the dank basement. He then untangled a garden hose from behind the water heater and hooked the spray nozzle on to a nail on the wall.

The Redhead informed the Short Guy that there was "no such thing as a free lunch", which angered him into shouts and tears, his face turning to bright neon pink, on the verge of a minor heart attack. The Big Dick replied to her free-lunch statement by grasping her throat, digging his nails deep into her soft flesh and cursing her with his eyes. She yelped in terror while he backed her up to the unfinished stone wall.

The Ugly Guy and the Factory Guy each grabbed one of the Blonde's arms. Though she fought with great passion, she stood no chance against them and their semi-muscular builds. The One with The Nine-Year-Old's Haircut ran for the wobbling rickety stairs, but had her calves snatched, one each by the two Welfare Leeches. They looked at each other, grinning over their prize. They had finally made a connection after all these years in Tommy's basement.

"Keep it near the drain," Tommy advised, pointing towards the fuse box. Beneath it was a drainage ditch that reached all the way up the incline of the uneven basement's floor. "And keep it quiet, grunts."

They dragged the hookers to the middle of the room, where they descended upon them like wolves, tearing at flesh and screaming with animal pulses of hatred and love. There were four men for each girl like a seventies swing party, and they shared their kills appropriately. Some came for the kill, others came for the food. Some came for both, and the steamy sex in between.

"Don't leave any bits behind." They growled, looking up at their host with fiery eyes. "Eat it or shove it down the drain, but don't leave it. Tell me if you need any tools."

The Drunkard grunted at Tommy, who handed to the man a hatchet in response. He nodded gratefully and went back to his work of ripping his woman—formerly Blonde One, the remainder of her scalp now stained bright red—apart.

"Keep it near the drain, men," he repeated, unhooking the hose from the stud on the wall, pummeling his customers and their prey with jets of cleansing water. Tommy found that if you didn't work them with water the whole time it started to dry and harden on the gritty floor by the time they were finished.

Though it irritated them at first, it became the norm very quickly, the unrelenting flow of crushing water in the guise of neatness. "Keep it near the drain, and please don't make any eye contact with me. You kind of creep me the fuck out."

Tommy withdrew a Camel from his chest pocket and smoked it so fast that his head hurt.

Business was good, and it was only getting better.

Go to Your Room

Shane McKenzie

"Y'all ready for this shit, or what?"

"Would I be here if I wasn't?"

Mike stood across the street from the home, staring at the lit windows on the second floor. A shudder ran down his spine.

"What about you Mike?" Chauncey said. "You're not gonna pussy out, are you?"

Mike didn't want to be there. He would have avoided any scheme involving Chauncey, but the eviction notice on his door that morning forced him out. He hadn't eaten a thing all day, barely anything the day before. He needed money.

When Chauncey told him they were going to rob Old Man McCook's, he almost did pussy out. He fondled the cold metal of the pistol.

"Nah man, I'm ready," Mike said. He couldn't peel his eyes from the brick house. A shove from behind snapped him from his trance.

"If you're so ready, then fuckin' act like it," Julius said. Mike couldn't stand him either, always trying his best to look tough in front of Chauncey.

"Let's do this," Mike said, strutting toward the house. He heard the other two talking behind him, and then their footsteps following.

The three of them pressed their bodies against the side of the home, searching all around for any witnesses. An orchestra of crickets surrounded them, chirping from the trees above.

Mike had always been scared of Old Man McCook, since he was a kid. There were rumors all over the neighborhood of how he was some kind of witch doctor or something. Nobody ever got near the house.

"Alright y'all," Chauncey said. "This is what's gonna happen." He grabbed Julius by his collar, and pulled him in close.

"You're gonna go knock on his door, and me and Mikey are gonna come in through the back." He slapped Mike's shoulder.

"Why do I gotta go to the front?" Julius said, eyeing Mike up and down. "This motherfucker should do it."

Chauncey got face to face with him, their chests bumping. "Cuz I just told you to, nigga."

Julius looked back over at Mike, and nodded his head.

"So once you got him at the door, keep his ass there, as long as you can," Chauncey said. "We're gonna be creeping up behind him, don't let him turn around."

Julius nodded as Chauncey spoke. He scowled at Mike. Mike hated the idea of him and Chauncey alone.

"Why'd we come to Old Man McCook's for? Can't we just hit one of them houses down the way?"

Chauncey glared at Mike, his gold tooth gleaming in the moonlight.

"Cuz Old Man McCook is loaded, and I'm trying to get paid. I know you don't believe the shit you been hearing."

"For real man, they're just some old wives tales, he ain't nothing but an old man," Julius said.

"Look man, we can split this shit two ways, we don't need your punk ass." Chauncey slipped on his ski mask.

Mike thought about this opportunity to escape, to get out of this mess before it started. His stomach growled, and he slipped on his mask.

"Alright man, get ready to knock on his door. Give us about a minute to get behind the house." Chauncey shoved Julius toward the front porch.

Julius edged forward, eyeing the door like a gateway to Hell. He looked back at Chauncey with doubt etched on his face.

"Get the fuck up there."

Mike watched as Julius walked out of sight toward the front of the house. Chauncey grabbed his shoulder.

"Come on."

A loud knocking from the front cued them. Chauncey pulled a crowbar from his backpack. Mike walked ahead of him and tried the knob. The door creaked open as the knob turned. They looked at each other and shrugged. Chauncey placed the crowbar back in his pack.

Another loud bang rang out, followed by talking. Mike recognized Julius' voice, but heard no response. Mike stared into the dark home, trying to listen. Chauncey grabbed his arm.

"Quit fucking around." He gestured Mike to follow him.

Mike used his shirt sleeve to cover his mouth and nose as the thick smell of sweat and shit hit him. His stomach heaved. He heard the buzzing of countless flies in the distance. The sound of Julius' voice grew clearer as he and Chauncey walked deeper into the darkness of the house.

Mike saw the front door, moonlight creeping in from the opening. The old man was facing Julius.

"Your friends need not be shy. My home is open to you all." The old man spun on his heels. He smiled at them.

Mike jumped and ran in the other direction. Chauncey grabbed hold of him and refused to let go.

"We're finishing what we started, nigga." He pointed his gun at the old man's face. "What's up ol' timer?"

Julius pushed his way into the door, his gun pressed into Mc-Cook's back. He stared at the old man, shaking his head.

Chauncey glared at Mike as he stood and watched. Mike drew his pistol, and pointed it at the old man.

"Please children, come sit with me. No need for those toys." Old Man McCook walked by them toward his living room.

"This motherfucker," Chauncey said. Mike could tell he was impressed at the audacity of the old man.

"Let's just get the hell outta here," whispered Julius. "Something ain't right."

Mike felt it too. A bad energy filled the air, every hair on his body stood on end. He wanted to end the charade, but Chauncey refused.

"Did I just hear you say that shit?"

"He said some things..."

"I don't give a fuck if he sang you a song, we're doing this shit!" Chauncey yelled.

Mike saw a single tear run down Julius's cheek as he nodded and steadied his gun.

"You boys have a seat here, and we can talk about this." The old man beamed at them from his cracked leather chair.

"You damn straight we can talk, and you can start by telling us where the cash is at."

"You don't need money," McCook said. "I have much better things to give you boys than money."

Mike stepped forward, "Like what?"

"Anything and everything."

"Shut your ass up!" Chauncey stepped right up to Old Man McCook and pressed the barrel to his forehead. "You need to start talking before it gets messy."

The old man's eyes stayed locked on Mike. His bulbous stomach bounced as he started to giggle.

"I ain't scared to plug you right now." Chauncey pushed the pistol harder against the old man's skin.

"Just listen to him, man," Mike said.

The old man continued laughing, his chuckling turning into a loud cackle. Mike noticed a slight movement from inside his mouth. He squinted as he tried to focus on what it was.

"Shut the fuck up!" Chauncey lifted the gun from the man's forehead and swung it back down. The metal smashed into the man's gaping mouth.

A loud buzzing erupted. A swarm of flies burst into the air, escaping the old man's cackling mouth. Mike felt the house shake as the laughter continued.

"What the fuck?" Julius screamed, swatting at the zig-zagging flies.

"Fuck this shit!" Chauncey yelled. He aimed his gun and fired. The laughter stopped abruptly as the bang of the gunshot echoed through the home. The old man sat motionless in his chair, blood dripping from the wound in his head.

"What did you do, man?" Mike peeled the mask from his sweaty head, watching as another fly crawled from between the dead man's lips.

"Can we get the fuck outta here now?" Julius continued swatting at the swarm of flies.

"The hell with that, we're searching the house first." Chauncey pulled his mask off and stared at his victim with a crooked smile.

"You just shot him, we gotta go!" Julius yelled. "Someone probably heard that shit."

"Man, you know nobody's gonna do nothing. The cops don't even come around here." Chauncey proceeded to search the man's pockets.

"This ain't right, y'all," Mike said. "Those flies were coming from his mouth."

"Why the fuck does it matter now? The motherfucker is dead."

"Y'all do what you gotta do, I'm outta here," Julius said, running to the front door. "What the fuck?!"

He shook the knob, kicking at the door. It wouldn't budge. He checked all around the frame, looking for some kind of lock, but found nothing. He smashed a window with the butt of his pistol, but found metal bars blocking his way. Julius looked over at the other boys, and ran toward the back. Mike heard him struggling and the string of cuss words that followed.

"We're stuck man. I wanna get the fuck out!"

"Quit your bitch ass whining and help us check the place. Once we get what we need, I'll get us out. Trust me."

"Something's wrong here," Mike said. "We shouldn't be here."

Chauncey backed away from McCook's body, pulling a wad of money from the old man's pocket.

"Y'all still wanna go?" He flashed the money. "We still got a whole house to look through."

Julius walked over to Mike as they both watched Chauncey peeling bills from the bundle of cash. Mike could pay his rent three times with that kind of money. Chauncey handed him his share.

"What happened, happened. Let's get this shit done so we can go, cool?"

Mike looked at the old man, motionless, blood dripping from his head. He pocketed the cash and nodded his head. Julius hesitated, but did the same.

"That's what I'm talking about, now come on."

They came to a stairwell, a dark room just beyond it. Mike strained his eyes to see, but it was of no use. Chauncey pulled a small flashlight from his backpack, and aimed it toward the darkness. Multiple chests and cabinets glimmered in the light.

"Alright, I'm gonna hit this room here. Y'all go upstairs and see what you can grab."

Mike and Julius looked at each other, both waiting for the other to lead the way.

"Get the fuck up there, God damn it."

"So what'd he say to you at the door?" Mike asked. His flash-light led the way as he and Julius ascended the stairs. Old crumpled photos decorated the walls of the stairwell. All photos of children.

"He said he knew why we came here," Julius said, staying one step behind Mike. "Said he knew y'all were at the back, even used your names."

"That's fucked up man, we gotta do this quick."

"What the hell is that smell?"

Mike smelled it, too. The same smell he noticed when they first entered the home. It was much stronger as they reached the top of the stairs. Flies buzzed all around them.

"Fuck this man, let's just go," Julius said. He grabbed Mike and started back down the stairs.

"Nah man, we're here, let's just get it over with." Mike pulled Julius into the hallway ahead of him.

Mike shot the light down the hallway. Nothing but doors on either side.

"I'll take this side," Mike said, walking to his left toward the first door.

"The hell with that, I'm right behind you."

"You wanna get the hell outta this place? Then let's get it done." Mike shoved Julius toward the other end of the hallway.

Julius stared at Mike, pleading with his eyes. It looked like he wanted to say something, but he just turned on his heels and headed toward his side of the hall.

Mike slowly nudged open the door and a loud creaking sound screamed from the hinges. He spat on the floor as the smell hit him. He covered his mouth and nose as he stepped into the room. The walls were alive with the movement of flies, their black bodies scurrying about. Mike spun in circles, in awe at the amount of them.

The only light source came from a television in the middle of the room, a Bugs Bunny cartoon flashing on the screen. A single wooden chair sat in front of it, and a bucket sat next to that.

"This is *my* room."

Mike shot his light toward the voice, quickly grabbing for his gun.

"My eyes!"

The flashlight shone on a filthy, scrawny child who screamed as the light hit his face. He crashed to the ground and kicked his legs, covering his face.

"Turn it off, I'll be good, just turn it off!"

Mike didn't know how to react.

193

It's just a kid, he thought to himself. *But what is he doing in this terrible room?*

Mike put his gun away and clicked the flashlight off.

"Shhh, I'm hunting wabbits," the television announced.

The boy jumped up and ran to the chair. He stared at the glowing screen.

"Haha, that's my favorite part!" He jumped up and down in his chair, pointing at the screen and laughing hysterically. He looked up at Mike, and smiled. "You wanna play with me?"

"Nah, just looking for a different room," Mike said. He backed away from the malnourished boy.

"Come on, you can stay," said the boy as he jammed his bony arm into the plastic bucket beside him. "I'll even share my grub with you."

Mike gagged as the boy displayed his food—dark fluid running between his fingers to drip onto the floor. A swarm of flies flew from the bucket, some landing on the stringy pink guts in his hand. The boy smiled up at him, and jammed the grub into his mouth.

"It's good," he said, small bits of chewed up meat falling from his lips.

Mike turned and flung himself from the room, slamming the door shut behind him.

Old Man McCook was supposed to be crazy, but this was just too much. Mike knew that after they were finished, he would have to call somebody to save that poor kid. He looked around the hallway, searching for Julius.

"Jules," Mike whispered. He got no response and walked to the next door. Julius must have found something good, probably stuffing his bag right now.

Mike hesitated as his hand wrapped around the next doorknob. This time, he had his pistol ready. He crept into the room, the hairs on the back of his neck standing straight up. A soft soothing music played as he walked through the door.

Dolls littered the floor, some of them life sized and very realistic. He walked past a small bed with frilly pillows and lacy sheets thrown about. A fancy dresser with a large mirror sat near the other side of the bed.

Mike grabbed a hairbrush with a golden handle, some pearl necklaces, and an ivory music box from the dresser. He tossed them all into his bag, the soft music still playing from within. He started

194

opening drawers, grabbing anything that looked valuable, doing his best to be quick.

Mike shrieked as he looked into the mirror to find a life size doll standing behind him. The head tilted to the side, watching Mike do his business. He spun around, facing the china faced doll in a pink Cinderella-type dress. It was a child, the doll mask strapped to her head. She stared at him, not moving, not saying anything.

"I'm not gonna hurt you," Mike said. "I just need to borrow these things, cool?"

The doll nodded, walking toward Mike. She had her arms stretched out as she approached him. She grabbed and hugged him, squeezing his leg. Mike just stood there and let her embrace him, not sure of what to do.

"I gotta go now, but I promise I'll be back, okay?" Mike did his best to sound friendly. "I just need to borrow these things, but I'll bring them back."

She nodded and ran to her bed, diving onto the mattress. She kicked her legs and ruffled up the sheets, all the while staring at Mike.

He backed into the door, reaching behind him to grab the knob, keeping his eyes on the strange girl. She waved at him, and then continued her flailing.

He stumbled out into the hallway, loosing his footing as he escaped the eerie room. Even though they were just kids, he was ready to get out of there.

Old Man McCook was one crazy son of a bitch.

As he got ready to approach the next door, he noticed that a door on Julius's side stood slightly open. Mike wanted to see his progress and compare their stash.

"Jules," whispered Mike, creeping toward the door. "Yo, Jules."

That familiar smell got stronger as he grew nearer. He pulled out his gun and used it to push open the door. The sound of loud buzzing erupted, thousands of flies covering the walls. He backed away as he saw the scene in front of him, pointing his gun toward the horror.

Julius hung from the ceiling, large metal hooks holding him there by his wrists and ankles. His stomach ripped open, entrails hung down like party decorations. Twin boys, naked and filthy, danced underneath him, circling playfully with their arms interlocked. They giggled as the blood rained down on them, the purple intestines slapping them in the face.

"Oh, Jesus!" Mike screamed. He couldn't peel himself away from the room. The boys stopped their twirling to look at their new visitor.

"We got another one, Lucas."

"It's my turn this time, Edgar."

The boy knelt down and picked up a bloody butcher knife. The boys held hands as they approached Mike.

"Y'all stay the fuck back! I swear to God, I'll fucking shoot."

"You hear that, Lucas? He said a swear."

"Did you hear him use the lord's name in vain, Edgar?"

"I think we got a devil in our room, Lucas."

"Maybe we can cut the evil out of him, Edgar." The boy swiped the air with his knife.

"This is your last chance, one more step and its over!"

They laughed at Mike's threat, looking at each other with delight.

Mike pulled the trigger, sending Lucas flying backward. Blood sprayed the wall behind him. The boy fell motionless to the floor.

"What have you done to my brother?"

"I warned you!"

The boy jumped up and ran at Mike with scrawny legs. Mike fired again, hitting the wall on the opposite side of the room. The bullet cut through the curtain of entrails, dark fluid exploding and splashing to the floor.

The boy jumped and latched onto Mike, biting down on his arm. Mike thrashed and slammed the boy into a wall. Edgar fell to the ground, blood running from his lips. He stared up at Mike with an animal-like ferocity in his eyes.

Mike fired, obliterating Edgar's head and decorating the room.

Blood pumped from Mike's wounded arm at a dangerous speed. He ripped off a large piece of cloth from his shirt and tied it around the wound.

He glanced up at Julius, the taste of stomach acid at the back of his throat. He never cared for him much, but nobody deserved to go like that.

Mike walked back out to the hallway. He shut the door and

turned around. A scream escaped his throat and he redrew his gun. Children surrounded him. Their soiled, skinny bodies closed in on him. Some of the children stared at him wide eyed, their lips trembling. Others growled and bared their teeth at him.

A girl, maybe thirteen years old, stood naked in front of him. Some of the smaller children hid behind her, looking up at Mike. Long needles protruded from the girl's grasp.

"All of y'all better not move." Mike kept his gun aimed at the girl. "I don't wanna hurt you!"

"You will never leave here," the girl said. "Nobody leaves this place."

"Get the fuck back!"

"Our father will punish you for what you did."

The other children gained courage from her words, and started to follow her toward Mike.

"Father will punish you," they chanted, taking the lead from the needle wielding girl.

Mike fired his weapon as panic took over his thoughts. The teenage girl flew backward onto the floor, her needles bouncing on the hardwood. A pool of blood formed around her still body.

The children screamed and ran as fast as they could to their bedrooms, doors slamming in unison.

"Mike!"

Mike jumped at the sound of his name, firing another shot into the ceiling. The voice came from downstairs.

"Mike!"

"Chauncey?" yelled Mike into the dark stairwell, "that you man?"

"Course it is, let's get out of here!"

Mike looked back at the dead girl in the hall. A feeling of pity for the children lay heavy on his heart. He didn't want to kill anyone, but they killed Julius. He wanted to leave and never think about this place again.

He ran down the stairs two at a time, the contents in his backpack rattling behind him. Chauncey stood at the foot of the stairwell, staring up at Mike.

"Did you find anything worthwhile?"

"Let's just get the fuck out of this place! They got Julius!"

"We can't leave I'm afraid."

"You alright, man?" Mike asked, looking at Chauncey up

197

and down.

"Never better." Chauncey smiled at Mike as his hands grabbed hold of his upper and lower lips. He pulled them in opposite directions, ripping the dark flesh apart.

Mike stared at Old Man McCook, blood dripping from his face. He smiled at Mike, bits of Chauncey still clinging to him.

"I'm so glad you came, my boy. I have a nice room ready for you."

Mike aimed his pistol. McCook just smiled at him, playing along with the charade.

"You stay where you are motherfucker."

A body sat in the leather chair, a gold tooth shining from the skinless face.

"Please don't shoot." The old man chuckled.

Mike ran to the front door and jiggled the knob. He pointed his gun and shot at it, but it still wouldn't budge.

"You let me the fuck outta here!" Mike's voice cracked as tears rolled down his cheeks.

"You killed my children. I'm going to need a replacement. You should do just fine, I think."

"Don't come any closer, God damn it! I'll kill you too!"

"You took my Ruthie away from me. My sweet, darling Ruthie."

A loud bang echoed through the home as Mike pulled the trigger. The old man stumbled backward, but never took his eyes off Mike. A buzzing emitted from the hole in his chest and a swarm of flies escaped his body. He smiled.

"I am growing tired of this game, son."

Mike fired again, and again. He ran by the fly-infested man, shoving him as he passed.

"That's a boy. Go to your room!"

Mike hesitated at the top of the stairwell.

Where the hell could he go?

A pale, white face with pink cheeks poked out of a door. She beckoned to Mike, her grimy hand waving him in. The Doll Girl. He ran into the room, slamming the door behind them.

She hugged him, jumping up and down with excitement. She grabbed Mike's hand, leading him toward her bed.

"Is there a way outta here?" Mike asked. The windows in the bedroom had the same metal bars.

The girl jumped up and down on her bed, paying no attention to the question. Mike pulled out his bag, and dumped the contents onto the sheets.

"Here, see, I told you I would give them back." He picked up the brush and handed it to the living doll.

She grabbed it with excitement, ran to her vanity mirror, and started brushing her hair. The sound of buzzing grew nearer.
"Please help me!" He jumped up from the bed and shook her by her bony shoulders.

She pushed him away, running to her bed and crawling beneath it. Mike could hear her sobbing, and walked over to the bed to sit. Flies zoomed around the room, coming in through the crack at the bottom of the bedroom door.

"I'm sorry I got upset. I just need to go home. Please show me how to get outta here."

Something wrapped around his ankles, a metallic clinging sound coming from under the bed. Panic filled his thoughts as he realized what had happened. Metal clamps locked around his ankles, a thick chain ran under the bed. He pulled on the chain, sweat running down his face. The chain wouldn't budge. Red blotches stained his socks as he struggled to get free.

The door swung open and crashed against the wall. The sound of countless flies erupted into the room, along with a low laughter.

"Good girl," McCook said, "who's my little sweet pea?"

The little doll girl ran to him, and hugged him.

"We have a new friend, don't we sweetie?"

She nodded, and ran back to her bed to jump up and down. Old Man McCook walked toward Mike, his arms outstretched as if in welcome.

"Please lemme go, I won't tell nobody about none of this," Mike said. His lip trembled as he spoke.

"Now now, just relax." He knelt down to Mike's level. "I think you're going to learn to love it here, my son."

As the man knelt down, flies swarmed all around him, walking up and down his face.

Mike pressed his gun to the man's head, and fired. Blood and flies splattered onto the ground. The old man stumbled backward, shaking his head.

"Have we not learned our lesson yet?"

Mike wrapped his lips around the barrel, squinting his eyes, and pulled the trigger.

Nothing happened.

He pulled the trigger again, and again. Nothing.

He looked up at the old man, the little girl still jumping on her bed next to him. Old Man McCook held out his hand to Mike, a twisted smile on his face.

"Let's get you to your room."

NREM SLEEP

A. R. Braun

"Is the real nightmare sleeping or waking?"
-- Bong Otto, a burned-out philosopher.

Wednesday

Adriana lay in bed, afraid of falling asleep, of having that dream again where she's in the nursery at church, about to...

She sat in the nursery, a couple of little girls sitting on her big-boned lap. It was the evening service and the full moon shone through the small, rectangular window. The smell of baby powder and piss invaded her nostrils. The children screamed. Waverly, the chunky, red-haired girl on her lap, cried while gulping down tears; Willow, a wisp of a girl with black hair bobbed up and down as she struggled to waddle away; and a blonde, slim boy named Huey threw toys to-and-fro.

The feeling of overwhelming responsibility consumed her. Adriana hefted Waverly up and walked over to check on Joey, the sleeping baby in the crib.

He lay on his chest, face in the covers.

Oh God, turn him over! Don't let him die of crib death!

She tried to set Waverly down so she could turn Joey over, but the former shrieked and thrashed like never before.

Fury mixed with fear came upon her as she turned Baby Jocy around—blue-faced, chest not heaving, dead . . . of SIDS.

"No!" Adriana shrieked. "Oh God, it's my fault, please, no!"

Waverly bit down on her leg hard enough to break the skin. A stinging pain encompassed her calf.

As if possessed by a beast, Adriana bent down and snatched Waverly by the hair, yanking her up and grabbing her neck.

No, I can't hurt that little girl! Somebody stop me and help her!

No one stopped her.

She shoved Waverly toward the wall . . .

Adriana woke thrashing and screaming.

201

A strange man gaped at her and then grabbed her shoulders. "Honey, it was just a dream!"

"No!" She kicked at him, hitting him a few times in the chest.

He fell off the bed with a grunt. Wide-eyed, the man lay on the floor, his short, brown hair mussed, his glasses hanging on his face sideways.

He rose and straightened his spectacles. "You're awake. Everything's all right."

Confused, Adriana rubbed her eyes and looked at the strange man in the room. Her eyelids felt heavy—if she could just get some more sleep. She lay on the pillow and closed her eyes.

Darkness covered her like a shroud.

Thursday

The sun shone brightly through the garden window, and the white glow blinded Adriana as she shielded her eyes with her hand. She rose and drew the curtains.

Spring has its drawbacks, she thought.

Sitting back down, Adriana drained her fourth cup of coffee while white strings of smoke rose and curled from the cigarette in her shaky hand. Her husband sat behind his plate of sausage, eggs and pancakes. His short brown hair, as mussed as it was last night, made him look younger than he really was. The glasses didn't help. He grinned, reading the newspaper. She envied his devil-may-care attitude; he'd never suffered from night terrors in his whole life.

As if in answer to her thought, he met her eyes. His brow furrowed slightly while he took a sip of coffee. "Hon, are you all right?"

She broke down and cried. The memory of the dream was too much.

Should I be working in the nursery?

Kerry rose, slipped his arms around her from behind and shushed her. A twinge of arousal asserted itself when his hard muscles intertwined with her flesh.

"Baby," he said, "What's the matter? Another dream?"

She nodded.

"What was it about?"

Her tears ran into the brown stains at the bottom of the white coffee cup. "I hurt . . . oh God, I hurt those . . ."

"Oh, sweetie." He kissed her cheek. "Hurt who?"

I can't tell him. He'll put me away.

"Honey, I think I need to see a doctor. These night terrors are driving me insane."

Kerry nodded and kissed her. "I'll make the appointment. We need to get you better."

He headed to the phone. The sleep clinic had a cancellation and was willing to take her tomorrow.

***

Adriana sat on the black leather couch with Kerry, one of her hands in a bowl of popcorn, the other wrapped around a chilled bottle of diet soda. Caffeine was her best friend now.

Kerry stretched his arms out and yawned. "Well, I've got a hard day ahead of me tomorrow. I'm fixing a school's A/C unit." He faced her. "Coming to bed?"

She shook her head and focused on the television. She'd insisted they watch shows as innocent as possible, programs that wouldn't give her nightmares. They'd started with a movie about babysitters and had ended up on a children's channel, watching pretty boys and girls fret over a musical audition.

He rubbed her back. "Come on, babe. Even though you can't see the doc until tomorrow, you need your rest."

She laughed. "Oh, screw that. I'm staying up as late as I can."

He sighed, let go of her and rose. "All right, goodnight." He bent, kissed her, and then made his way to the bedroom.

Adriana watched him go, then returned to chugging the calorie free, yet artificially sweet soda. The episode playing on the widescreen bored her, but boring was just fine.

Just fine, she told herself, *just fine* . . .

Her eyelids drooped. She shook her head and slapped her cheeks.

The room's walls suddenly changed from white to sky-blue, accompanied by fluffy, white clouds. The TV morphed into a crib—Joey's crib.

Oh God, please don't let this happen.

She felt the couch move, looked to her right and, on her knee, Waverly reached into the popcorn bowl. They sat in a wooden chair with bars at the back. Willow sat on the floor trading slaps with Huey, snot hanging from her nose.

Baby Joey lay on his chest and face again. Waverly wailed,

and Adriana turned to look at her. Tears ran down the child's face.

"You gonna hurt me! You're not my mommy!"

Adriana rose and put Waverly down. She darted around Huey and Willow to get to Baby Joey. She turned the baby over, relieved to hear him gulp and then cry.

Thank God.

Something hard pushed its way up her skirt with enough force to nearly go up her rectum. Adriana wheeled around and saw Waverly with a small toy truck in her hands. The child laughed. Her tears had stopped blurring her red face.

The fury and turmoil built again.

Make it stop, oh God, make it stop!

Adriana's hand went into the air as if possessed, then balled into a fist.

No! Don't hurt the kid!

The red-haired child's eyes grew wide. Adriana couldn't stop it, as much as she tried. Adriana caught Huey and Willow rolling on the floor in the corner of her eye, yanking out each other's hair.

Brats!

The haymaker swung Waverly's way . . .

Adriana woke up thrashing on the couch. A loud whistle—a teakettle?—rang in the background until she recognized her own high-pitched scream. She beat at the pillows and spilled the popcorn and diet soda all over the rug.

A stranger in a blue bathrobe ran into the room and stared at Adriana. His eyes had grown wide. The man walked toward her.

The rage again. *How dare this strange man try to comfort me! Where am I?*

She bounded up off the couch, ran at the man and buried her head in his stomach, knocking him over the TV. The set crashed, crackled and set off sparks. The strange man rolled over and held onto the back of his head.

That's what what's-his-name gets.

Friday

Adriana sat on a bed waiting for the doctor to come in at The Sleep Medicine Center in Mowquakwa, Illinois. The trip from the suburb of Wampum had been silent. Thank God her husband was all right. She had no memory of throwing him over the TV, but he'd said his head only hurt a bit—just a nasty bump on the back of the

204

noggin and a minor backache.

She sat in a room with glass windows, one black, where they probably evaluated her while she slept. A stocky man with receding, black hair and glasses walked in, shutting the door behind him. He carried a clipboard and smiled at her as he made his way over.

He held out his hand. "I'm Professor Conover of the Department of Neurology."

She took his firm hand in hers and squeezed. "Adriana Berry."

"So, you've been having some nightmares, I take it?"

She nodded, thankful that her husband was not present.

"Can you tell me what they're about?"

She sighed, gripping the sides of the bed with white knuckles. "I'm in the nursery, as I always am on Sundays, at church." She sobbed. "A-And instead of being gentle like I usually am, I find a baby. He's not moving . . . he's . . . you know. SIDS, I think. And I . . . and I . . . hurt a little girl." Adriana couldn't stop the tears.

The doctor put a firm hand on her shoulder. "I'm sorry," he said.

Adriana blinked, trying to see the doctor through the veil of tears as she looked up at his face. "Am I going crazy?"

He shook his head. "Not at all. You have a condition called 'night terrors.' It's hard to pinpoint exact causes, but they can range from stress and poor sleeping habits to poor nutrition. Have you been cooking healthy meals at home?"

She sighed, looking at the yellow tiles of the floor. "I'm always on the go, so I eat fast food for lunch every day. By the time I get home I'm usually too tired to cook. We had pizza last night and Chinese the night before."

"I see." He made some notes on his clipboard. "Were they good about giving you the time off at work?"

"I guess they had to be."

He nodded. "When do you usually go to bed?"

She met his eyes. "I try to go to bed at eleven every night, but I just lay there forever. It feels like someone's turning a screw in my mind."

Dr. Conover nodded and made some more notes. "Night terrors usually attack in the 4th stage of sleep, non-REM sleep, where the eyes' movement under the lids is slow. Your husband told me you thrash around, wake up screaming with no idea where you are—

205

even get violent—which are all symptoms of the condition. We'd like to keep you here overnight to monitor your sleep habits, put you on a nutritious diet and get your sleep cycle back to normal."

Anxiety pricked her mind and she swallowed hard. "Overnight?" She ran her hands through her hair and fidgeted. "Is that necessary?"

Doctor Conover nodded. "If you want to get better, we need to do a sleep study." He rubbed his eyes and slipped his glasses back on. "We can start monitoring you tonight. I can even give you a sedative so you can fall asleep right away. We'll take a look at you tonight and tomorrow night. Then we'll need to get you on a healthy meal plan for when you go home."

She nodded. *Anything to make the child-murdering dreams stop.*

The doctor handed her a form on a clipboard. "If you'll just sign here."

She scrawled out her best John Hancock. Adriana caught a glance of the doctor as he turned to leave the room. If she hadn't known better, she would've sworn that the doctor had a shit-eating grin on his face and beady little eyes as he stared down at the form.

That Evening

Adriana's eyes opened. Confusion at first. She lay in the institutional bed, electrodes hooked up to her forehead like the Lovecraftian pseudopods of an underwater creature.

Clicking footsteps walking into the room roused her senses. She closed her eyes to try to focus. When she opened her eyes, Doctor Conover loomed over her with a scalpel in hand. Two nurses clad in short, white lab coats stood on either side of her. Their legs were bare and so long under the coats that they seemed to go on forever.

Adriana wanted to ask what the hell the scalpel was for and why the nurses weren't wearing pants, but she couldn't move. The slim woman on the right had blonde, straight hair that fell across her head and onto her shoulders like running water. Glitter speckled her high set cheekbones which framed full, pouty lips. She'd generously applied eye shadow above her blue eyes, sparkling with desire, and her deeply-tanned skin bronzed her frame like a statue. The brunette on her left sported heavily-applied gold eye shadow above wide, green eyes that led to a slim nose, fine-structured cheekbones and thin lips; her slender neck exposed milky-white skin, and strands of curly black hair hung just above her shoulders.

Both nurses held needles at least fifteen inches long. They primed them, sending jets of liquid flying from the tips.

The doctor's grin turned into a frown, then a scowl. He flashed white teeth, big enough to belong to a horse, and ground them together.

I'm in a madhouse! God help me, they're going to kill me!

The nurses unbuttoned their coats and slid them off. The blonde's huge, tanned breasts couldn't be natural. The nipples looked like baby bottle-tops in the center of her twin peaks. They were erect. She rubbed the shaved vagina between her legs, spreading apart the pink lips.

Are you kidding me? Lord Jesus Christ, get me out of here!

The brunette's small breasts barely jiggled, they were so firm. She fingered the brown labia that hid underneath a triangular thatch of black pubic hair.

Adriana tried to speak, tried to rise up off the bed, but again couldn't move; only inaudible sounds gurgled from her lips.

Doctor Conover twisted his face. "You know what we do to baby killers around here?" he yelled.

No, I'm not a baby killer! I'm here for treatment!

The nurses laughed and moved forward, undoing Adriana's shirt and running their hands over her breasts.

My God, am I dreaming? Is that what's going on?

She willed it to stop, with no luck. Not only did it continue, Adriana found her nipples getting hard underneath the nurses' soft clutches. The brunette ripped Adriana's pajama bottoms off and spread her labia apart with her fingers, sticking a couple digits inside her sex. Though every fiber of Adriana's being was against the slutty adultery that ravaged her, blinding shock waves of excitement pulsed through her, making her undulate and moan.

The wide-eyed blonde slapped Adriana's left breast, then her right one. "Child-killing whore!" she said with a chirpy voice.

The brunette stuck her fist inside Adriana, causing her to convulse. Unsure of which feeling took precedence, pain or pleasure, Adriana shuddered.

"This is what you get for being a kid-killing slut!" the brunette cried.

The blonde smirked up at Dr. Conover. "Hurt her, doctor!"

He leaned forward and shoved the scalpel into Adriana's

right eye, half blinding her and causing white-hot jabs of pain to pulse through her socket. The throbbing agony gave way to hellish, excruciating torment as the good eye saw dark red squirt all over the blonde's hair and face. The nurse laughed, took her hands off Adriana's breasts and stuck her tongue out, squealing as she lapped up the blood.

Adriana screamed, and felt a sharp, jabbing pain in her sex, as if someone poked her with broken glass. She raised her bloody head off the pillow to see a red face eating her pussy. The visage belonged to what looked like a cartoon version of Satan, cat's eyes glared up at her and curling horns stuck out of his forehead. The Devil's pointy, serrated teeth bit into her clit. Her blood made his face turn from bright red to dark crimson. Adriana couldn't bear much more. She passed out as Satan laughed, chewing and swallowing her clitoris.

***

Adriana woke thrashing and shrieking like never before. She didn't recognize her surroundings. She kicked her legs so vehemently that she fell off the bed and slammed hard against the floor. A door opened and footsteps ran into the room. Hands helped her up and a light came on. It was a balding man in glasses and a red-headed, heavy-set nurse. A woman with long, white hair stood at the door, her hand still on the light switch.

The man and the woman helped Adriana back into bed, and the woman pulled out a small needle which sent Adriana keening as loudly as she could—though she didn't know why. All Adriana knew was that everything became blurry and a peaceful calm claimed her as she shut her eyes and drifted off.

Saturday

"What did you give me?" Adriana yelled, her knuckles white as she gripped a warm cup of coffee.

The doctor sat across from her in the white-walled cafeteria of the hospital. Chatter and clatter from the hospital staff and the other patients stopped.

"Just a sedative," Doctor Conover answered. "It's your night terrors. You had another nightmare."

She slammed her free fist down on the table. "I want out of this place!"

The doc moved his head back a couple inches and then

sighed. "Mrs. Berry, it was just a dream. I'm sure they'll dissipate after you catch up on your sleep and your diet is changed."

Adriana looked into her cup of black coffee and saw a fun-house reflection of her plump face. Her visage was oblong, and matted hair flanked her frown. She met the doctor's wide eyes. "I dreamed you were all devil worshipers, and you had X-rated nurses."

The doc chuckled. "It's all part of your illness."

She let out a panicky breath that stopped and started over and over. "What am I saying? When I woke up, your nurses were normal." She breathed deeply. "Will I really get better?"

"You got twelve hours of sleep yesterday and have eaten nothing but healthy food the whole time you've been here. I'd venture a guess that you'll sleep well tonight, probably with no nightmares."

She nodded. "I hope you're right." *Because church is tomorrow, and I have to run the nursery.*

Sunday

Adriana was woken up by the rotund nurse. The doctor smiled down on her. She blinked at the harsh glow of the overhead lights.

She yawned and rubbed her eyes. "W-what time is it?"

"It's six a.m. on Sunday morning," the nurse answered.

The nurse helped her sit up, putting her hand on her back.

Adriana stretched. "Did I have a nightmare?"

Doctor Conover chuckled. "I'm glad to report that you had no night terrors. You didn't thrash around, and there was no trace of anything but good dreams. Looks like the change in your diet and sleeping habits worked."

Joy filled her mind. "Really?" She giggled like a schoolgirl. "You mean I'm cured?"

"I think so," the doctor pointed toward the door. "You have an anxious husband that can't wait to see you."

She rose and hugged Dr. Conover. She couldn't help it. "Thank you so much!"

"Just doing my job."

She sobbed tears of joy.

***

After a healthy breakfast at the sleep center with her husband, they'd headed home. She'd explained to him that Doctor Conover had cured her, and Kerry had been overjoyed. Now they walked out the door of Bible study room, headed . . .

Toward the nursery.

The chatter of the other members seemed to echo, as did the laughter and screams of children and the band practicing in the sanctuary. As she moved closer to the danger zone, her legs became like jelly, her nerves rattled and her hands shook. Adriana stopped.

I can't.

Adriana looked at her husband, whose eyes were wide. "Honey, I—" She just shook her head.

He rubbed her back. "What is it, sweetie?"

"I can't run the nursery. I never told you, but I had nightmares about...about..."

He hugged her. "Aw, baby. The doctor said you were cured."

She broke down, crying on his shoulder. When she'd pulled herself together, she raised her head and saw Pastor Wilkes, a middle-aged, graying man with a jutting forehead looking at her. He wore a white polo shirt and khakis instead of a suit—a typical Southern Baptist uniform.

"Are you all right?" Pastor Wilkes asked in a deep voice.

"I'm sorry, pastor, I've been sick lately. I don't think I can run the nursery today."

He put a hand on his chin and held her stare. Then he sighed and let his arm drop. "That's okay. I understand." He looked toward a tall, brunette teen staring into the nursery while resting her forearms on the half door. "Cali? Would you like to run the nursery today?"

She smiled and nodded.

"Thank you." He eyed Adriana again, putting a comforting hand on her shoulder. "Maybe next week. Enjoy the service and get some rest after church, you hear?"

Adriana nodded. "Thanks so much. I will."

The pastor walked away, probably to another of a hundred duties.

Kerry moved Ariana towards the sanctuary with his hand on her back. "Let's go worship."

***

After church, Kerry eyeballed her surreptitiously while driving to McDonald's, where they always ate after the service. "You sure you're all right?"

She hit him lightly on the shoulder with her palm. "Oh, quit coddling me. I'm fine."

"I suppose you're going to have the Southwest Chicken Salad while I scarf down on a Third Pounder?"

She pulled the sun visor down to shield her eyes from the blinding spring sun. "No. I saw on one of those shows about celebs losing weight that it's okay to cheat a little, about twenty percent. I want Chicken Nuggets—a ten piece."

Her husband laughed. "That's my girl. A ten piece it is. I would've felt like crap grubbing down in front of you while you ate roughage."

She laughed and, suddenly, everything felt right with the world.

Later they played tennis and celebrated her recovery by going out to a fancy dinner at The Supper Club. Adriana ordered a chicken salad with white wine. Then they hurried home and made mad, monkey-love until midnight. They would have continued all night, but they had to go to work in the morning.

Lying on her husband's sculpted, muscular arm, Adriana shut her eyes and let herself drift off without fear.

***

"You worthless fucking cunt!"

Shots of terror fired off inside her veins as she eyed Pastor Wilkes at the foot of the bed. He wore the same white polo shirt, but no pants or underwear. His huge, erect cock bobbed against his covered belly.

Adriana wanted to scream but couldn't speak—couldn't move. She looked at her snoring husband out of the corner of her right eye. Why didn't he wake up?

The pastor scowled, crossing his arms. "Just like the rest of the leeches," he said. "Twenty percent of the members do eighty percent of the work."

She finally found her voice. "I meant to run the nursery, but I was afraid I'd hurt the children." Though the room felt cool, her face broke out in beads of sweat.

He dropped his arms and clenched his fists. "Well now you're hurting the church! And now I'm going to hurt you!"

She struggled with all her might to turn and rouse her husband, but still couldn't move. Pastor Wilkes tore the coverlet and sheets from her side of the bed. She shivered. Her mind squirmed as the strong parson lifted up her legs, spread them, and poised his massive cock at the opening of Adriana's vagina, just letting the fist-sized head throb against her labia. The pastor smiled and rammed forward, splitting Adriana in half.

The pain sent shocks of torment into her stomach.

God help me, the pastor's turned evil! Why doesn't my husband wake up?

She felt herself go mad as his large face shoved into hers, his tongue sliding past her teeth. He reeked of recently-eaten quiche. He bit her lips, drawing blood, and rammed her so hard that her head banged against the headboard. Still her husband snored on. The sensation of being ravaged with broken glass returned as he continued to thrust into her.

Pastor Wilkes pushed off of her with wide eyes and his mouth formed into an 'O.' He pulled out, scooted his crotch up and came all over her face. The man's salty, fish-scented spunk sprayed into her mouth as she gurgled, cried, and screamed in that order.

Adriana woke, thrashing her feet and punching the head of the man next to her. He—whoever he was—grabbed her arms as he rolled over onto her.

Big mistake.

"Honey, you had one of those dreams again! The nightmare's over."

Who was this man, and how dare he mount her after . . . after what? Who was she? Where was she? It didn't matter. All she felt was the rage.

She lurched forward and bit into his throat, chomping down with all her might. With teeth firmly clamped she shook her head, and pulled his larynx out. Hot, metallic liquid flooded her throat along with fresh meat and hard chunks of cartilage.

The victory tasted good. That's what the bastard gets. Adriana masticated the flesh in front of his red, wide-eyed face. She spit out the larynx, hitting him on the nose. He sat up and grabbed his leaking throat, which continued to spout dark blood. His face went from red to blue while she laughed.

Her snickering was cut short as he fell on top of her, his cold lips brushing hers.

Fucking men!

She cackled as her brain went haywire, no hope, no love,

only conquest and sickness. She reached down and played with the man's soft cock while she made out with his dead lips. Adriana could feel herself getting wet. She thrust her hips forward and stuck the tip of his penis into her vagina. Adriana rocked the man's dying body against her. His bowels released at the moment of death and hot piss filled her vagina while the man's shit clumped out and rolled down her ass.

Squishy.

The smell didn't bother her. Nothing did, except for this disease, this insanity, all that was wrong with the world. After she came, she rolled the man off of her and went back to sleep.

***

Adriana woke when her husband shook her shoulder. "Honey, wake up."

She stirred on the bed, blinking her eyes against the sun shining in the window. She remembered killing him now.

Must've had two night terrors. I'll call Doctor Conover tomorrow and tell him I need to go back. "What time is it?" she mumbled.

"You've got an hour before work." He got out of bed. "Can I take a shower before you?"

"Um-hmm." She rolled over. "Wake me when you're done."

"Sure thing."

She lost consciousness.

***

Adriana woke after the sun had set. *Did I sleep all day? Oh shit, I pulled a no-show!* For some reason, she lay on the edge of the bed. She felt slimy between her legs. *Wow, we must've really gone at it last night.* Adriana wrinkled her nose at the putrefying smell, recognizing one of her hubby's almost-lethal methane gas farts. He must be home from work.

Adriana got out of bed. She needed a cigarette and some coffee.

Adriana stumbled into the bathroom, turned on the light and stared her reflection in the mirror.

Her chin was covered in blood. Yellow piss crusted on her legs. Wide-eyed, she turned around to check her ass to see what felt sticky back there. Traces of dark-brown shit caked her butt cheeks. Adriana's eyes goggled, her frame shook, a nervous breakdown poked at her mind with ghostly, bony fingers.

213

She looked at her watch. It read five a.m.

She could barely walk back into the bedroom. Creeping, stumbling, she turned on the light . . .

Daddy

Uri Grey

Bear:
Below is the full transcript of a tape removed from a 'Talking Teddy Bear' which was found in the woods by one of our reporters, completely by chance.

After mama and papa died in Bergen my crazy uncle took me and Mr. Bear but he asked us to call him Daddy. Daddy loves me a lot and he even let me do things mama and papa never let me do and he buys me a lot of new toys none of the kids in Bergen have. Daddy doesn't live in Bergen. He lives in the woods and he is a hunter. Daddy lets me sleep with him and in the night he loves me a lot. Sometimes he loves me too much and it hurts to pee after it but after that he always says sorry. Daddy is the greatest.

I tried to play with a boy in school but he was scared and went away to cry to his teacher. The teacher looked very sick and then took me to the principal's office and they didn't let me go home until a policeman came and we all went home together. Daddy was very angry and he screamed a lot and the policeman screamed too and then Daddy took an axe and put it in the head of the policeman and there was a lot of blood. The teacher started running but Daddy shot her with his gun because he's a hunter. I cried a lot and it really hurt when Daddy loved me tonight. But I was scared to tell him to love me more carefully because I was afraid he will put the axe in my head too. Daddy said we must move to a new cabin and we gave the policeman and the teacher a Viking funeral.

Daddy said I don't need school because he bought a TV and I can watch it and learn all the things in the world. I learned from the TV that what he calls love is not what everyone calls love. But Daddy says I must love him if I live in his cabin and it is very cold outside and I am not a hunter, so it will be OK.

Daddy says a woman doesn't need a teddy bear so bye-bye Mr. Bear. It's cold outside but you won't mind because you're warm and made of fur.

215

The following text has been transcribed from a badly deteriorated manuscript found in the woods by a local hunter.

Daddy bought me an empty book and told me to write in it everything that happens to me, every little thing. He likes to read it with one hand down his pants.

I met a young man in the forest today and when I told him about Daddy he said he will take me to his parents' home tonight and tomorrow morning we will all go to the police station down town and have Daddy arrested. I really like him and I hope he will marry me and I hope Daddy will be taken to Bergen and be hanged from a tree. I hate that son of a bitch!

Daddy came tonight very quietly. I didn't see or hear him come but when I woke up I stepped in something wet. I opened my eyes and there was light in the room and I saw that everyone except me didn't have a head and the beds and the floor were painted sticky red. I screamed and tried to run through the door but a hand caught my ankle and dragged me under the bed and I was all smeared in blood and got it in my hair; even tasted some and it was horrible. There were five heads under the bed; one of them was Daddy, "Surprise!"

We had to move again. Daddy said that the woman's place is in the home and that there is no need for her to walk too much. I promised I won't leave the house again but he looked me in the eyes and said, "But how do we make sure?" I said I swear by Baby Jesus but he said "Fuck Jesus" and hit me on the face and then he set on my back and I couldn't breathe because he grew so fat. He held my foot and cut my ankle with his axe and I screamed and then he cut the other and I screamed again and since then I can't run, only limp.

Blog:
The below web journal has been kindly brought to our attention by a reader who asked to remain anonymous. The last post was made about two years ago.

Daddy bought a computer with internet so that he could watch movies and talk with other hunters. In his movies girls just like me are raped by many men at once and sometimes they are killed afterward. When Daddy brought home a little camera I was very afraid, but in the movies he made he didn't kill me.

I observed how Daddy typed his password and when he was away I used the internet myself. I opened an anonymous blog (how can I open any other blog? I don't even know my name, or Daddy's). I write everything I can't write in the book. And as for the book, I just reproduce old chapters in the book now in the blog. Daddy won't know the difference because this is how his life looks like; he fucks, kills, eats and fucks in an endless cycle. I'm the same, only on the receiving end. Every evening I envy the bloody carcasses he drags home and orders me to dismember. At least they don't have to shamble around like disgusting invalids. At least they only die once. At least they have fur or feathers to cover their nakedness from that horrible man. But no, I undress them, not only their hair, but their skin, their muscles... it's horrible! I wonder what Daddy will do with me when I die... I don't care; just let it come as soon as possible.

I celebrated 10,000 page views today. It's funny really. It seems the whole internet knows about that poor girl, but no one can help her because she doesn't know where the hell she is, not even what country!

More and more people leave comments like "stop complaining bitch, and do some cutting!" or "kill that fucker already!" I think they are just being mean, but maybe being mean is the right thing to do in a mean situation. I can barely walk, but I think I should give him a fight. Since childhood, since I saw him killing all these people, I convinced myself that he was invincible, that he was Satan himself, but you guys showed me that he's just an ugly and horny freak. He always takes his guns with him, but I think my carving knife should do nicely. Wish me luck guys, here goes nothing!

Damn! It was like in that Seven Samurai tribute I saw on YouTube, when that guy just knows he's about to be attacked. Maybe he saw my shadow or something, I don't know. I was really quiet. He didn't look very angry but he said the internet gave me bad ideas, so I think this is goodbye guys, thanks for watching and for all the support!

Daddy returned and said that if I spend the whole day sitting in front of the computer anyway I don't really need my legs and besides, if I don't like his cock I might as well not feel anything at all down there. It will be best for the both of us. So tonight when he finished and I was still on all fours he took his bowie knife and slid it into my spine and fumbled in it a bit, like he does when a can won't open. It felt like a tetanus shot in the small of my back and then there was nothing, as if my legs and privates just disappeared. I toppled foreword and heard him going to shower.

Well, maybe it really is for the best. It's true that now I can't walk at all, only crawl around like a run-over cat, but at least his prophecy came true; when he's doing his thing in me, I can just look at the ceiling and plan my next web post.

The meaner guys told me to kill myself so I'm going to do just that. Some guy wrote that freezing felt like falling asleep so I thought it would be the best way. Tomorrow, when Daddy goes to hunt, I will crawl out into the snow, find some nice and quite spot and lie there and die. Hopefully, the wolves will find me before he does, but what do I care? Meat is meat is meat, and half of me is meat already.

Ciao guys!

Blood:
The below text has been transcribed from graffiti found on the inside walls of an abandoned hut in the Morskogen forest.

If Daddy wasn't Satan, then he must have been guided by him. As soon as the feeling of nothingness started creeping up my belly, delightfully erasing the sensations of filth and shame that tainted every inch of my body, Daddy's shadow fell over me. A fat and ugly shadow that smelled of carnage and lust. Without saying anything, he took me by the hair and dragged me all the way home while I was powerless to offer even token resistance. He put me to thaw in a hot bath and I felt tingling all over my torso and arms and feeling started to return to them. The feeling of pain, of course, because the water was too hot. All the while he was hammering something and I was pretty sure it was the computer, the only piece of earth in my Hell. After a while he returned, naked, like a great big hairy gorilla and sat behind me in the bath. "No more internet for you, young lady." I felt his thick fingers playing with my breasts and then sliding up and closing on my neck. It hurt more and more, as if bolts of fire were shooting up and down my body, even into my legs and pelvis, which were just extra luggage as far as I was concerned. I tried to pull his paws away but just then I heard a loud crack and my useless hands dropped into the water.

The hammering was not the computer. The computer is safe

and sound. Instead, Daddy nailed two large hooks into the wall of the tools shed. He put a bucket under them, and hanged me by my armpits, like a coat on a rack, to be used when needed and hung back when not. I felt like a marionette in the puppeteer's suitcase, paralyzed as she is expecting her next humiliation. Sometimes I felt like a tiny person trapped inside the head of this dead thing. Yes, I no longer feel this body is my own; it is wholly Daddy's. I'm just the caretaker that keeps it running for the owner. I still stare at the ceiling when the owner's inside, enjoying the services, while I'm outside, wondering between stars (I haven't seen the sky for so long I had forgotten how it looks), humans (did I ever see any? I only remember corpses and monsters) and the internet (I visited so many sites, but never enough!).

Daddy was tired one night and after he finished, he just remained on top of me, snoring while slowly suffocating me. After I got tired of the ceiling and the smell of stale sweat and the white dots started dancing, I examined him closely, possibly for the first time. He didn't look like a God, or a demon, or even an animal. Just an aging man, mumbling obscenities in his sleep, his Adam's apple going up and down irregularly, just like his butt does when he's fucking me. I closed my teeth around it and pulled it with all my strength. There was a squishy tearing sound and it came out with his entire larynx and some veins and nerves dangling from it. With the bloody cylinder still clenched in my teeth, I watched as he woke up and fumbled for his neck. When he didn't find it, he started staggering around, bleeding and vomiting all over the place. Eventually he fell on his back and looked at the ceiling. He looked really scared. I wondered what he saw in there. I wondered what such a primitive man could see in anything. Probably just a ceiling going dark, and dark, and darker...

After he stopped breathing, his monstrous cock shrunk until it turned into a harmless little thing, even smaller than his larynx, which was now mine. I think it was the first time I saw him without an erection and for me, this was the moment of ultimate victory—he will never rape anyone again, not with that fluffy little worm.

I used his larynx as a pen to write my story on the white sheet of his bed. When I ran out of ink I bit my tongue and when I ran out of space I pulled myself with my teeth. Falling didn't hurt at all. "Look Daddy, I can go with no hands!" If someone ever comes upon this cabin, all he has to do is to read the writing on the bed and the floor, follow it to the still running computer, find a little book shoved under the mattress and recover the long lost teddy bear of a fucked up child. Then he'll learn the story. Then he'll be fucked up too.

I don't feel hunger.
I don't feel shame.
I don't feel pain.
I think my story is over now.

Good Girls

R. Warren Smith

Jessica and Britney were twins. They were five years old and wore designer shirts and shorts under fashionable bib-style overalls. Each pouting, round face was framed in long brunette hair that set off their grim expressions and twinkling, brown eyes. Without a sound, they stood in the corner of the classroom kicking little Joe Hibberts into submission. He had stopped screaming and squirming several minutes ago, but the two girls continued kicking his limp body. After some time, they became bored as they realized Joe's flattened head would no longer ooze out anymore blood or brains no matter how hard they kicked. Angered at the loss of a new toy, the twins turned and walked back to their desks. The rest of the class sat motionless and unaware in their seats.

Sitting side by side in their own chairs, the girls chewed on their lower lips as if in great concentration and suddenly the rest of the children began to move, squirming in their chairs as the young teacher, Miss Figg, began to read aloud to them again. The entire class had sat like statues the whole time the twins had been killing Joe, not even seeming to breathe. And with a single thought, the twins had set their world into motion again. A little girl sitting directly in front of the twins turned to look at them. Her green eyes swept past them to Joe's still form. With a shriek, she stood up and pointed to his body. The rest of the class turned and Miss Figg stood to look as tiny cries escaped a few of their lips. Miss Figg gasped. She dropped her book and ran to the lifeless boy.

As she moved past the twins, Jessica stuck her leg out and sent Miss Figg flying to the floor. Britney turned and locked her gaze on the rest of the class as Jessica jumped on top of the teacher. She grabbed Miss Fig by her long blonde hair and beat the teacher's head against the floor.

While Miss Figg's brutal thrashing continued, the rest of the class seemed to be hypnotized by Britney as she slowly walked from one child to another and stabbed each of them in an eye with a long letter opener that she had withdrawn from one of her overall pockets. After a few minutes, every child was sprawled on the floor in expanding pools of blood.

Miss Figg screamed in pain and fear as she fought to get Jessica off her back. Finally, she managed to get to her knees and throw Jessica off only to have Britney jump onto her and claw at Miss Figg's eyes. Britney forced her back to the ground and slammed the teacher's head against the hard floor. Jessica quickly returned to her sister's side with a pair of scissors and stabbed the teacher over and over again in her abdomen, smiling broadly as ear-splitting shrieks filled the room. Both girls kept up their assault until the teacher lay as still as the rest of the class.

The lights dimmed throwing the dead children into the shadows as if they had never existed. The light shrunk till it surrounded the two blood-drenched girls. They stood up in the spot of intense light, each holding the other by a hand. In the surrounding darkness, a door opened and several men wearing white lab coats entered. A few went to Joe, while another team surrounded Miss Figg. They probed both bodies with various pliers, scalpels, and digital equipment.

As the teams worked, two more men entered and stood before the twins. Both were bald, wore dark sunglasses, and were attired in sharp, black suits with white shirts and dark ties. They stared down at the twins with blank expressions. The twins returned the gaze. In the moment of silence that followed, the surrounding technicians looked uncomfortably out of the corners of their eyes at the four figures standing in the intense light. But none of them stopped working.

Suddenly, the taller of the two men stepped forward and slapped Britney to the ground.

"Don't try your head games on us, girl!" he ordered in a sharp, controlled voice. "You're games work on the weak, but never make that mistake with me or my associate. Do you understand?"

"Yes, sir," Britney whispered as she stood back up, tears welling in her dark, brown eyes. Silently, Jessica reached out and hugged her.

The two men turned and conferred in hushed voices for a minute before turning back to the girls. The shorter man crouched down and removed his sunglasses. There was a smile on his lips, but his stark blue eyes were as cold as ice. The twins trembled silently before him.

"You both did a great job," the man stated affably. "Mrs. Cleckley?"

A very prim looking woman wearing a subdued skirt and immaculately pressed blouse strode through the door on shining, high-heeled shoes. She gazed sternly at Jessica and Britney through horn-rimmed glasses.

"Why don't you go with Miss Cleckley and have a bowl of ice cream?" the crouching man offered. "I think you've earned that, don't you?"

"Yeah!" both girls shouted gleefully, their tears and the blood seemingly forgotten, and headed out the door, being shepherded by the redoubtable Mrs. Cleckley, who was already directing them toward the bathroom to get cleaned up.

"Well, what do you think, Dean?" The crouching man stood back up and looked around the room.

Rubbing his temples, Dean replied, "I think we've got the perfect weapon in those two, Don. Britney is becoming adept at hammering into my mind. I wonder how long it will take them to surpass us?"

Looking at the bodies being carted away, Don stated "Who knows? In the end, they've got to be the best at what they are expected to do." Looking at the two girls walking out of the room, he added, "The possibilities are limitless. At this age, they'll be useful for anything. After all, who's going to suspect little girls?"

With a smirk on his face, Dean observed, "When you put it that way, they certainly seem like good girls."

Looking around the blood soaked room, Don stated, "They'll be more than good enough for our needs."

Without another word, the two men walked out of the room and closed the door.

Saving Ralph

Alec Cizak

Billy Lloyd expectantly looked at the baby, sitting at the table. He had named it Ralph, despite the fact that it was a girl. He found her the same way he found all the children he had saved.

While looking for scraps in a dumpster behind the McDonald's on Seventh and Western, he heard a rustling among the discarded wrappers and trays. Digging through the trash, he saw that someone had thrown out an infant girl. He guessed she was somewhere between six months and a year into her life.

"I'll call you Ralph," he said as he pulled her out.

Ralph was the name of a boy who used to dunk Billy's head in the toilet in gym class, way back in grade school. Ralph laughed at him, made fun of the fact that he was overweight and that he smelled terrible because he couldn't stop sweating. He insisted that Billy would never amount to anything but a slob on a couch, counting the sands in his own particular hour glass to the rhythm of crunching potato chips.

"Billy Lard-ass, Billy Lard-ass!" Ralph had gotten the whole school yard to chant it, over and over again.

Billy was a killer on the offensive line of his Pop Warner football team, but he never harmed anyone off of the field. Even jerks like Ralph. But when sixth grade rolled around, he finally confronted him:

"What's your problem, Ralph?"

It was in the boy's restroom and a crowd had gathered.

"My problem," Ralph stated, "is that you take up too much space. You're fat and ugly and slow and stupid."

'Slow' had been a word attached to Billy by many. Teachers, psychologists, even his parents. He believed them and never tried to prove them wrong.

"Further," Ralph continued, "when the rest of us are married and raising our children, we're gonna be paying tax dollars to keep people like you comfortable in a trailer home somewhere just outside of town. So even though I won't have to watch your worthless life vanish like bag of corn chips, your grubby hand will be taking money out of my wallet."

Billy decided to end the torture right there. He rushed forward and swung his massive fist at Ralph's bony face. Stepping aside to avoid the slow moving punch, Ralph stuck his foot out and simultaneously tripped and pushed Billy into a stall where he smacked his face against the back wall and fell down, right onto the bowl of the toilet. Ralph leaped over Billy's massive frame and dunked his head into the water and brought his foot down on the flusher.

The other boys in the bathroom laughed and laughed and laughed.

Billy fought his way back up. "I'm gonna kill you!" He clenched his fists and charged for Ralph. A teacher walked in and broke up the fight and Billy never got his revenge.

"I wish I could see that son of a bitch today," Billy explained to the newest little Ralph, sitting quietly and patiently, awaiting dinner. "I'd show him the difference between an asshole and a human being."

Billy turned from the infant back to the pot of rain water he was heating over a stove fashioned out of a broken, twisted shopping cart. A small fire heated the wire meshes of the shopping cart and, in turn, brought the water to a boil.

"Almost ready," he assured the little girl.

Billy should never have made it to college. He was a D student at best, usually passing because the coach at Beaumont High frequently threatened to beat the crap out of any teacher who might fail his star center. The University of Texas ignored all the rules governing who was eligible to attend and recruited Billy on a full scholarship.

Ralph's middle school prediction that Billy would never get laid was put to rest the moment he told girls he was going to play football in Austin.

"Coach says I'm gonna start right away."

And with those simple words, he managed to sleep with a dozen different young women his freshmen year all while knocking defensive linemen five yards backwards every time the Longhorns ran the football.

"Where's Ralph when you need him?" he had joked to his friends and parents as TV cameras showed up after games to ask him why he was so brilliant.

"Well," he'd smile, thinking how far away that toilet in the sixth grade was, "I guess I'm just good at what I do."

The Longhorns almost won a national title his freshmen year. The quarterback and running backs and wide receivers got most of the attention, but it was Billy's punishing blocking that brought the team to the edge of glory.

"You shoulda' seen me," he said to little Ralph, "girls, media, they all loved me." He beamed as he dropped some old, dirty vegetables he found in a dumpster behind Von's Supermarket into the stew he was preparing.

His professors were forced to pass him despite the fact that he never studied and never came to class. He met June Walker, the daughter of a state congressman. She was proper, beautiful and dutiful, and promised to make him happy once he made it to the pros and brought in healthy million-dollar paychecks. They were going to be married and create babies and visit relatives on holidays and live out Norman Rockwell's wet dream.

His face soured. He thought about summer camp, just before his sophomore year. A freshmen named Barry Brown hit him square on the head in a downhill drill. At first it was diagnosed as a concussion. When Billy tried to stand up after the hit, the world spun around him and he fell back down. He was out for almost a minute.

As camp continued, Billy's performance on the field deteriorated. His memory began to vanish to the point that he often had to ask June who she was in the middle of a date. Medicine at the time managed to deduce that he had suffered severe brain damage.

Billy picked up an old salt shaker and seasoned the broth. "You'd be amazed," he explained to little Ralph, "how quickly life will take everything away from you."

Within a month, he lost his girlfriend, his scholarship, and was sent back to live with his parents in Kansas.

"We can't afford to mind you," his father announced one day, and then allowed Billy to pack a suitcase full of his clothes, dropped him off at the bus depot with three hundred dollars and wished him well.

He rode the Greyhound to Los Angeles simply because the road ended there. He lived on the streets from that point on. Alongside veterans and drug addicts and other unfortunate folks who had made the trip to the land of gold only to be disappointed by the reality that those who had the wealth weren't giving it away.

The house he currently squatted in was a rundown number on Serrano, just above Fifth Street. The Korean owners had given up on trying to restore it as the wood was rotted beyond repair and rats and mice nested by the thousands in the walls.

Billy had learned how to digest rodents long before he moved in, so they didn't bother him. If he saw a rat waddle across the floor he would catch it, kill it and cook it. Soon they figured out that he was the most dangerous predator they had ever encountered and stopped showing their tiny snouts when his scent was in the air. It was about this time that Billy took to saving discarded infants.

When he had pulled little Ralph out of the dumpster, she was covered with grime and filth and grease and cried non-stop.

"It's alright," he had assured her, "I'm gonna make things better for you." It broke his heart every time he found a baby like that.

"Let's get you washed up." He had jumped the Red Line to McArthur Park and dunked the infant in the lake until the dirt was gone. He held her under water, waiting for her to stop crying and fidgeting, assuring him she was ready to be saved.

"Looks just about right." He smiled at little Ralph, still staring blankly at him from the table. He picked up her purple, stiff body, and put her in the pot for dinner.

Stacy Bolli is a busy single mother to three incredible children and hails from the beautiful sun soaked state of Florida. Stacy has several works published in anthologies and on-line magazines including: Bonded By Blood II: A Romance In Red, Best Of House Of Horror: 2010 and Sins & Tragedies, to name a couple. She is also a proud staff member to the on-line magazine "The Dark Fiction Spotlight."

Uri Grey is a game writer, translator, humanist, twitterist and storyteller from Israel. A D&D instructor by day and a freelance writer by night, Uri has written games and short fiction for numerous publications, including Wizards of the Coast, Paizo, Mongoose, Bull Spec and Brain Harvest. He lives in urigrey.com and rather enjoys the view, particularly during the sunrise, to which he likes to refer as 'bedtime...'

Quinn Hernandez hails from the Quad Cities where he is a full time family man. His work has appeared in the anthologies, Through the Eyes of the Undead, Back to the Middle of Nowhere, Oh, the Horror!, and Dark Things 3. Upcoming publications include, Shadows Within Shadows and Fearology: Terrifying Tales of Phobias. He thanks you for reading his bio, and he hopes to see you again.

Adrian Ludens is a member of the Horror Writers Association. He will have a story in the upcoming HWA anthology "Blood Lite 3: Aftertaste", edited by Kevin J. Anderson. Look for other stories by Adrian in the Blood Bound Books anthologies "NightTerrors," "Unspeakable" and "Seasons in the Abyss." Visit his author page on Amazon or find him on Facebook for updates and links.

John McNee is employed as a reporter for a local newspaper on the west coast of Scotland. In his spare time he writes horror fiction. He is a firm believer that the maxim "truth is stranger than fiction" only applies to those suffering from a severe lack of imagination. His work appears elsewhere in the anthologies Ruthless and Gospels of Blood, Psalms of Despair, as well as in the online and print versions of Sex and Murder magazine.

A. R. Braun has eleven publications. His short works have appeared in Horror Bound, Micro Horror, Downstate Story, the Vermin anthology; the Heavy Metal Horror anthology; Bonded by Blood 2: a Romance in Red, and the up-and-coming Complete Guide to Writing Horror. He has been published three times in SNM Horror. A. R. lives for death metal and records with a studio project where he performs everything but the drums. He also records audio comedy for fun, but will release professional podcasts later. A. R. just finished his first novel and is looking for an agent. Contact him at http://arbraun.com.

Somewhere in southern California lurks a creature by the name of **Robert Essig**. This beast is known to have a macabre fascination with horror and is fortunate to implore an imp of whom whispers dark delicacies to him in the night. Robert’s fiction has been in over 30 publications including Bards and Sages Quarterly, The Scroll of Anubis (Library of the Living Dead), Tales of the

Talisman, Everyday Weirdness, and Withersin. He is the editor of the anthologies Through the Eyes of the Undead (Library of the Living Dead) and Malicious Deviance (Library of Horror).

Calie Voorhis has over 15 short story publications, including stories in Ray Gun Revival, Beyond Centauri, Fusion Fragment, Andromeda Spaceways Magazine, and stories in the print anthologies Anywhere But Earth, Dead Set: A Zombie Anthology, Farspace 2, and Space Sirens. She holds a BS in Biology from UNC-Chapel Hill, an MFA in Writing Popular Fiction from Seton Hill University, and is an Odyssey workshop alumnus. She lives in North Carolina, where her official "day" job is at Thalian Hall Center for the Performing Arts as Assistant Technical Director.

Kenneth Yu is a writer from the Philippines whose work has seen print in his country's various publications, including the Philippine ezines Usok and Best Of Philippine Speculative Fiction 2009, and in the anthologies Philippine Speculative Fiction IV, V, and VI. "Cherry Clubbing" placed 3rd in the Neil Gaiman-sponsored Third Philippine Graphic Fiction Awards in 2010. Elsewhere, his stories have been accepted in The Town Drunk, AlienSkin, and Innsmouth Free Press. He also won Fantasy Magazine's 2009 Halloween Flash Fiction contest. He also has fiction podcasts due out in 2011 at Pseudopod.org and at Dunesteef Audio Fiction Magazine.

Teaching prose at a university in the sleepy Costwolds, **KJ Moore** is equally grateful and surprised to be employed, published and read.

Glynn Barrass has been writing fiction and poetry for just over four years. His favorite genres being zombie fiction and the Cthulhu Mythos, he intends to write a lot more of both in the future. Glynn apologizes if upon reading Plague Hulk you develop a strong aversion to eating either mushrooms, or apples, but secretly hopes the story has just that effect. Hailing from the North East of England, he shares his home with his cat Sisko, and a few friendly ghosts he's met over the years.

C.M. Saunders began writing in 1997. His work has appeared in numerous magazines, newspapers, ezines and anthologies, including Fortean Times, Enigma, Urban Ink, Nuts & Record Collector. His latest novella Dead of Night is available now on Damnation Books, along with his critically-acclaimed Apartment 14F: An Oriental Ghost Story. When not writing he teaches at a media college in Hunan Province, southern China.

James L. Grant is currently a computer tech for a major company by day, cartoonist/novelist by night. His best-known work is Two Lumps, an online comic about cats that has resulted in 7 collections published by Stonegarden Books. His short fiction has appeared on Gothic.net, Bloodlust UK, and Weird tales, as well as various other magazines. Grant lives in Dallas, Texas, with his wife and conspirator, Mel Hynes.

Matthew Keville is thirty-four years old and lives in New York City, where he spends his time reading, writing, watching creature features both old and new, sublime and ridiculous, and exploring those parts of the city that tourists usually can't find. His favorite New York activity is watching midnight showings of cult movies at
arthouse theatres.

JW Schnarr is the evil mastermind behind Northern Frights Publishing. He currently resides in Champion, Alberta Canada with his daughter and a grumpy turtle. When not writing, editing or publishing, he can be found scheming. And watching sports. A member of the HWA, he is the Editor of Shadows of the Emerald City and War of the Worlds: Frontlines. Look for his Short Fiction collection Things Falling Apart as well as his novel Alice and Dorothy, a fairytale of sex, drugs, and murder. Both will be available in 2011.
JW Schnarr wants to be your friend on Facebook.

Tonia Brown lives in the hills of North Carolina with her fantastic husband and an ever fluctuating number of cats. She has an identical twin sister, who also happens to be her bestest friend. She likes fudgsicles and coffee, though not always together, and has probably seen more corpses in her lifetime than she cares to admit in certain company. You can learn more about her and her moniker, Regina Riley, at www.thebackseatwriter.com

Craig Saunders lives in Norfolk, England, with his wife and three children. He used to have three black cats, but they were unlucky. Craig started out writing fantasy, followed by science fiction, then humor. It took eight novels before he figured out that he was a horror writer, but Craig hasn't wasted any time since, with thirty horror shorts and four horror novels under his belt.
When he's not writing, Craig pretends to listen to his family while making up stories on scraps of paper. Follow his blog at www.petrifiedtank.blogspot.com.

Forrest Ingle is twenty-four years old. He currently lives in Shelby, North Carolina. He is a graduate of Cleveland Community College. His fiction has previously appeared in Twisted Tongue and Rage Machine Magazine.

R. Warren Smith lives in the Flyover Realms (aka Missouri), loves to read and write and read and write some more.

Chris Reed's fiction has appeared in a variety of small press magazines, including Black Ink Horror, Tattered Souls, and Midnight
Echo. When not writing horror, he enjoys making the underground mini-comics Used Addictions and The Adventures of Lil' Pube, available at www.usedaddictions.com and www.lilpube.com.

Alec Cizak is a writer from Indianapolis. His work has appeared in Beat to a Pulp, A Twist of Noir, Powder Burn Flash, Thuglit, Niteblade, Static Movement, Farmhouse, Etchings, Genesis, zygote in my coffee, and Altered Perceptions (R.I.P.) His work has also appeared in the anthologies Ruthless: A Collection of

Extreme Shock Horror, Niteblade: Nothing to Dread, and Pale House. He is also the editor of the crime fiction journal All Due Respect.

Eric Dimbleby lives and works in Maine. He is married with one son, and a second child is on the way. He has been published in dozens of magazines and anthologies. In 2011, his first novel, called "Please Don't Go" will be published by Pill Hill Press. To learn more about Eric's collected works, visit www.ericdimbleby.com.

Michael Cieslak is a lifetime reader and writer of horror, mystery, and speculative fiction. A native of Detroit, he still lives within 500 yards of the city in a house which is covered in Halloween decorations in October and dragons the rest of the year. He is an officer in the Great Lakes Association of Horror Writers. His works have appeared in a number of collections including three GLAHW anthologies, Dead Science, Vicious Verses and Reanimated Rhymes, and the Nightmare Fuel 2: Silent Nightmares podcast. His mental excreta can be found on-line at thedragonsroost.net.

Shane McKenzie isn't real. He's an old wive's tale. They say he lives in Austin, TX, the land of armadillos and chainsaws, but nobody can be sure. They say if you say his name three times in the mirror, he'll come. They also say, whoever *they* are, that you can visit him at his blog, www.shanemckenziewriter.blogspot.com.

Piper Morgan has been published in Night Terrors, Dark Things II, Daily Flash 2011: 365 Days of Flash Fiction and Daily Flashes of Erotica 2011. You can catch her bitching and ranting at: http://pipermorgan.blogspot.com or drop her a line at piperdmorgan@gmail.com.

Atris Ray is a new writer with a primary interest in fantasy and horror though he dabbles in many genres. His fiction has been published in MicroHorror, Macabre Cadaver, and Sorcerous Signals. He is currently working on his first fantasy novel. He lives just outside of Atlanta, GA with his wife, toddler son, and pets.

Chad McKee is a biologist who moonlights as a writer of fiction and poetry. His contributions have been published in the anthologies 2012 AD, Day Terrors, The Best of House of Horror (2009), Seasons in the Abyss, and The Garden of Life. He has also published scientific articles in a variety of medical journals. He is an American Southerner who currently lives in Oxford, England."

Michael Bracken is an active member of the Horror Writers Association. His horror fiction has appeared in Hot Blood: Strange Bedfellows, Midnight, Northern Horrors, Weirdbook, and many other anthologies, periodicals, and online publications. He can be reached at Michael@CrimeFictionWriter.com.

Edward R. Rosick has had a number of short stories published in magazines, webzines, and anthologies including: Pulphouse, Marginal Boundaries, and Little Green Men.

231

www.ingramcontent.com/pod-product-compliance
Lightning Source LLC
Chambersburg PA
CBHW022205170626
46807CB00005B/2352